PROJECT EXORCISM
Book One and Two

By

Mandy M. Roth

Futuristic Paranormal Romance

New Concepts   Georgia

Be sure to check out our website for the very best in fiction at fantastic prices!

When you visit our webpage, you can:
* Read excerpts of currently available books
* View cover art of upcoming books and current releases
* Find out more about the talented artists who capture the magic of the writer's imagination on the covers
* Order books from our backlist
* Find out the latest NCP and author news--including any upcoming book signings by your favorite NCP author
* Read author bios and reviews of our books
* Get NCP submission guidelines
* And so much more!

We offer a 20% discount on all new Trade Paperback releases ordered from our website!

Be sure to visit our webpage to find the best deals in e-books and paperbacks! To find out about our new releases as soon as they are available, please be sure to sign up for our newsletter (http://www.newconceptspublishing.com/newsletter.htm) or join our reader group (http://groups.yahoo.com/group/new_concepts_pub/join)!

The newsletter is available by double opt in only and our customer information is *never* shared!

Visit our webpage at:
www.newconceptspublishing.com

Project Exorcism Book One and Two is an original publication of NCP. This work has never before appeared in book form. This work is a novel. Any similarity to actual persons or events is purely coincidental.

New Concepts Publishing, Inc.
5202 Humphreys Rd.
Lake Park, GA 31636

ISBN 1-58608-795-9
© 2006 Mandy M. Roth
Cover art (c) copyright 2006 Eliza Black and Dan Skinner

All rights reserved, which includes the right to reproduce this book or portions thereof in any form whatsoever except as provided by the U.S. Copyright Law.

If you purchased this book without a cover you should be aware this book is stolen property.

NCP books are available at special quantity discounts for bulk purchases for sales promotions, premiums, fund raising, or educational use. For details, write, email, or phone New Concepts Publishing, Inc., 5202 Humphreys Rd., Lake Park, GA 31636; Ph. 229-257-0367, Fax 229-219-1097; orders@newconceptspublishing.com.

First NCP Trade Paperback Printing: July 2006

Dear Readers,

Each book in the Project Exorcism series is written to stand alone, though the author recommends reading them in order to maximize reader pleasure. To aid any who have not, as of yet, read the other book(s), or any who simply wish for a refresher, the author has included a small summary for ease of readability.

Series background: Year 2206--Man has long since achieved space travel. Almost all planets in the known universe are part of the Commission, an intergalactic governing body that oversees the well-being of all within its quadrants.

Supernatural creatures were discovered among us in 2055 and immediately a witch-hunt began to rid Earth of them. A battle broke out and Earth's human population dropped. In the end, humans were victorious, but only because a few select figureheads in the supernatural world agreed to the terms of a peace treaty. The terms were simple. They (the supernaturals) were to be escorted off planet Earth and relocated on other planets, ones that were not part of the Commission's territory. Ones that were agreed upon ahead of time, and ones which the supernaturals would not be a threat.

Thus began Project Exorcism. Five vessels set out on this mission. Only one arrived at its chosen destination. The others were thought lost during the meteoroid shower that occurred shortly after take off. Man now faces a new threat, only they are unaware of it. By shipping the supernaturals off, they unknowingly gave them access to other planets' resources, including added magical abilities, the ability to breed with their natives, and so very much more.

Welcome to Project Exorcism.
Mandy

PARANORMAL PAYLOAD

Dedication:

To my dad for being a science fiction fan and subjecting me to it all those years ago. I have finally stopped hiding with one eye peeking out from behind a pillow and started spinning dark stories of my own. All the years of pizza, over-sized headphones, movie marathons and laughing until we made ourselves sick still put a smile on my face. And to my mom for having to deal with us after a weekend full of junk food, up all nights and scary movies.

Prologue

Sevan moved slightly, getting a better angle on the beauty below him. Lorelei had haunted his dreams now for months and although he'd come to understand that he'd wake to find his sleep quarters empty and the raven haired goddess below him only a memory, he still caressed her tenderly. For the time being, she was his and he'd use that to his full advantage. He circled her belly button with his tongue as he looked up the length of her perfect body. Letting his eyes linger over her ample breasts and dark nipples, he could find no imperfection unless owning his heart was considered one.

The Fates themselves must have taken pity on him. Loving someone wasn't an option for him or others like him--the ones who carried the tiniest bits of supernatural DNA. Thankfully, Sevan's blood carried so little that the

Commission's screening didn't catch it. Only he and his family knew. Humans from Earth had thought they had wiped out all traces of the monsters of night long ago during Project Exorcism. While humans did succeed in escorting the majority of the supernaturals off the planet in 2055, a small percentage remained, hiding among the humans or simply hiding. Now, a little over a hundred and fifty years later, supernaturals still existed, though finding a full-blood was almost impossible.

Hiding under the Commission's nose was the best place to be. The only problem was, should Sevan ever be lucky enough to find his mate, that one special person made just for him, he would have to disappear. If the Commission ever learned of his ancestry they would court-martial him if he was lucky. Death would be the alternative. Not just for Sevan but for his mate as well.

Now, coming upon the phase in his life where he wanted a family more than life itself, he found himself daydreaming about his mate, what she would look like, who she might be. It was then that the dreams of Lorelei began. No part of Sevan believed she was truly the one for him. No. She was too perfect. Too beautiful. Too glorious to be real. He now looked forward to sleeping in hopes of seeing her. So far, in the six months since the dreams began they'd been together each and every night.

Licking his way down her flat stomach, Sevan stopped when he reached the thin well maintained strip of black hair covering her mound. He parted Lorelei's slit, revealing her pink bud and smiled wickedly. "Baby, you're gorgeous. The sight of you all spread out before me makes my dick so hard that I can't stand it."

"Please, Sevan," she whispered.

He couldn't help but smile at Lorelei's soft pleas for more. This woman his mind had created was so far beyond faultless that it was immeasurable. The idea of waking terrified him. Inching lower, Sevan dropped his head down and captured her clit, flicking his tongue back and forth over it.

She inched up on the bed, doing her best to try to escape him. Knowing that she loved it when he did it, Sevan continued, hooking his arms around her thighs and pulling her to him. He licked, sucked and caressed her, bringing about tiny gasps and sweet moans from her lips.

"Please."

Sevan sucked gently, his heart beating wildly. He knew she wanted him in her but he wanted her to come first. Her happiness meant everything to him. Of course, his need to please her was part selfish as well. When she came he was able to lick it, taste it, enjoy it coating his tongue as he shared in her joy, forever committing it to memory. Sliding a hand around, he inserted a finger into her tight channel as he continued to run his tongue over her clit.

Lorelei cried out and laced her fingers in his hair. The knowledge that she was close to hitting her peak spurred him on. He increased his pace and added a second finger. The second her legs drew together, effectively clamping his head, he knew she'd reached culmination. Her pussy convulsed around his fingers and cream trickled freely from her. Sevan's dick jerked painfully, needing to find solace in her and soon.

Crawling up the bed quickly, Sevan took hold of his rigid cock and aligned it with her heated core. He entered, instantly burying himself to the hilt. Lorelei bucked beneath him, grabbing hold of his ass and pulling him to her. He increased his thrusts. Her body took hold of his, fisting his shaft as he worked in and out of her. It was heavenly. Every dream always was. It was as though Lorelei were made especially for him. His subconscious had created a woman so perfect that no woman in his waking hours could compare to her. Sadly enough, he doubted that even his true mate would measure up next to Lorelei and the place she'd taken in his heart.

"Do you like that, baby?" he asked, already knowing she did.

Nodding her head, Lorelei bit her lower lip and stared up at him with eyes so blue they didn't look natural. The walls of her pussy grabbed him tight, holding his cock in her as she came again. This time Sevan joined her, pushing down and locking to her tight. Unable to stop himself, Sevan gave in, emptying his seed deep within her, filling her to the point she couldn't possibly hold it all.

Lorelei's grip on him loosened slowly, making way for tiny caresses. She ran her hands through his hair and hugged him tight, giving him the reassurance he needed that she was still there. "Thank you."

He let out a soft laugh. Normally, it was him thanking her. It had become a running joke between them. The first time he'd experienced the joy of being in her he'd repeatedly thanked her while he fucked her. "Mmm, you are most welcome."

"Sevan?"

He kissed her lips as he stared down at Lorelei, not wanting to pull out. The second her lips began to tremble Sevan knew she was on the verge of tears. "Baby, what's wrong? Did I hurt you?"

"No," she said, her voice weak. "I don't want to want to wake up and find you're not there with me."

For some reason his mind had been having the woman he'd invented react with the same emotions as him. The same fears of waking and the other not being there. No part of Sevan wanted to wake to find himself alone in his quarters, his arms empty and his heart heavy. The idea of remaining in a dream-like state for all eternity had occurred to him more than once. Seeing Lorelei teetering on the edge of tears only added to that. "I'll come back."

"How do you know you will?"

"Because I've come every night for almost six months, Lorelei."

She swallowed hard. "What if the dreams just stop, Sevan? What if this is our last time together?"

Hearing her voice his ultimate fear left him needing to kiss her. Dropping down, he did just that, tasting her mouth as if it were the last time he'd ever be permitted to sample it. The fear of waking at any moment struck him hard and he drew back a bit. "Lorelei, I love you. Know that in case this is the last time."

It didn't matter that she was a figment of his imagination. He'd fallen in love with her upon first sight and it had only increased. In the waking hours he tried to find a real love, someone to fill the hole in his heart but he couldn't even stomach the idea of touching another woman. She was all he wanted.

The stunned expression on her face was priceless. He kissed the tip of her nose and chuckled. "That wasn't the response I was expecting."

She touched the side of his face and locked gazes with him. "And I wasn't expecting to fall in love with you either."

Suddenly, it felt as though he'd been stabbed through the heart. The news of her loving him should have been joyous. Instead, it only made matters harder for him. He was in love with a dream. It was sick and he knew it but he couldn't stop. Too many nights they'd spent together, talking about their pasts, their people, their futures and too many times they'd fallen into one another's arms, making love until it was time to wake.

"Did I say something wrong?" she asked, running her hand over his bare chest.

Taking hold of it with his own, Sevan brought her hand to his lips and kissed it gently. "I want to claim you, Lorelei. Make you mine for all eternity."

"This is only a dream, Sevan. Trust me, I want it too but it can never really be."

"Then what does it matter?" He shifted a bit. "I want to know that I claimed the person I love in my life not just the person I'll be forced to."

"Do it."

"What?" he asked, shocked by her response.

Lorelei reached down, cupped his cock and squeezed it gently. "Fuck me and make me yours, Sevan."

Needing no further encouragement, Sevan adjusted himself over Lorelei and chuckled. She gave him a questioning look and arched a black brow. "Something funny about this?"

"Only that I can't claim you the way it should be done. I can't fully shift, Lorelei. I only possess the strength, speed and skill of a lion. I can't actually shift forms or have my teeth grow long enough to bite you, mark you as my own and taste of your blood."

Running her hands through his hair, Lorelei managed to soothe him. "This is a dream, Sevan. Anything is possible."

His cock responded instantly, seeming to find her wet core all on its own. It wanted her as much as he did. Never one to tell his dick no, Sevan pushed into her instantly finding the pleasure he sought. Lorelei met him thrust for thrust, taking all that he had to offer while begging softly for even more.

"Uh, Sevan, please."

It was on the tip of his tongue to protest and tell her that he truly couldn't mark her when he felt his mouth begin to burn. His gums seemed to light with a painful fire and he felt a change in his mouth occurring. Knowing his teeth were lengthening, Sevan did nothing to try to stop them even though his mind told him to panic. Somehow, his body knew it had been created to do this very thing.

Staring down at Lorelei's creamy smooth neck, Sevan watched with a supernatural eye as the veins seemed to pulse. Unable to control himself, he began to drill into her, striking the head of his cock against her cervix. Lorelei thrashed beneath him, clawing at the backs of his arms and staring up at him with her beautifully blue eyes.

"Mine, Lorelei. Mine," he growled out, his voice suddenly lower than it had ever been. He fucked her harder, knowing she not only could take it but demanded it during the mating ritual. "I claim thee as my mate, my soul, my love for all eternity. Take my seed as proof and taste of my blood as I taste of yours."

He struck out fast, sinking his newfound incisors into her tender shoulder. Lorelei cried out a second before Sevan felt her biting him back. The sweetly coppery taste of her warm blood filled his mouth. The man who had ruled his body all the years of his life was repulsed by the events. The beasts who'd spent that time caged rejoiced in the knowledge that she now belonged to him, real or not.

A spasm tore through Sevan's body as his balls drew up tight and semen shot forth from his cock, filling his mate fully. She wrapped her legs around his waist and held him to her as they continued to drink of each other's blood.

Slowly, she released her hold on him. "Mine."

A wind came out of nowhere, whipping around them, yanking on them yet leaving them joined. A strange force slammed into Sevan, entering his body from behind and coming out the front. He knew the second it hit Lorelei because she jerked and cried out. Fearing he'd done something to hurt her, Sevan released his hold on her and felt his teeth recede. "Are you hurt?"

"No," Lorelei said, shaking her head and smiling. "It was supposed to happen, Sevan. It means we're true mates."

Laughing softly, she shrugged beneath him. "Well, I guess in our dreams anyway."

"I'll never take another, Lorelei." Shocked by his own proclamation, Sevan just stared down at his mate--his wife.

She kissed the tip of his nose quickly. "Don't make promises you can't keep, Sevan. Let's just enjoy what we have now."

"I meant what I said. You are my wife now. And I won't...."

Pressing her fingers to his lips, she silenced him. "You will not live for a dream. You will enjoy your life as you were meant to. I love you and understand this. Who knows, Sevan, maybe the fates have bigger plans for us yet."

Chapter One

Lorelei Janelle plopped behind the control panel in the central observation deck to see what vessel had sparked the warning probe's alert system. She didn't like the idea of intruders in their vicinity, but it only happened every now and then so she couldn't complain. As much as she disliked worrying about outsiders, she did enjoy the company. Her nights had been filled by erotic dreams of a man too good to be true and her days were a rude awakening to the harshness of her world. Her nocturnal lover hadn't come to her in two weeks and her fear that her mind had finally given up generating him was great. It would, of course, wait until she'd mated mentally with him to pull the plug.

"Unit One, this is Captain Vasil of the Alpha Brig Three requesting permission to enter atmosphere and dock. Emergency commission code 327 has been initiated," a deep, familiar voice said in her earpiece.

Her inner thighs damped and for one brief moment, her breath caught in her throat. Who was this man that sounded so very much like her secret lover? How had he elicited that shocking response from her body with nothing more than his words? Fearing he was another Dsendiyun, she sighed. Lorelei was beginning to think the sex starved planet they came from encouraged them to 'get lost' as close to her people as possible. It wasn't like they got any sort of sexual stimulation while they were here. Not unless they considered being chained together good fun.

Some men do.

Lorelei glanced up at the glass ceiling. Seeing no sign of a vessel nearby, she double checked her radar to be sure she hadn't imagined the entire thing. There was no way she could have received a hail signal yet have the radar detect nothing. The electromagnetic waves that a vessel put out in a non-cloaked state would have shown up before. None did.

Having had many unauthorized vessels attempt to dock in her lifetime, Lorelei knew exactly how to handle them. She tweaked the computer's controls, demanding a more precise reading. Varying the frequency of the waves being sent off, she hoped to initiate a reflection of some sort, allowing the radar system to accurately pinpoint the vessel's location. It didn't work. Tweaking the calibrations even more, Lorelei set the control tower's sensors to ultra in hopes of catching a pattern of bounce backs consisting of the direct opposite waves than they were sending out. If the outsiders thought they were going to get away with active cancellation, they were wrong. Dead wrong.

Much to her surprise, nothing showed up on radar. Having never had one elude her, Lorelei tried another approach. She shifted to the Commission based recognition systems they'd installed many years ago after a sanctified vessel crashed into their red sea. Instantly, a blip appeared on the screen. Zeroing in on it, she brought it up closer and began to run a remote diagnostic on it. The main fuel tank had a crack so large that she knew they'd lost the majority of their liquid fuel as soon as it happened. Their life support systems were dangerously close to giving out and their alternate source of power seemed to be having issues as well.

Who would be stupid enough to enter our atmosphere with that amount of damage?

As soon as the question formed in her head, Lorelei knew the answer. The Dsendiyuns. Once located on radar, they were easy to spot with their flashy crafts and telltale too strong pick up lines. They would certainly have announced themselves to her by now. The tiny bit of thrill they got from trying to make her work at pinpointing their point of entry would have long worn off and she'd have gotten it right within seconds. Not to mention their ability to stay cloaked for long intervals within the planet's atmosphere was almost non-existent. No. Who or whatever approached them couldn't be the notorious romancers from Dsendiyun.

Disappointment shot through Lorelei, catching her by surprise. It had been a long time since she'd been touched by a man her mind did not create. The two weeks that she'd gone without Sevan coming to her nightly felt like an eternity. She missed the feel of his strong arms wrapped around her, the feel of him buried deep within her and knowledge that even though she'd invented him, he loved her. Her body was reaching the point where the desire to reproduce was almost on her. The only problem being, it had transcended her normal boundaries and infected her mind with a make-believe man whom she mated with in a dream.

It was as absurd as it sounded and although she truly did love the idea of Sevan, she couldn't live her life married to a fantasy. Waking up and crying every morning would get her nowhere and she knew it.

Irritated, Lorelei stared at the radar, watching the blip approach. "No way would a Commission vessel venture into uncharted territory. The ship's probably stolen and I bet it was those damn traders again. Probably want to try to nab off with more of our artifacts or to try to sell us more household cleaning equipment. I will not have my people's legacy sold to the highest bidder, nor do I need the latest and greatest debris remover. Do I look like a domestic goddess? No. I swear I will shoot them on sight if they attempt to take one thing." She wagged her brows and smiled. "If they've come to take me to bed, I'll reconsider. Mmm, bloody hell I'm horny."

Lorelei groaned as her nipples hardened. As much as she wanted to sneak away and 'handle' her current problem, she didn't. Thinking about sex was the worst thing she could do. It only seemed to intensify her craving for it--for Sevan. And there truly were only so many times she could masturbate before her fingers pruned and her wrist hurt. Sadly enough, she'd hit that state long ago.

"Excuse me, Miss, but I am no trader, nor am I a thief. Not to sound shallow here but I tend not to agree to fuck someone until I've had a look at them. As shocking as it sounds, not all men stick their dick in whatever moves. Plus, as overly romantic as this sounds, I'm the last guy you want. I'm holding out for a dream, honey, and to date no woman can stack up to her." He cleared his throat and the sound wreaked havoc on Lorelei's body.

She wanted desperately to come back with a witty comment but the tingling in her pussy fogged her mind enough that she didn't know or care how to respond to his comments. All she knew was that his voice was divine and so familiar that she was positive she knew him somehow.

"My ship's run into a bit of a snag and I need to work on it. If you'd be so kind as to tell your people to open the loading doors I will be out of your hair in no time flat. I'll require some fuel along with the use of some of your tools. I can assure you that each one will be returned in pristine condition. Though, I have been wanting a new set of torch acceleration adjustors."

Lorelei cursed herself for forgetting, yet again, that her voice transmitter was on. She had a bad habit of failing to remember to deactivate it after leaving the main tower. The teasing tone in his voice told her his comment was lighthearted, yet it was easy to tell she'd offended him. Why that mattered to her, she didn't know. But it did.

"Need I remind you that I have just initiated a code 327?" The frustration was evident in the heavy sigh that followed his comment.

Not one to fall for a sexy voice or succumb to guilt, Lorelei readied her inborn defense mechanisms. "Need I remind you that we are not part of the Commission and we do not recognize their laws? If you're seeking Commission friendly territory, you will not find it here. We are not a repair station nor are we prone to allowing arrogant arses to dock for giggles. And for future reference you will not take that condescending tone with me again or you will sit there until your ship gives out. I am not one of your disciples, nor will I ever be. And, I'll have you know that basing the choice of having intercourse with someone off appearances places you below a lechranki worm in my book."

"Less than a blood sucking worm that eats its own vomit?"

"Mmmhmm." Lorelei grinned from ear to ear as though she were just a child again. Goading this man had to be the highlight of her month. Why? She wasn't sure but it felt good all the same.

There was some mumbling and then she heard another male laughing. "Shut up, Jordan," the sexy man said, his voice reminding her of Sevan's.

"Always good to know that you are an arse with everyone, not just people you are trying to sweet talk into allowing you to dock. And in case you should have the misfortune of needing repairs this deep into space again, might I suggest you pretend to be mute and allow someone to speak for you. Perhaps sending a holographic image would even work. Just be sure not to model it after yourself or it too will find a rather cold reception."

"Listen lady, you better check that ... ouch! Hit me again and I will toss your ass out into space, brother or not."

Feigning glee, Lorelei clapped her hands together. "Oh goodie, mummy, they come in pairs. Do you think I could have a set of slime lechranki worms to go with the arrogant, ill-mannered boys that wish to dock here? Oh, please, mummy. I've been such a good little girl this year."

Captain Vasil laughed and the seductive sound of it rolled over her, caressing her in places she never dreamed a voice could. Places she hoped he really would touch her. Shocked and a bit embarrassed by her sudden state of need, Lorelei lashed out at him. "Oh my, my, he has a sense of humor. Be still my bored out of its mind heart."

He was quiet for a moment and Lorelei was almost sad that he had no comeback for her. Suddenly a bit panicked that she may have been too harsh, Lorelei took a deep breath and prepared to apologize to the stranger. That in itself should have tipped her off that something was amuck. Before she could get a word out, Vasil beat her to it.

"My apologies. My crew and I have had a rough go of it. We would like to clean up and get our ship fixed before heading onward." Captain Vasil was sincere. Her powers picked up on that immediately. It was a bit disheartening that he'd decided to end their back and forth but understandable due to the serious condition his ship was in. Still, giving in to him could cost him his life.

Knowing the risk he and his crew would be in if they docked here this late in the day and were unable to leave before the suns set didn't sit well with her. The man may possess the sexiest voice she'd ever heard but it would get him nowhere in life if he didn't have his head attached to his body. "Sorry, Alpha Brig Three, permission to dock denied. Seek assistance in the next quadrant over. I'll monitor your ship until it reaches the new destination. Two units will be sent up to refuel and escort you. Control tower out."

Lorelei went to cut transmission when she heard the mysterious man on the other end sigh--again. Her gut twisted and her stomach flipped at the very sound of his breath exhaling in her earpiece. She hated giving in, but disliked the thought of never hearing that voice again.

Am I confident enough that I can keep him safe?

Hating herself for her instant inner 'yes', she rolled her eyes and tossed her hands in the air. "Can you be in and out by suns set?"

There was a moment of silence followed by a low whistle. "Yes, we only need a couple of hours to get everything operational again."

It was Lorelei's turn to sigh. "If you promise to not cause any trouble, take full responsibility for whatever may come from docking here and be out by suns set then you may dock. No exceptions."

"You've got yourself a deal, little lady."

"Refer to me as little lady again and you will rot in space. Are we clear?" Lorelei bit back a tiny smirk as she envisioned the look on the man's face. The only problem was, she tended to insert the face of the sexy stranger who had plagued her dreams for months into every fantasy she had.

"Yes, ma'am."

Chapter Two

Captain Sevan Vasil glanced over at his brother and second in command, Jordan. "What?"

"Nothing," Jordan said, his lips pursed and his arms crossed.

It didn't take a genius to tell him his brother was pissed. "Spill it."

"I'm not so sure we should dock here. The planet is not marked on the map and you yourself heard that they are not in the business of giving leave to Commission vessels. And what was that about assuming full responsibility for docking and…?"

"And," Sevan interrupted. "We don't really have much of a choice here. Our fuel tank cracked somewhere back near Margaidia and unless you want to chance piloting a vessel with no fuel and limited life supports all the way home, I'd suggest you get real comfy with the idea of docking here. We'll never make it back to Earth unless we do and you know it."

"Captain, I did not mean to question your authority."

"Cut the shit, Jordan! Don't go all military on me. You and I go back too far for you try to be stuffy now. I can still remember you in diapers!"

"You're three minutes older than me. Of course you remember. You were there too, moron. If you want to start flexing your three minute older muscles, let's go…."

The main screen flickered and interrupted Jordan's little rant. Static covered it for a split second before a vision so beautiful that Sevan had to fight to breathe appeared. Angelic didn't even begin to cover her. Instantly, his heart hammered.

It couldn't be. No. It wasn't possible. She wasn't real, was she?

Sevan couldn't think, couldn't move as he stared at her. The woman was identical to Lorelei. Overwhelmed by emotion, he sat there breathing heavy and trying to stop the obvious hallucination before him.

The goddess on the screen looked up at him, her royal blue eyes wide and then glanced down at the control panel before her. "Bugger! How the hell do you turn it on again? If I don't figure it out soon they'll end up stuck in orbit and I am not in the mood to fetch them. The last thing I want to do today is go and tow an arrogant, cocky, too sure of himself man, who thinks the universe should bend at his very command ... errr ... Commission officer's vessel in. I would rather wallow through pikineius dung than retrieve them."

Nice to know where we rank, Sevan thought, chuckling silently.

The hint of an old Earth British accent came through, reminding Sevan of home. They didn't spend nearly as much time among the Free World people on Earth as they'd like. No. Now their days were spent in the Commission going where they demanded.

The woman before him narrowed her gaze on the control board before her. She was obviously oblivious to the fact that she already had the visual communicator working. The thought of telling her he could both see and hear her crossed his mind for a millisecond before he decided to just take in the show until she figured it out. Besides, his cock had joined in the spectacle now and its rather hard state demanded he remain still or risk ejaculating in his pants.

Not an option he wanted to take. Though it was hard to keep from yelling out the name Lorelei-- the very idea that it wasn't her terrified him. If she were real and if she too shared the dreams then she could be his mate.

Neither man said a word as the vixen before them leaned forward. Her long black hair fell into her face, looking so silky and smooth that Sevan could almost feel it. Bringing a toned arm up, she lifted it away. Her luscious lips pouted outward, as if she were in deep thought.

You're fucking killing me here. You're a hallucination that's it.

Scolding his mind for placing the vision of his dream lover in place of the actual woman didn't seem to stop the hallucination. Watching the woman only served to make it worse. Sevan had always been a sucker for women who were animated, especially when it came to their lips. Just thinking about how full and lush hers looked made him picture his cock buried in her mouth, as he held tight to her silky hair. Flashes of the erotic dreams he'd been having for months flooded back to him. It was her face he'd seen beneath him as he sank into the paradise of her warm depths. But how could that be? Had their ship blown up after the fuel tank cracked? Was he dead now and left to dream of Lorelei forever?

If you've got to go, ending up envisioning her for the rest of eternity isn't so bad.

The gorgeous woman punched the controls a few more times before rising slightly from her seat. Wearing a tiny black top that came to just above her navel, his eyes widened as it pulled up to just under her ample breasts. His cock dug painfully into the top of his pants. It would tunnel through the material soon and demand attention from her. Having her with him in bed was the only way he was used to dreaming of her and while this little tit for tat was amusing, he wanted her pussy milking him as he came in her.

Sevan heard Jordan draw in a deep breath and knew that the vision of beauty on the screen was having the same effect on him. A surge of jealousy went through him. Glaring over at his brother, he dared him to have a sexual thought about his woman.

My woman? Great, now I've laid claim to a fantasy woman--again. Next I'll be pulling up various versions of my own harem.

As horny as he was, he'd most likely pop anything inflatable and the holograms, while stimulating, couldn't take the place of a real woman so he pushed the thought from his mind. Shifting in his seat, Sevan tried his best to distribute the mass between his legs. If he continued to stare at her, his cock would be hard for a week. No amount of jerking off would ease the pain she would no doubt bring him. As if it wasn't bad enough that he already woke each morning to find his dick so hard he could hammer a steel panel into a wall with no further aid, now he would be forced to live out his death staring at her from afar.

She looked so real. Never before had anyone been in his dreams other than the woman on the screen before him. Always ready for him, she appeared to him out of nowhere and with one look they knew what the other wanted. He'd fucked her so many ways that he felt himself blush. He wasn't shy but he wasn't prone to dropping to his knees and licking the sweet pussy of a gorgeous woman who suddenly appeared to him either. He'd done things with Lorelei that he'd never dreamed of doing in real life and she sparked things in him that no one else did. The worst part of it all was that he'd actually fallen in love with her--a dream, a figment of his overactive imagination, a vision that now appeared before him in what he hoped was waking hours. And he hoped beyond hope that she truly was the mate he sought.

"Blasted thing doesn't work! If that lil' Bagardo demon that claimed he fixed this pulled a fast one on me, I'll pull his purple head off and shove it up his lime green...." Jerking her hand away from the control panel in front of her, she winced as a blue spark shot out at her catching her upper arm and burning it instantly.

No baby, don't ever cross those wires.

Sevan went eerily still. He'd never worried over a woman before. Well, no woman that wasn't related to him or a member of his crew. His cousin had accompanied them on their journey and he worried like hell every time she left the ship.

It shocked him how real and how human the woman on the screen appeared to be. One, if she was real then some deep shit was going on. Dreaming of a woman galaxies away had to have some sort of cosmic ramifications. Mating with her only intensified that. For two, all planets with human or human-like life forms had been mapped out by the Commission ages ago, at least in this quadrant. His luck she was projecting an image that they'd feel comfortable with long enough to lure them in and then he'd find out that she was really an alien with six heads. That had to be it. She was picking his brain and came up with Lorelei's likeness.

Ah, I hope not.

She tried again to fix the panel. Another blue spark shot out and caught her creamy cheek. Hissing, she grabbed hold of it and winced. Sevan stood fast, reaching for her as if he could really touch her through the viewing screen.

Glancing down, he found Jordan staring at him with an odd expression on his face. Wisely, his brother didn't comment on his concern for the beautiful creature before them. She reached out to try it again but pulled away at the last second allowing Sevan to exhale.

"Christian, can you get this thing to work? I can't seem to get it to respond to any of my commands. I swear it bit me twice already and if it does it again I will shoot it and then recycle its parts into a waste receptacle. The damn thing has a mind of its own and I'm frankly tired of dealing with it. I hate technology and it hates me. It's a rather mutual agreement that is best not tampered with."

"Promise you won't bite me if I get close enough to fix it. Though, there are certain places you could nibble if the urge should strike," a very male voice said from off screen.

Sevan's blood ran cold as the beast within threatened to surface. It would control his temper or rather, leave him uncontrollable. He had no right to feel the pang of jealously that now rode him, but he did. He watched as a large arm appeared first, followed close by a handsome man who looked to be in his mid-thirties. Tattoos covered the man's arms. And upon closer inspection, Sevan saw that the woman had similar markings on her arms as well although hers were a degree lighter than the male's. In his dreams, Lorelei didn't have any sort of markings on her.

Maybe she just looks a lot like Lorelei--a hell of a lot like her.

The man near her looked as though he'd won the strong man of galaxy contest several years running. Sevan was not a small man by any standard, but he wasn't quite the barbarian that stood by the tiny woman now.

Christian moved his body around the woman's and let his eyes linger over her cleavage longer than Sevan could stand. His jaw tightened and he felt Jordan's hand on his shoulder.

"Easy now, brother. We've only come to fix the ship."

"Here you go. Just push this button here." The man put his mouth to the woman's ear, whispering something only she could hear. Her cheeks flushed and her body tensed. "Follow that procedure and you'll be up and running in no time. Not that you need any help in the getting things up category."

"Thank you, Christian," she said, shifting in her seat. She glanced up at the screen and apparently was able to see them now as well because she froze. "No." Her tongue darted out and over her bottom lip. That simple act sent chills of pleasure throughout Sevan's body.

"By gods, she's even more beautiful in person."

Her brow creased as her cheeks flushed. Jordan cleared his throat and Sevan realized that he'd not only said that out loud, but she'd heard every word of it. It was his turn to blush.

"Control tower, this is Alpha Brig Three, requesting permission to dock," Jordan said, laughing slightly.

"Perm … permission granted." Her blue gaze locked on his. She seemed to study him, tipping her head slightly and narrowing her eyes. Something clicked and she shook her head as she hit another button and backed away from her seat. "Navigation will now be controlled by our tower. Please refrain from attempting to override this or irreparable damage to your vessel will occur. We will meet you in the loading area momentarily."

Stunned by her rather cold tone, Sevan stared mindlessly at her. She went to cut transmission and Sevan leaned forward fast not wanting lose sight of her. "Wait! What policy do you have on outsiders?" It was best to know if they regarded them as hostile or not right off the bat. Not that it mattered what she thought, his dick already thought of her as the only place it wanted to reside and there was no overriding that.

She gave a tiny smile that tugged at his heartstrings before answering. "I think you will find that we're friendly enough. We'll see to it that you're taken care of during your time here today. Come suns set we will not tolerate any excuse causing you to stay on our planet. I take it from the lack of my need for a translator that you speak Earth-English, as do we. That's always comforting. It's rare that any passersby speak our language. Our atmosphere is rich in oxygen so respirators will not be necessary. Our digestive systems are identical to yours so you will find our food adequate to sustain you. All of this leads me to believe that your visit will be most enjoyable." A sad look passed over her beautiful features and Sevan wanted to kiss it away. "Be sure to remain armed though. We are willing to allow you to do so in good trust. We shall not harm you and we expect the same in return."

She cut transmission before he had a chance to ask why he and his men should remain armed. That was an odd request. Most planets they stopped at required them to check their weapons and deactivate any of the Brig's defenses.

"That's interesting," Jordan said, reading Sevan's mind.

"You heard the lady." Sevan pushed the button for the intercom that ran throughout the ship and looked at Jordan. "This is the Captain. We're docking now. Be sure to leave your weapons on and maintain a state of readiness. Travel in groups of two and do not engage without my permission. Anyone who disobeys this command will not have to worry about a court-martial. They won't be alive to stand before the committee."

Chapter Three

"I hope you know what you're doing." Christian bellowed.

Lorelei let out a small laugh. "Like I had a choice. You saw the diagnostics screen. They've cracked their fuel tank and are running at eighty percent life-support. The ship's climate control is damaged as well. They would never have made it to the next repair station without assistance regardless how many ships I sent up to escort them."

"My, my." Christian touched her shoulder. She tensed. "Aren't we quick to defend our actions?"

Lorelei didn't care for what he was implying, but didn't bother to go into it with him. Christian was known for his jealous streak and that was just one of the reasons why she'd refused to marry him even though law ruled the marriage to take place. It wasn't as though he was a bad man, just not the man for her. There was a time he acknowledged that as well, but those days were fading fast, being replaced by endless sexual banter and tiring tries at bedding her. The Christian she'd known and loved made rare appearances. Today, he seemed to be in hiding.

"Are you coming down to meet our guests or are you planning on standing there sulking all day?" Lorelei asked, annoyed with having to deal with another one of Christian's temper tantrums.

Giving her a nasty look, he put his weapon on. "Oh, I wouldn't miss an opportunity to meet the man you practically drooled over, my dear."

"I did not drool over anyone. And even if I did, what business is it of yours?" She had little desire to go into the fact that when she'd looked into the outsider's eyes she'd been unable to breathe. Never in her wildest dreams had she thought the man she craved nightly was real. The only thing that worried her was that Sevan didn't do much of anything when she looked at him. In her dreams he'd declared his love for her, claimed her as his own, given her pleasure like no other man had and made her feel as though the two of them were all that existed in the universe. Perhaps the outsider just looked like Sevan.

Her chest tightened. Every bit of her body ached to be touched by Sevan, to know the pleasures his body could bring her in the waking hours and to see what she could offer him in return.

Christian held the door ajar for her and let out a wicked laugh. "Perm ... permission granted. Please, Lorelei. Your nipples were so rock hard that you could have impaled me with them. Do me a favor and try not to fuck the outsider before they leave today. I would not want to have to raise another man's baby. That does seem to run in your family. Your grandfather was a better man than I. He raised your father knowing he was not his and knowing that he held the blood of the others in him."

She spun in the hallway to strike him and he caught her wrist. His olive eyes lit with a fury she'd only seen reserved for battle. Christian was beyond jealous and that made him deadly.

"Let go of me."

Leaning down, he put his lips next to hers. "Give me what I want and I will." A low growl trickled from his throat and he didn't sound like himself. "I was chosen to be your mate after Samson gave into the others' pull. Honor what our elders have deemed to be law. Give in and all will be well."

"I am not going to marry you and how dare you bring him into this, Christian. Your brother didn't give in. No more than you did." The urge to strike him was great, Lorelei held back.

"Marriage is not a word our people use. Stop trying to be more like your very unhuman ancestors. You want me. I can smell it. You might as well rub your cream all over my face. You reek of desire."

"Who said it was you I'm wet for?"

He tightened his grip on her wrist and she cried out. Christian's eyes widened as he came back to his senses. More and more Christian was falling prey to the darkness they'd put in him. Losing him wasn't an option. Though marriage wasn't on her mind, it didn't mean she had no love for him. On the contrary, she loved Christian and always would. "Lorelei. I'm sorry. I didn't mean for...."

Lorelei backed away from him and he made another move to reach for her. She shook her head no. Visions of the nightmare they'd suffered through only seven months before came flooding back to her. They'd lost so much and in the end had overcome it all. None of the memories were pleasant and the thought of reliving that terrified her.

Christian grabbed hold of her and brought her body close to his. "Let's get you to the infirmary. I can harness the power I need to heal you there. The idea of leaving the slightest mar on you sickens me, Lorelei."

Lorelei heard his words, but they made little sense to her. Her mind was still planted back in time, seven months ago, when they'd been sent out to try to negotiate peace with 'the others' only to find it was a trap. 'The others' had used Christian against her. They'd manipulated him and forced him to do things that no man would ever knowingly do to the woman he loved. He had no memory of it nor could he be faulted.

Her brain told her that they were safe within the compound walls and that no evil could befall them, but her body reacted with fear. She dropped to the ground and spun her leg around, sweeping Christian's feet out from under him. Thankfully, Lorelei had the element of surprise on her side, or she would never have been able to budge Christian. His six foot five inch frame crashed to the floor. She sprang to her feet and took off running in the other direction. It was easy to feel the shift in the air around her signaling that Christian was moving at the same speed.

"Lorelei! No!" Christian tackled her to the ground and held her tight, pinning her with such a force that she could barely breathe. Her body shook and the realization that he could hurt her again hit her. From the moment 'the others' had touched his mind, he'd been forced to fight back the demon within. The darkness their leader had put in him wanted to cause pain and suffering. He smelled of it. The taint. The hatred. The evil. None of the smells that were normally associated with Christian. No. The Christian she'd grown up with was kind, caring and protective.

"Christian, no. Fight him. Don't let him win again." Her voice sounded weak, even to her.

Chapter Four

"Thought they said they were meeting us in the loading area," Jordan said, glancing around the large, empty area.

On cue, a door opened and a woman entered. At first, Sevan thought it was Lorelei and almost ran to her but the closer she got the more differences he noticed. Her hair, although as long as Lorelei's was several shades lighter. This woman was a brunette, not a coal black beauty like Lorelei. Her features were strikingly similar, giving her that same heart stopping capability. But she wasn't the one he wanted to hold and never let go. She wasn't the one who made his heart ache to just see her one more time.

She smiled at them as she approached. Jordan made a small choked sound. When Sevan looked over at his brother he saw that he was taken aback by the woman who now stood before them.

"Welcome," she said extending her hand to Sevan. "I'm Nina. You spoke with my sister and she granted you permission to dock. I'm sure she explained our policy on you needing to stay armed and the importance of you leaving prior to suns set."

"She did," Sevan said, looking past her for signs of her sister. His chest tightened in anticipation. He needed to touch her, find out if she was his Lorelei, know she was real and then pull her into his arms. No part of him cared if his advance would be welcomed or not. After being subjected to non-stop dreams of knowing her body every possible way, then declaring his love for her, he needed to hold her, if only for a moment.

The very idea of Lorelei had ruined him for other women. In six months, he hadn't touched a woman carnally. His cock ached to be caressed only by Lorelei. His entire body burned to be buried deep within her as he released his seed. His fantasy woman was real or at least appeared to be. As good as fucking her upon first sight sounded, Sevan knew that he had to know how she managed to invade his thoughts to begin with.

Nina glanced at him and her smile faded away. "This way ... our men will see to your ship. Let us see about filling your bellies while you wait."

Sevan touched his wrist communicator. "Brig crew, stay alert and remain in docking bay. I'll call you all soon for eating shifts."

They followed Nina as she walked out the double doors and into a large corridor. Jordan seemed to be paying special attention to her backside and he couldn't fault his brother's taste in women. Nina was beautiful. It was apparently genetic.

"If you stare at my arse any harder, it may burst into flames," she said, in a low hushed tone.

Sevan hid his laugh as Nina looked over her shoulder at Jordan.

"Christian. No!" someone yelled, breaking the jovial feeling that had only just begun.

Sevan turned to see the onyx-haired temptress from the visual communicator pinned under the large hulk of a man called Christian. His entire body lit with fury as he shot forward to help her. Jordan seized hold of him and thrust him against the wall. "We are offworlders and this is not our business."

Nina gasped when she saw her sister and Sevan took that as a sign that all was not well. "Let me go!"

Jordan pressed against him hard and whispered, "I know what you're thinking. I didn't forget the description you gave me of the woman from your dreams. That girl isn't her. She's not your Lorelei."

Sevan stared at the raven-haired goddess and lunged for her again. Jordan, of equal strength, kept him in place. The woman twisted in Christian's arms and touched his cheek. The urge to see the man's head on a stake grew by the second.

"Christian, we need to get up now. You have to pull yourself together," she said, putting her forehead to his.

"What?" The man shook his head, seeming to come out of a daze.

The woman shot up and headed straight towards them. Her head was turned, her attention on the hulk of man behind her. She was too fixated on Christian to notice them. Jordan stepped back, allowing Sevan freedom. Sevan put his arms out just in time to catch her. For a little thing, she packed a hell of a punch. They tumbled backwards in a mass on the floor. He landed first, followed closely by her. She smelled of vanilla and he couldn't help but to draw in a deep breath--savoring her scent. It was identical to his dreams.

"Ommpf," she murmured, as she attempted to roll off him. He held her to him, enjoying the feel of her body pressed against his. She was even better in the flesh and he hadn't thought that possible. Her royal blue eyes narrowed on him as she tipped her head slightly, appearing to survey him.

"Lorelei, get off our guest," Nina said, sounding like she wanted to laugh.

Lorelei?

Sevan's gut clenched tight as he lay beneath her. She was real.

Jordan leaned over them and arched a brow. "Not to interrupt you, Sevan, but the ship needs tended to."

Nether one of them moved from their spot.

* * * *

Lorelei stared down at Captain Vasil, unable to form any sort of witty response to him. It was him! The man she'd assumed was her subconscious' answer to her need for comfort. Unable to stop herself, she touched his face, running her fingers over his stubble and tracing the hard edge of his jaw line. It was easy to relish being close to his chiseled perfection so she did. The gods were good judges of her idea of the perfect man. They had to be. They'd sent her a mate that was made to order.

A mate?

She dismissed the thought of mating quickly. It was just a dream. Having been close to being mated once before, Lorelei had no desire to repeat the horrific events that put an end to her engagement to Christian nor did she intend to give her heart to another. No. Her life was her own and she would never willingly hand control of it to another person. Not again.

As much as she wanted to believe herself, Lorelei knew that resistance to the fates' choice for her was futile. Her body was on the cusp of a reproductive high and already the effects left her in cold sweats with a burning need to be filled with seed.

Staring down at the man below her, Lorelei couldn't stop the feelings that ran through her. So many nights she'd dreamed of his kisses, his touch, his body sweetly invading her in every way possible. To have him here, in the flesh was almost too much. Before Lorelei realized it, she was grinding her hips against his rather impressive erection. The thin layers of material between them did little to prevent her clit from striking against his bulged member. Heat flashed through her cheeks as she thought about the countless nights she'd opened herself for him in her dreams, allowing him to do things to her body she hadn't even thought possible. The feel of his long, wide cock sliding in and out of her pussy still made her wet. Now, with Sevan under her, she wanted to tear their clothes off and fuck him until she could go no more.

The emerald green eyes that stared back at her from under a shaggy veil of blond hair had consumed her thoughts for months. Having them focused on her now, seeming to soak her in, was nothing short of pure torture.

Sevan looked as stunned as she felt. Reaching up, he touched her lips softly, causing heat to flare through her body. Long strands of her hair fell forward, encasing them in a wall of black, giving them a moment away from the prying eyes of the others. A slow, lazy smile moved over Sevan's face as their gazes locked.

Lorelei licked her lower lip out of habit and Sevan moaned softly. It was then she knew the attraction went both ways. Could it be he'd dreamt of her as well? If so, did that mean he truly was the one--her mate, her husband?

Are you the one?

Sevan's brow creased. "What one?"

Shocked that he'd heard her thoughts, Lorelei drew in a sharp breath and searched his handsome face for any clue that might unravel the mystery that had plagued her for so many months. All she found was the face of the man she'd not only come to be addicted to dreaming about but the man she dared to say she loved. Thinking him only a figment of her imagination, Lorelei was ashamed of her growing need for him, for his tender caresses and his overwhelming feelings of protectiveness.

Now, as his straining erection pressed firmly to her swollen clit the shame she felt began to fade rapidly, leaving only carnal lust in its wake. The steely contours of Sevan's body only served to drive that feeling on, increasing to a dangerous point. Her magic began to pound as hard and fast as her heart--thumping to the point it teetered on the edge of release along with her sex starved body.

Someone cleared their throat, breaking the moment.

* * * *

Sevan did his best to focus on anything but the need to fuck the beauty above him. His cock had already begun to slink towards her cunt knowing that it would bring him salvation like no other would. He would have acted on it, taking her and fucking her into submission, assuring himself that she would never leave his line of sight. Too long he'd spent thinking he was going mad desiring a woman that didn't exist. Finding out she did changed all the rules of the game. He'd fallen in love with her and there was no way he'd let her go. The only question he needed answered was whether or not she dreamed of him as well.

Not wanting to assume anything, Sevan took a laid back approach to breaking the ice. The only problem was that it came out harsher than he expected or wanted. "That's quite a welcome you have there. Do you greet all your visitors this way?"

"Hardly," Lorelei said, rolling off him, but not before he felt her erect nipple brush past his hand.

He wanted to comment, but as she sat up, her hand ran over his now rock hard erection. Drawing in a ragged breath, he tried to steady himself to avoid coming in his pants. That not only would be messy, it would mortify him. No. The amount of semen he had built up was going to be released into Lorelei not his pants, that much he was sure of.

Sevan smiled, and cocked an eyebrow knowing he was being an ass but unable to stop himself. "I'd be more than happy to accept a greeting like that every time we cross paths."

Stop being such an ass to her. You love this woman, idiot.

She cast an angry look down at him and he cleared his throat. "Considering that you are leaving our planet by suns set, I doubt we will cross paths again."

Don't be too sure of that.

She dusted her firm backside off. Rising to his feet, Sevan purposely lost his balance just so he could use her to steady himself. The second he took hold of her upper arms his entire body lurched back into a state of mind numbing need. Lorelei gasped and he could only hope the feeling was mutual.

"Thank you," Sevan said softly as he caressed the backs of her toned arms, hoping that she would catch their private joke line. She didn't react to it.

Instead, Lorelei's blue gaze raked over him and he wanted to see it above him once more. He wanted to feel her in the flesh while they reenacted the dreams that had haunted him. The call of her lush lips was too much. Bending down, Sevan went to capture them and felt the heavy weight of so many stares that he halted in mid-motion.

"Dare I ask what the two of you were bickering about this time?" Nina said, appearing next to her sister and motioning to the hulk of a man. "And why in the world were you on the floor?"

Lorelei turned a bit, still staying close to him but focusing on her sister. "It was nothing. Christian and I seem to do that for sport now."

Christian crossed his large arms over his chest, doing his best to look intimidating. "That is the only sport I seem to get from my wife anymore, Nina."

Wife?

Nina laughed. "Watch your tongue, Christian. If you keep calling her your wife before the ceremony actually takes place you're likely to jinx it."

Lorelei was to marry Christian? No. That couldn't be. Sevan stared at her, desperate for her to announce it wasn't true, that it was some sort of joke. No way could she ever take another man into her, not after what they shared. Not after she'd allowed him to lay claim to her. His chest tightened as the realization that the dreams were quite possibly only one-sided hit him. What force would bring her image forth in his sleep, allowing him to experience a love like no other only to give her to another the moment they met?

"Christian." Lorelei shook her head slightly, exhaling as she went. "Please refrain from discussing marriage in front of others. There is a time and place. This is not it."

"Please refrain from bringing your human terms for what occurs. You share their blood but you share ours as well. Never forget that, Lorelei. And try not to forget the sins of your ancestors. I am not in the habit of raising other...."

Lorelei pulled away from him and directed her attention to Christian. Sevan would have been jealous had he not sensed the rage within her. Nina apparently sensed it as well because she moved next to her sister quickly and offered her a small smile.

"Jacquelyn listens," she whispered to Lorelei.

Lifting her hands up, Lorelei tipped her head back and forth. He watched in awe as a slight wind began to twirl around her. Jordan gasped but Sevan just stared at her, already knowing how very special she truly was. Her hair lifted slightly and the oppressing feeling of rage dissipated instantly. She went to Christian and cupped his face. The second she pressed her lips to his, Sevan saw red.

He moved fast to snatch Lorelei away from the man but found Jordan seizing hold of him. "Captain."

The warning fell on deaf ears. The only thing that mattered was Lorelei and the fact that she was in the arms of another man. A small spark of light passed from her lips to his, causing Sevan to stop his struggle against Jordan's grasp.

Lorelei drew back from Christian as he shook his head slightly, seeming to come out of a daze. He looked down at Lorelei with wide eyes. "It happened again, didn't it?"

Sevan wanted to know what the man was talking about but held his tongue.

Nina touched Christian's arm. "How much can you remember?"

"I knew what I was saying was wrong but I couldn't stop. Lorelei, I didn't mean to pin you to the ground. I...."

Lorelei smiled and Sevan's heart beat madly in his chest. He wanted that directed at him, not the psycho before her. "Christian, we will beat him. I promise you this. See how far you've come in seven months? You're now able to recall what you do during the spells and even fight him. I watched you hesitate a little bit ago and when you tackled me you should have crushed me. You didn't. See, we will beat him."

Christian snorted. "Is that before or after he uses one of us to kill you, Lorelei? I am a threat to you and shall remove myself from the premises. Change all of the access codes and give the information only to the females. It might be wise to section the males off and quarantine them again until the passing of the moons. His power weakens after that and will take some time to recover."

Lorelei shook her head. "No, Christian. You will stay with us. Your place is here."

"It's getting to the point that I'm over reacting to every tiny thing you do. I know that the elders arranged a marriage between us even though we both know it wasn't to be. I cannot replace Samson. Yet I can't stop the hate that burns when I think of you with another man. I want you to be happy, Lorelei. I do. Why am I suddenly jealous of every aspect of your life?" Christian cupped her cheek and Sevan wanted to beat him until he lost consciousness. "I will never forget waking to find you the way I did and I will never forget knowing it was I who caused it."

Nina moved forward fast and pushed him hard. "You did not cause anything. He could just as easily manipulate the men standing among us now and attack her. He picked you to prove a point. The man is a lunatic, Christian, and wants to make the biggest statement he can. Having you, the Chieftain, destroy Lorelei would be the ultimate irony. The only thing that could top that would be for Lorelei's true mate to arrive and slit her throat because he deemed it so."

Sevan stiffened.

Lorelei laughed. "Always a ray of light, aren't you, Nina?"

"I'm honest."

Jordan sighed. "Brutally so."

Everyone just stared at him. Nina cast him a dirty look and Jordan winked at her. For a moment Sevan thought she might actually punch Jordan. He wouldn't stop her. Seeing his brother get his ass kicked by a girl would be hilarious.

Christian nodded. "I shall take my leave of you all now."

Nina and Lorelei grabbed hold of him. Nina shook her head. "He can manipulate any man's thoughts at will. It is a risk we both know and watch for. We know that we are only truly safe with one another, carefully removed from the male population but we also know that these men he uses are our friends, brothers, husbands or fathers. They aren't monsters. They are people we love. Removing ourselves from them means he wins yet again."

Sevan glanced at Jordan and found him staring at Nina with possessiveness in his eyes. Was it possible that his brother was as taken by Nina as Sevan was with Lorelei? Could it be that fate had intervened and caused the rupture in the fuel tanks to get them here on purpose?

"Uhh, is there something we should know about?" Jordan asked, eyeing Nina carefully.

It was Lorelei who answered. "Nina, see to it that our men are aiding in the repair of their vessel and that they are stocked with food and any additional supplies they require. Captain, what is the ratio of females to males aboard your ship?"

Curious as to why her tone was now so cold, Sevan tipped his head and watched her carefully. "I believe it about seven to three, males being the majority. Why?"

Nina stared at him. "Alert your females that they are to watch their male crewmen carefully. It would be wise to suggest they go to a portion of your vessel that they can seal themselves in if need be. We have such locations here and they are most welcome to use them. I can assure you that the facilities are extremely comfortable and quite safe from attack."

"From attack? Watch the male crewmen? What the hell is going on here?"

Christian stepped forth. "My apologies for my lack of manners, Captain Sevan. I am Chieftain Christian Beauden. You have already met two of my head advisors, Lorelei and Nina Janelle. Nina is head of security and defense and Lorelei's skills do not have a particular label but it is safe to say she is a powerful leader among our people. While it is nice to have visitors among us this is not the best time. To explain it would take longer than you are permitted to be here. It is safe to say that should you or any of your men begin to feel a tugging, the slightest of mental pulls, perhaps a driving suggestion or urge then you should hand your weapon to the nearest female and back away fast. Notify whoever is closest that it has occurred and expect to be placed in restraints until it is clear you no longer pose a threat to anyone."

Sevan's mouth dropped open. "What? Neither I nor my men pose a threat to anyone who isn't trying to kill us."

"Captain," Christian said, softly. "As much as I would love to debate this matter with you, it's pointless. Do as I instructed or live with the knowledge that you may hurt or possibly murder someone against your will." Christian glanced at Lorelei. "From your responsiveness to Lorelei, my guess would be that you are a prime target for manipulation. Currently, it is Lorelei he wishes to destroy. That being said, no females are safe when he strikes so all males pose a risk."

"Who the hell is he and what do you mean prime target for manipulation?" Sevan asked, confused and concerned for Lorelei's safety. "I would never hurt her. I've thought she was a figment of my imagination for…." He stopped instantly, not wanting to reveal that he'd dreamed of her.

Lorelei locked gazes with him and his body tightened. "Captain, please do as Nina asked. I don't want anything to happen to you or your crew. Had your ship not been in such a dire state of need I would have had it escorted to the next planet over for your own safety. You and the people who have come with you are my responsibility to keep safe. I was the one who allowed you to dock. I never expected that Stegian and the others would attempt to strike out during the day. All I can ask is that you take every precaution necessary to assure your safety and that of your crew."

No longer did Sevan feel the need to argue for answers. The raw emotion in Lorelei's eyes told him that the steps were needed. He pressed the communicator chip on his waist and kept his eyes on Lorelei. "This is the Captain, all female personnel are to report to level two and are to lock it down at the first sign of trouble. No males are permitted on that level. Non-lethal force is permitted to ensure they stay off it. This remains in effect until a native female from this planet notifies you otherwise. Captain out."

Jordan moved forward. "Sevan, why in the hell are you only allowing females from here to tell them to come out?"

"Because he realizes that should any of you be compromised, himself included, that you would have access to the females and could possibly harm them," Lorelei said, as she teared up. "Thank you, Captain. Should the worst happen I can assure you that we will see them to safety and do everything within our power to break the hold on any males that have been used."

Nina glanced at Sevan and then Lorelei. "I think it best that we get them in and out as fast as possible. I can feel your energy circling them all, protecting them from Stegian. He's powerful, Lorelei. You can't keep that amount of energy up for an extended period and you know it. You already exude enough strength just to keep Christian semi-guarded at all times. You sleep longer than you should and eat less than needed. It's not healthy and our concern for you grows daily. If you fail and your personal shields crumble, he will have open access to your mind. I don't even want to imagine what he'll do to you. He hates us, Lorelei. But mostly, it's you he blames for not winning the last massive strike. And I think we all know that you are the first one he wants to see dead, Lorelei. In his eyes you pose the biggest threat."

"I will never submit willingly to him, Nina. I'll leave him no choice but to kill me."

"What?" Sevan asked, suddenly panicked.

Lorelei smiled. "Tell me, Captain, if you found yourself in hostile territory and in the enemy's hands would you submit to them or not?"

Sevan's brow creased. "No I wouldn't submit to them."

"Neither will I."

Sevan went to question this but stopped when Lorelei put her hands in the air and closed her eyes. Nina and Christian stiffened. Her breathing grew shallow as her lip began to tremble. She faced him fast. "No, he knows that offworlders are here. He fears this group for some reason," she said, staring at Sevan with wide eyes seeming to search for something. Her eyes flickered closed briefly and she gasped. "He believes that many mates for our people reside upon the vessel. He's not waiting for suns set to attack. He's doing it now."

A loud howling noise sounded all around them. Sevan watched as the women grabbed their sides, each one

PROJECT EXORCISM 39

touching weapons that were slightly different from his own. He grabbed his sidearm, uneasy about how close the animal sounded. "What was that?"

Lorelei and Nina exchanged weary glances and Christian moved in closer. "Nina, do a full security sweep of the perimeter and I'll double check that the compound computer system is still in operation. I don't want a repeat of last time."

Nina looked towards the corridor junction and put her hand out. A small panel slid back, revealing controls. "All guards on full alert. This is not a drill. I repeat. This is not a drill."

Christian nodded before turning to leave.

"Christian, wait," Lorelei said, taking a step closer to him. Sevan wanted to sweep her up in his arms and take her as far away from the blond Adonis as he could but he held back. He didn't expect to compete with a man who looked to be cast from stone. Sure, he was fit. In fact, he was rather bulky in the way of muscles too, but nowhere near Christian's size. "I'll check the computers. You know who you need to protect. Jacquelyn needs you near. I'll be fine and you know I can do it. Or at least get them all to spit blue sparks at me." She laughed softly and rubbed her cheek where the mark had been.

Nina stopped dead in her tracks, and spun around to face Lorelei. "Do you think that's wise, Lorelei?" There was an edge to her voice that told Sevan she knew damn well that it wasn't wise, but wasn't about to call her sister out on it in front of the group.

Red lights flashed in the hallway and an alarm went off. Nina shook her head. "We have a security breech."

"Captain Janelle, this is Until Leader Essen. I have three injured and one missing. We're in the fourteenth sector along back climate control boosters. We don't have a visual but they're near us," a voice said over the compound sound system.

"UL Essen, I'm on my way." Nina glanced at Christian and then Lorelei. "If they've made it that far they could make it to the education facility."

Lorelei gasped. "The children are still in session."

Nina nodded. "Christian and I will head to section fourteen. Lorelei, you'll need to check on the computer system. We'll cover the children." She lifted her hand toward the open panel. It was then that Sevan noticed the slight buzz in the air. "Jacquelyn, I know you're listening. Lock down your room and allow no one to enter until you are told otherwise."

Christian pushed past Nina and grabbed Lorelei's arm. "Promise that you'll be careful. You know what he's after and what he will do to get to you."

Sevan saw the array of emotions move over Lorelei's face and knew that whatever came out of her mouth would be a lie. He felt so connected with her and he didn't even know her. It was unnerving to say the least. "I promise. Be careful."

The large man ran off in the other direction and Sevan noticed that Nina had left as well. He looked at his brother and found him staring off in the direction Nina had gone. "Stay here and supervise the repairs and our men."

"What are you going to do?" Jordan asked.

Sevan met Lorelei's gaze and smiled. "I'm planning on going with her to check the compound's computer systems and see to the children's safety."

"Right. Then I'm going with Nina and Christian," Jordan replied.

Chapter Five

Lorelei ran down the corridor, followed closely by Sevan. Why she'd let the outsider follow her was still unclear. She should have ordered them off the planet, or never allowed them to dock in the first place. Her instincts had been right. This was no place for them. It wasn't a place for anyone.

"How much farther?" Sevan yelled over the sound of the alarm.

She slowed her pace and let him catch up to her. Reaching out, she touched his arm lightly. The compulsion to just feel his skin had been on her since she'd first laid eyes on him. Part of her still couldn't believe that the man she'd dreamt of for the last six months was real, the other part wanted to test just how real he truly was.

Sevan moved in closer to her, dwarfing her frame. At five foot six, she wasn't short but he seemed to tower over her. His mouth twitched and it took everything in her not to touch his full lips. She wasn't used to men like him, men who ran around in full officer fatigues and who didn't have hair as long as hers. Christian hardly ever wore a shirt, more often than not opting only for a vest for warmth. Her people tried to wear the least amount of clothes, leaving their protective markings free to do what they were created to do--heal, guard, and draw power from the land.

Sevan looked down at her hand on his arm and ran his finger, lightly over the first of her faint markings. "Did it hurt?" He asked, taking yet another step closer to her. "Getting these tattoos ... did it hurt?"

She knew what tattoos were. She'd studied enough about the human culture and Earth to understand, and her markings weren't tattoos. "They aren't what you think they are."

"You're beautiful ... errr ... I mean they're beautiful."

Smiling, Lorelei studied Sevan closely, not wanting to feel anything for him but failing miserably. Too many nights he'd come in the form of dreams and had taken her to levels of ecstasy that she couldn't just turn a blind eye.

"Thank you. We're all born with them. Each person's means something else. Some declare their owner to be a warrior. Others mean scholar, healer, leader and so on. The list is endless. Many of the markings are forms of protection or good wishes. They come from the Shamenian side of my ancestry."

"What do yours mean?" Sevan asked, moving closer to her.

"A number of things. These," she pointed at her upper arm, "are for my status. These announce that I am supposedly wise although the burn on my cheek would likely state otherwise. The ones on my torso are blessings for fertility and pleasure."

Sevan's breath caught. "So, the marks are some form of population control, too?"

Lorelei couldn't help but smile. "Trust an outsider to simplify it for us."

"So, I'm right?"

Shrugging, Lorelei lifted her tiny vest a bit, revealing even more of her faint markings. "In a way. My markings in particular tell that the gods and spirits of the land will offer the blessing of children when the pairing is with my mate. In short, if they up and decide I found Mr. Right there is no means of population control that will prevent me from conceiving a child."

He took a step back as though she were contagious. "Oh."

"Relax. I'm not any different than a full blooded human female. I can't get pregnant by breathing the same air as you. Coupling is no different for my people than yours. Though we know fairly quickly when we are with child. The marks either disappear or change significantly."

Something moved over Sevan's face. His eyes narrowed. "Would anything else make them disappear?"

"I honestly don't know. It changes with each individual. I've seen some people's fade when they meet their significant other and then completely disappear when they conceive a child. They do return in some fashion, be it a tiny mark on a thigh to a full blown return."

Lorelei took a moment to laugh softly at Sevan's facial expression. He appeared so caught up in their discussion that she worried his forehead would remain permanently crinkled. "Don't quote me on any of this. Like I said, everyone is different. Take me for instance. Six months ago my markings were several shades darker. One morning I woke up to find them faded to what you see before you now."

"Six months ago?" Sevan asked, his voice cracking slightly.

"I understand that to you they may appear a bit off-putting but to our people they're not only important but a thing of beauty. In my eyes, it's odd to not see the markings on you. Here, when a man bears no markings declaring him a Shamenian he is considered the enemy until he proves otherwise."

"Lorelei, they are anything but off-putting. They're captivating." His warm thumb ran over the circular sign for power near her wrist and she felt her magic rise up. Knowing that not all outsiders possessed the same gifts as her people, she tried to pull her arm away, but it was too late. The power within her surged forth.

Images from the reoccurring dreams she had poured forth along with pictures of things that were altogether new. Lorelei's body jerked with each vivid picture of Sevan thrusting himself into her, his hand cupping the back of her neck as she rode him. Her pussy quaked with need and dampened as her mind shot to images of him nibbling on her breasts, taking each nipple in his mouth and spending equal time teasing them. Her knees went out from under her as yet another image hit her, this one of him buried deep within her, releasing his seed.

Strong arms wrapped around her, keeping her from hitting the floor. She blinked, the visions finally fading away and found herself staring into intense green eyes.

Sevan looked down at her. "What...?"

Lorelei tried to regain her footing, but her inner thighs still twitched as though from the orgasm the vision brought on. "I'm sorry. I think I might be coming down with something."

"Something that involved us fucking?" Sevan shook his head as though he were trying to absorb all that was going on. "The dreams were real weren't they? You had them too. Didn't you?"

Her mouth opened, but no sound came out. The thought of him sharing one of her visions and her dreams was absurd. Not even Christian could do that and he was the greatest Shaman they'd ever had.

Sevan brought his mouth to her neck and let his hot breath move over her skin as he spoke. "Is that really what it feels like to be inside you? I gotta tell you, baby, you are all that I think about. Tell me that I'm not the only one having the dreams."

Lorelei averted her gaze. "You're not."

The feel of his warm lips on her neck made her sigh as her breasts heaved upwards. "What's happening to me? Is it your doing? Did you invade my head so I'd come here and help you?"

"No," Lorelei said fast, hurt that Sevan would suggest such a thing. She tried to pull away but he held tight to her. "Let go. None of this was my doing. I would never lure anyone into this situation. Especially not someone that I...."

"That you let sample every inch of your body? That you let fuck you so many ways that I lost count? Is that it, Lorelei?"

"Stop it." She pushed lightly on him, not wanting to harm him in any way but hating his accusations. Knowing it was for the best, Lorelei focused on putting a wall between them, hardening herself to him so she could send Sevan on his way and not die of a broken heart. Finding out he was real only to have to send him away already ripped at her gut. Letting him love her in the flesh would kill her. "Get away from me. They were just dreams. They meant nothing. I need to see to it my people are safe. Go back to your own kind, fix your ship and leave."

"Don't," he whispered, brushing his lips over her neck. "I'm not sure what to think. My ship, which has passed every inspection with flying colors, suddenly has more problems than I can count when we're passing by your planet. I radio for assistance only to find the woman who has invaded my dreams staring back at me. Now, I'm told that I might be used by some madman to hurt her. This is too much for any one person to absorb. Don't pull away from me just because I questioned it aloud. I need to understand what's going on."

Lorelei shook her head slightly, still needing to put distance between them. "How can I give you answers to things I don't even understand? All I know is that he believes your vessel contains our mates or potential mates." She glanced towards the gray wall not wanting to reveal it all to him but finding it hard to leave important pieces of information out. "Stegian believes you are my mate. He made sure to leak that to me when he was scanning the facility to pinpoint our location. That means he will either attack you to draw me out or use you to attack me."

Sevan snorted. "I won't hurt you." He didn't go into detail on the subject of her being his mate and that scared her. Did he not mean his vows? Did he want to take his claim back? He was human, so he could. And why would the fates give her a human mate? Why not a supernatural to match her strength and speed?

Lorelei closed her eyes and thought hard about all of the human customs, words and phrases she'd been taught of as a child. "Umm, he thinks you're my soul mate. I can't change that and trust me, Sevan. If he decides to use you to hurt me there will be nothing you can do to stop him."

"What? Some insane guy believes there is this one perfect person for everyone and that I'm yours?" Disbelief laced his voice, causing Lorelei's heart to feel heavy. "That's it. I'm heading back to my ship. This is a little too convenient for my taste. You show up out of the blue. Invade my dreams. Let me claim you and make me fall in love with you. Whatever game you're playing ends here, baby."

He loves me? He really does?

Lorelei took a moment to collect herself knowing she had to send Sevan away for his own good. "Wonderful, go. I'm almost sorry that you aren't here to loot us. At least then I'd have started out with low expectations."

"I'm out of here," he said, turning to head in the other direction.

Something howled loudly, signifying just how close it truly was to them. The compound walls were thick. That meant it was just outside of it. The second Sevan stopped dead in his tracks, Lorelei's body tensed. "Go. You're sick of my game and I'm sick of you. I'm glad the nightmares of you have ended." It was harsh and a lie but she needed him to go for his own safety.

Sevan glanced back over his shoulder at her, his eyes betraying his words. He was worried and her powers allowed her to sense that his concern was for her. As heartwarming as that was, he couldn't be allowed to stay.

Aiming her weapon directly at him, Lorelei drew in a deep breath as she stared down the barrel. "Captain, you are to report back to your vessel immediately. I hereby revoke your status of honorable guest. You are no longer permitted to roam freely. Do as I say or...."

"Or what? You'll shoot me in the back?" he asked, his voice low, his eyes still locked on her. "Is that what you do to someone you've spent how many nights with? Is that what you do to a man you allowed to take you as his wife, even if it was only a dream? Is that how you return affection, Lorelei? The second we meet in the flesh you threaten to shoot me?"

Closing her eyes, Lorelei thought of all the nights they'd spent together. The memory of Sevan declaring his love for her, claiming her, had plagued her for two weeks straight. Every second of not being with him had chipped away at her heart. Now, as she held a weapon on him, shame filled her. She couldn't shoot him. Raising her weapon high, she let off the trigger and sighed. "Sevan."

"Was it all a lie, Lorelei?" His green eyes stayed locked on her. "I have to know."

"No," she said, shocked by her own admission.

A wolfish grin appeared on his face. It faded away quickly as another howl filled the air. Sevan moved to her quickly and pulled her behind him. "Stay close."

The thought of Sevan going up against an enemy such as the one waiting for them made her smile. "Excuse me, Captain, but I think it's you who had better stay close to me."

Lorelei didn't wait for his comeback. Putting the code in to open the exterior door, she shook her head. The door opened. Sevan tried to push in front of her, but she held her weapon out towards him and arched a brow. "Want to see if your charm works two times in a row? I should warn you that I have no problem setting my weapon to knock you out rather than watch you kill yourself by running head first into a situation you have not been briefed on."

He froze.

Smart man.

She handed the weapon to him butt first and nodded. Shaking his head no, he touched his own sidearm. It was a cute thought, but unless he was packing ammunition with liquid silver nitrate in it, he might as well walk out unarmed. Her people had spent years synthesizing it for protective purposes since it had first arrived with the humans long ago. Lorelei thrust her weapon into his hand. He tried to hand it back to her. She growled. He smiled. Instantly, she caught the scent of a lion shifter as Sevan touched her arm lightly. It wasn't exuding a smell indicating dominance and danger it was more of a sexual calling.

Confused, Lorelei's brow furrowed as she stared at Sevan. A slow lazy smile remained plastered to his handsome face. "Something the matter?"

Placing her finger to her lips to indicate the need for silence, Lorelei shook her head no and pulled her pant leg up. Sevan gave her a suggestive look and glanced downward. When he caught sight of her backup weapon, he nodded his head and squeezed her arm gently. Tiny shockwaves of desire radiated from beneath his fingertips and Lorelei had to concentrate hard on listening to their surroundings. Something was close and if she didn't stop ogling the outsider, they'd be too dead to act on their mutual feelings.

Another howl sounded and Sevan attempted to push past her. Grabbing his arm, she pulled him back to her and nodded in the direction of the nearest line of black bark trees. The yellow leaves that draped down provided enough coverage to make it difficult to see very far beyond the first couple of rows. A shadowy figure moved around and Lorelei knew what it was. She could only guess how many of them had actually come to test the strength of their safeguards.

"There has been a breach in section twelve," Christian said over the intercom.

Sevan leaned down and moved in close to her. "Where's section twelve?"

Putting her mouth against his ear, she noticed how tiny flecks of white ran through his otherwise jet sandy blond. "You're standing in it."

Sensing the presence of something evil before she saw it, Lorelei grabbed her backup weapon from her ankle and spun around fast. She let off two shots. A large brown blur appeared out of nowhere and crashed down just outside of the doorway.

"It's a wolf!" Sevan shouted. He pulled on her shoulders as she headed towards the large creature. "It's the biggest damn wolf I've ever seen. My gods, it's as big as me."

It was Lorelei's turn to give him a suggestive look and she did. His gaze met hers briefly, before she concentrated on the bulge in the front of his pants. Licking her lips, she brushed her hair out of her face and turned her attention back to the creature on the ground. The fact that it didn't shift into human form told her that it was a hybrid--one of Stegian's new breeds of fighting 'machines'.

* * * *

"Devi!" someone shouted.

Sevan spun around quickly with the weapon that Lorelei had equipped him with drawn. He centered it on the two men running towards Lorelei. Their eyes were wide as they caught a look at the scene before them.

"Are you hurt?" one asked, as they slowed their pace.

Lorelei stepped in front of him and put her hand out towards the wolf on the ground. The men stopped instantly. "Please inform the Chieftain that the threat has been eliminated. I'll need you both to stand watch here for any more. I'm not sensing any, but Stegian's tricks have gotten to us before." The way her voice trailed off at the end left Sevan wondering who this Stegian was and why the hell he had mutant wolves attacking his woman.

My woman? The thought of that made him smile. She would be his, of that he was sure.

"As you wish, Devi," they said in unison, bowing their heads slightly.

Devi?

Lorelei took him by the arm and the men gasped. He tried to jerk away, afraid that he'd somehow violated something sacred to them but Lorelei yanked him to her.

Damn, she's strong.

In an instant, she had his face cupped in her hands and was pulling his lips towards hers. Hearing the men's shocked responses, he tried to stop her, but he was too late.

Her full lips met his and the world around him was lost. The only feeling left was that of Lorelei's lush body pressed tightly to his. His cock throbbed and his body ached to toss her to the ground and ravish her. When she raked her nails lightly down his back, he groaned in her mouth.

She pulled back slowly, leaving his lips tingling. He dared a sideways glance at the men who'd arrived and found them with one knee on the ground and their heads bent. He looked at Lorelei and she smiled down at the men.

"You shall act as my witnesses."

"Yes, Devi," They answered, rising slowly to their feet. They looked at him and for a second Sevan almost checked to see if he'd sprouted markings as well.

Lorelei bit at his lower lip, leaving his cock twitching and his body aching to find release in her. Bending down to meet her head on, Sevan gave into the urge to pick her up. Being face to face with her only made his hunger grow. Now, the need to fuck her actually bordered on painful. "I need to be in you."

Pulling back slightly, Lorelei pushed on his chest and dropped to her feet. She glanced at the men before them and smiled. "Bear witness that this man is not my mate."

An uncontrollable urge to peel his shirt off hit him. It was so spontaneous that Sevan gave into it without a fight. He pulled his black shirt over his head and turned his backs to the men, hoping to get Lorelei to speak with him alone. The men gasped.

Lorelei's smile faded. "What is it?"

Sevan noticed her markings fading before his eyes to the point they were almost gone and his breath hitched. "Lorelei?"

"What?"

"Say you were to find that mate of yours and things were to happen, you know, progress further."

Lorelei cast a wary look at him. "You mean we fuck?"

"Yeah, that will do. Say you were to find him and be intimate with him. How long would it take for your markings to fade?"

"I don't know. I've seen them fade instantly on women who simply stand next to their mates. I imagine they would...." She stopped suddenly and looked down at herself. Her blue eyes widened. "No. You can't be him."

Slightly offended, Sevan raked his hot gaze over her tight body. "Why not?"

"Because you're human and ... and, well I don't know why but there is no way that you are my mate. Stegian and gods who brought us into the same dream plane are all mad."

"Hold on," Sevan said, putting his hand up. "What do you mean dream plane? Are you telling me that," he stared at her stomach and watched as the circular markings there began to regain their color quickly, "Lorelei, what does that mean?"

She followed his gaze and covered her mouth fast. Shaking her head, she tried to run past him. Not wanting to let her out of his sight, Sevan grabbed her arm and pulled her to him being careful not to harm her. "No. You will stay here and answer my questions."

"No. You don't understand. I have to get to Christian." Lorelei's blue eyes stayed glued to her stomach.

"Why?"

One of the men stood quickly and came to her. He stared at her stomach in awe. "Devi, the legends are true."

"What legends?"

The men looked at Sevan with nothing short of wonder in his eyes. "The legends that speak of the powerful ones being given great signs when the time came for them to reproduce the next line of leaders." He pointed at Lorelei's stomach. "The symbols stand for fertility. When brought out as they are now, it means that now is the time that she is most fertile. Her body thirsts for the seed of her mate."

Sevan let the man's words sink in. "Why in the hell are you trying to get to Christian?"

She looked at him like he was insane. Since the thought that she might be had crossed his mind, he let it go. "Captain...."

"Call me Sevan, Lorelei. I think we're way past pleasantries."

"Fine. Sevan, I need to get to him so that he can assure the coming of the next line of leaders. It's not something that should require an explanation."

Instantly, it felt as though Sevan had been kicked in the chest. The idea of Lorelei running to another man to give her a child not only sickened him, it infuriated him. "You will not let any other man touch you. You are mine. I have spent six months loving you and I am not about to let you lie with another man."

The two men gasped and stared at him with wide eyes.

Lorelei shook her head. "Don't give him that look. He's not my mate. He can't be my mate."

One of the men moved behind Sevan and touched his upper right shoulder blade. "Look, Devi. He carries you on him."

"Huh?" he and Lorelei said.

Turning his head, Sevan strained to see what the man was pointing at. "How is my tattoo of a woman with a black panther painted on her leg lying cuddled with a lion a symbol of Lorelei?"

Lorelei lunged at him, twisting him around fast and making a noise that was a cross between a yelp and a cry. "Bollacks! Get the Chieftain now. Tell him that he'll need to perform a bond breaking ceremony immediately. Sevan cannot be permitted to stay on our planet any longer than necessary and I'm not about to allow him to remain bonded to me any longer than necessary."

"Bonded?" Sevan asked.

"Would you stop asking so many questions? I'm trying to fix this."

"Hey, lady, don't start yelling at me because I don't understand your lingo for soul mate haven here. I'm just trying to get by. You know, friendly alien relations."

Lorelei snorted. "Bloody hell, if I'm an alien what are you? Oh, I know. A lower life form."

"A lower life form? Is that why you keep saying human like it's a dirty word? Do you think you're better than us?" Sevan asked, his anger with her growing but somehow channeling into the need for sex. "I saw your little magick trick in the corridor Lorelei. You may be gifted but you aren't the only one with special qualities, honey."

"Are you trying to tell me something, Sevan?" Lorelei arched a brow. "I'm all ears. Are you ready to tell me why in my dreams I just knew something was different about you, that there was something more? When you bit me, it was with the teeth of a shifter, not a man. Yet, when you set foot on my planet I sense nothing more than human in you. How is that?"

"Because I told you once already, Lorelei. I am not full-blooded. I carry a small bit of lion DNA in me. I don't know how the hell I shifted in the dream. But I can tell you this. From the moment I entered your atmosphere the beast I carry in me has wanted out. It's wanted to destroy Christian for daring to touch you and it's wanted to fuck you as bad as I have. So you can check that holier than thou attitude at the door, sweetheart."

The men exchanged knowing looks and smiled. "It's good to see that you and your mate love one another."

Sevan stared at the men, unsure if he wanted to shoot them or hug them for bringing the love word up.

Lorelei shook her head, sending black tendrils cascading over her shoulders. "We are not mates and we are not in love. We only just met and he's leaving very shortly." She pushed past him fast, nearly knocking him over.

She's really fucking strong.

Rushing up behind her, Sevan turned her to face him and stared into her blue eyes. "I'm not going anywhere. Do you mean to tell me that by claming you in the dream, I've claimed you in real life? Are we husband and wife?"

She let out a soft laugh. "All evidence is proving that theory though I personally think it's ridiculous. If you were able to successfully claim me in a dream why is it that I didn't end up with child? It's not like we didn't join enough. Bloody hell, I've lost track of the amount of times we spent the night banging away."

Walking into her, Sevan forced her against the hallway wall, pinning her in place so he could speak to her without fear of her running. He didn't have all the answers but he did know that he loved her. "I'll admit that I'm a little lost here. I don't have all that great knowledge of the dream plane things like you do. I do, however, know that you are in no way, shape or form allowing another man to touch you. I told you once already, you are mine, Lorelei. My woman. My love. My mate. And my wife, if we believe that what happened in our dreams is real. I believe, Lorelei. I fully believe that I took you in my arms, marked you while I offered you my seed, my essence, making you my mate. I'll do it again right now if it will make everyone feel better but you said it yourself, your markings began to fade six months ago. That is the exact time that the dreams started. I am your mate and you are mine. I'm the one who will handle what you need, not some muscle bound guy with hair like a girl. I am the man who will plant the seed deep within...." As the words fell from his lips, Sevan's body tightened along with his stomach.

One look at Lorelei told him that she was as shocked by his declaration as he was. She shook her head. "Take it back, now!"

"It is too late, Devi. We have borne witness to the marks and the gods' sign but have also heard his vows to you. It is official."

"No, it is not. You can't count that. He's an outsider. A cocky one at that." She tossed her hands in the air. "There is no way that can count. He didn't know what he was doing."

"What did I do?" Sevan asked, concern still gripping his stomach.

"You stated before witnesses that you claim her with a bond in place." The man was so matter-of-fact about it that Sevan actually felt a little slow not getting it.

"Huh?"

Lorelei glared at him. "Tell them you didn't understand what you were doing and we can get this taken care of. I want to keep you for a husband like I want a gabaetion rash."

Sevan balked. "You would rather have a flesh eating rash devouring you than be my wife?"

The realization of what he'd just said hit him hard. Joy tore through him. "I'm your...? You're my...? We're...?"

"Married, yeah, now that you're up to speed can you take it back? I need to find Christian and...."

Sevan dropped his lips down on hers, rendering her silent as his tongue did what it wanted to do, memorize her mouth. He heard the sound of the exterior door closing and planted his palms on the wall along the sides of Lorelei's head. She tasted so sweet that it was intoxicating. The more she wiggled against him the stiffer his dick became.

"Sevan, please," she whispered, sliding her tongue over his lower lip. The small action told him how much she wanted what he wanted. If that was true they'd both be very happy very soon. The idea of waiting another moment to touch her, to take her was ludicrous.

Chuckling into her mouth, Sevan continued his invasion of her mouth, not caring who watched him do it. He inched his fingers down her arms and over her smooth stomach. Aching to be in her, he went for the top of her pants, no longer able to wait or take it slow. The tops of his fingers grazed the tiny thatch of black hair he knew she possessed and need slammed throughout him. His pulse sped while his body tightened. "I need to be in you, Lorelei."

Instantly, her body began to heat up, so much so that Sevan had to take a step back. As soon as he opened his mouth to question her, some sort of power shot forth from her, hitting the wolf on the ground and lifting it high into the air. Sevan watched in awe as it burst into a ball of red fire before vanishing. He would have questioned her on it but he already knew she was beyond special. She was magnificent.

"There," she said, lowering her blue gaze and smiling with wanton wonderment. "Now we're alone."

"Mmm, have anything special in mind?"

Lorelei's tongue slid out and over her lower lip, teasing him to the point the beast within threatened to rise. Doing his best to hold it down, not liking the surge of power it seemed to now carry with it, Sevan took a step closer to her. He couldn't fight the desire. He didn't want to.

She smiled. "You should let me go, Sevan. Christian has understood that when the time was right he'd be the one to fill me with his seed and that we would have a child together. It doesn't matter what my feelings or his are. All that matters is that our kind be able to once again conceive children. We are a dying race, Sevan. Please."

He clenched his fists, doing his best to squelch the beast within. It had never been this strong or this close to the surface in his waking hours. "Lorelei, you are mine. And I don't share my things with anyone."

"I'm a thing?"

"You're my wife."

Shaking her head, she moved in even closer, running her hands over his bare chest. "Sevan, you can renounce it in front of witnesses and be free of me--of this place."

The idea of taking his claim back was absurd. "No. You are mine forever, Lorelei."

She bit her lower lip as tears welled in her eyes. "If I don't get to Christian soon the window of my fertility may close, Sevan. I can't let that happen and I sure in the hell cannot allow you to father a child with me only to leave. In the end it will be Christian who raises the child so it should be he who fathers it," she said, whispering the last part so softly that Sevan knew that she didn't believe her own words. She wanted him but had been conditioned to believe that if the time came she should run to another.

Growling out, Sevan pulled at Lorelei's vest, freeing her ample breasts to him. He cupped one harder than he should but he didn't care. She needed to hear him. "Lorelei, I am not going anywhere. I've spent six months thinking I was going mad. Thinking I was in love with a dream. Now that I've found you, I'm never letting you go. If you decide that here is where you want to be then here is where I'll stay. No man but me will raise my child and trust me when I say it will be my child that grows in you."

"Sevan," she whispered, raking her fingernails over his skin, sending his cock into duress. It needed in her soon. "It's too deadly here for you."

"Do you want me to go? Do you want to push me out of your life?"

"No."

Exhaling, Sevan rolled her nipple between his thumb and first finger. "I'm not going anywhere, baby. When the ship is fixed Jordan can take it over."

"You'd say goodbye to your brother so easily?"

He shook his head. "It won't be easy but I can't leave my mate behind. I can't. Especially not since she'll be carrying my child in her very soon." Dipping his head down, he captured her nipple with his mouth and moaned.

* * * *

Stegian raked his nails over his desk, channeling the fury that burned inside him. The Janelle girl had managed to elude him yet again, this time finding her true mate. The moment he'd sensed the vessel enter the atmosphere he knew it had begun. Endless dreams of the Janelles mating, growing stronger in both strength and number as they mated one by one. Seven in all, he had never assumed he'd have so much grief over the only three who remained on the planet.

They were nothing more than women. Their brothers had been forced into exile long ago, leaving them defenseless. Well, all except for the Chieftain and his brothers. Samson had taken some effort to sway but when he finally managed to find his weakness, Lorelei, he broke the man quickly. The nameless, faceless elders--the ones who managed to exist beyond his grasp had deemed Samson worthy of Lorelei's hand should her mate not show himself. No one held out much hope of finding their one true mate on Sargaidia. Its sister planet, Margaidia was more a vacation paradise, held under tight control by the Commission.

Having crashed aboard a Project Exorcism vessel over a hundred and fifty years ago, Stegian had reveled in the fact that the planet's natural resources began to immediately enhance his already superhuman qualities. No longer requiring daily feedings, Stegian could go for extended periods of time and not lose his strength or powers. Being both a vampire and a sorcerer had left him in need of replenishing his system often while on Earth.

The human officials who had come to an agreement with the traitorous heads of the supernatural committee never planned on an accident throwing their vessel off course and they never planned on how much stronger the supernaturals would be on account of it.

Sensing Lorelei's power riding the air, Stegian narrowed his eyes and sought to connect with her mentally again. He'd been doing it on and off for six months each time managing to stay a bit longer before she noticed he was there. In his mind he could see her mate, his blond hair and green eyes staring down at her as he caressed her body slowly.

The smell of arousal managed to transcend the distance between Stegian and Lorelei, allowing him to catch the scent of her damp pussy. Need slammed through him and his dick hardened instantly. She and her sister, the captain of the Shamenian guards had always made his cock thirst to be buried in them. Now, as he stayed linked to her, viewing the events in third person, Stegian couldn't help but reach down into his pants and stroke his rapidly growing erection.

"Yunoc," he called out, knowing his loyal servant would come immediately.

He heard him standing quietly behind him but didn't bother to turn around. "Bring me one of the Shamenian mixed females we have. I want one with black hair and an appetite for rough sex."

"Yes, Master."

Stegian concentrated on Lorelei again, mentally tracing the contours of her body, wishing it was he touching her now not that dreaded Commission Captain whom he'd tried desperately to block from her dreams with no success. The man slid his hand down the front of Lorelei's pants and cupped her mound. Stegian could almost taste the cream the smell was so great.

Warm hands moved over his arm and he knew the woman he'd sent Yunoc for had arrived. Looking up, he smiled as he found her wearing nothing but a collar. Being part wolf and part Shamenian left her an outcast in both worlds. Stegian knew she'd have been better off staying with her own kind but when he'd first spotted her, he had to have her. The female reminded him of Lorelei and Nina, making her a perfect bed partner when the mood struck him.

Taking hold of her waist, he pulled her before him, still sitting in his chair and still smelling Lorelei's cream. He stared into the female's well maintained black thatch between her thighs and snapped out at it, not biting but wanting to. Parting her folds, Stegian leaned forward and licked her, instantly picturing Lorelei's pussy before him. Not the woman there now. "Mmm, you taste sinfully delicious."

When Stegian watched the Captain before Lorelei drop to his knees, pull her pants down and mimic Stegian's actions he couldn't hide his joy. The man was sensing his presence and reacting to Stegian's lead.

Wanting to test the theory, Stegian pushed two fingers into the slut before him and began thrusting them into her with superhuman speed. The Captain followed suit. Still wanting to push it further to know for sure, Stegian stood fast, licked the cream from his fingers and immediately spun the woman around. Grabbing her hips, he bent her over exposing the globes of her ass to him.

He freed himself from the confines of his pants and fisted his cock. The Captain continued to do exactly as Stegian did. He rubbed the head of his penis over the female's wet core twice before grasping her hair and ramming himself to the hilt in her. She screamed out and tried to get away from him. Tightening his hold on her, he kept her in place. Slowly, her tight channel loosened for him and she began to rock back onto his dick.

"Do you like that, slut?" he asked, shocked to hear the Captain ask Lorelei the same question.

Lorelei nodded as best she could, moaning and arching her back, leaving Stegian drilling into the female before him, fucking his desires away and not caring how rough he was. The woman didn't seem to mind. She continued to cream on his shaft as he fucked her and began to knead her fingers into her thighs, panting as she went.

"Yes. Take it, slut. Take it."

He fucked her harder, bending her over more, exposing the pink rosette of her ass to him. The need to take it hit him hard. Knowing that he couldn't let Lorelei's mate spill his seed into her, Stegian pulled his cock free from the female's pussy and pressed it into her ass quickly, allowing her little to no time to prepare for it. She bucked against him, taking the full, massive length of him into her tight ass.

It felt too good to stop. It wasn't the woman from his never ending harem bent over before him in his mind. No. To Stegian it was Lorelei's ass he was in. He searched out and to his shock found the Captain still fucking her pussy, still thrusting into her. Each of them panted as they stay locked together. The second Stegian saw the Captain reaching around to tweak Lorelei's clit, he let his rage out.

"No! Obey me. Pull out and do not release your seed into her."

"Master?" the woman before him asked, sounding as though his dick was filling her to the point she bordered on pain.

"Speak only when spoken to." Unable to stop himself, Stegian continued to thrust into her, enjoying the feel of her tight passageway around his shaft.

"Pull out!"

PROJECT EXORCISM 59

The captain ignored his command. Infuriated, Stegian thrust harder, needing to find the ever elusive release he thought sure would come. As the smell of Lorelei hitting her peak hit him, Stegian gave into the need to ejaculate, instantly bathing the woman in his come. It was then he knew that the captain, Lorelei's true mate was filling her with his seed, fertilizing the egg that had come forth demanding his seed.

Raking his dagger-like finger nails down the female's back, Stegian smiled as she cried out. Pulling his dick free from her, he turned her quickly and bent her over his desktop. The blood that welled to the surface on her back called to him. He dropped his face down and lapped it up slowly. Stegian's cock returned to a need of sex almost instantly as the blood of the woman filled his veins, breathing new life into him.

In mere seconds he had his cock shoved back into her ass as he bent down, licking her wounds. It was exactly what he liked--a fuck and a suck. As a vampire there was no greater high. Well, the Janelle sisters would certainly improve that.

Stegian focused on the female before him, breaking away from Lorelei just as she began to sense him. "I shall deal with you later. Know that I will not permit a child to be born from you."

* * * *

Lorelei's head snapped up as she felt the presence of evil all around them. Holding tight to Sevan's thigh, she continued to feel him coming in spurts deep within her, fertilizing the egg that her power assured her was there. "Sevan?"

Running his hand over her low abdomen, Sevan sighed in her ear. "I'm sorry our first time was like this, Lorelei. I couldn't seem to stop myself. The need to be in you was unlike anything I've ever felt before."

Every alarm bell in her went off. Stegian. It was his presence she'd sensed. "He touched your mind, Sevan."

"Who touched my ... oh, gods. That's why I wanted to pull out in mid thrust and ram my cock into your...." He stopped in mid-sentence.

"Into my what?"

Sevan hugged her tight to his chest. His cock was still in her, partially sated but there all the same. "I had the strongest urge to pull out and come in your ass."

Lorelei nodded as she drew in a deep breath. "He didn't want you to release your semen into me. The last thing he wants is another generation of Janelles standing in his way of owning everyone on this planet."

"It was hard to resist, Lorelei. All I could think about was missing our window of opportunity for a child together. I couldn't do it. I couldn't give that up. Not when you want it so bad. Hell, I want it too. I want a life with you. I want a family. There is no way in hell that some crazed lunatic with some half cocked gift of mind control is going to stop that."

It hit Lorelei then. Sevan had stood up to Stegian without even knowing it. Somehow he'd managed to keep from falling completely under his spell. If he'd found a way then that meant the others might be able to as well. "You did it. You blocked him from taking full control."

"No. I didn't allow him to take my chances at a family with you, Lorelei. That's all I did."

He didn't understand. He couldn't. Sevan wasn't raised with the fear of Stegian in him. No. She understood that and she almost felt sorry that he couldn't appreciate what an accomplishment he'd achieved.

Opening her mouth to comment, Lorelei stopped when her stomach cramped. She took hold of it, cradled it tight and cried out as heat flared through it. Sevan's hand which still rested on her lower abdomen pulled her back into him more.

"Baby, what's wrong? Why are you so hot?"

Lorelei glanced down and watched her markings fading fast. "Oh gods, Sevan."

"What?" he asked, sounding as panicked as she felt.

"It worked."

"What worked?"

Placing her hand over his, she smiled. "We created life."

He held her so tight that Lorelei thought she might burst. The feel of Sevan's large arms wrapped around her and the sense that he was as happy if not happier than her made it all perfect. Granted, being bent over outside and fucked hard and fast wasn't how she envisioned their first meeting to be but in truth, this wasn't their first time together. Six month's worth of dreams had placed them in one another's arms more times than she could count.

Holding tight to her husband's hand, Lorelei let it all sink in. "You're here. You're real and you're here."

"And I'm not going anywhere, honey. I promise you that."

Chapter Six

"Yeah, back at you, lady," Jordan bit out glaring at Nina as she stormed off in the other direction. Her tight little ass sashayed even though she struck him as a woman who would never do it on purpose. Naturally sexy and everything his cock could hope to dive into, the woman could bring him to his knees if she tried hard enough. Christian laughed and Jordan snarled. "What's so funny?"

"I have not seen Nina take a real interest in a member of the opposite sex ever."

"She's into women?" The thought, while exciting, worried Jordan. He'd already made a fool out of himself by opening his mouth and inserting his foot when he suggested that someone with breasts was hardly qualified to lead an army but the idea of Nina not even giving him a second thought because he had a penis scared him even more.

Christian laughed again. It seemed to be what he'd done most since they'd gone to assure themselves that the children were safe. "Jordan, she more than likes men. The problem is, Nina views them as disposable. She can bed one and move onto the next. She has unlimited access to the unmated males and they adore her."

He swallowed hard at the implication that Nina fucked her entire army. "She hasn't, um…?"

Christian pulled a box of tools down from the cargo bay container and arched a sandy blond brow. "If you are asking if Nina has pleasured the entire legion of men under her command the answer is no. Even she needs to pace herself." The smirk on his face told Jordan he was kidding but that didn't stop the jealous streak that threatened to consume him.

"Have you been with her?"

"No."

Jordan kept a close eye on Christian, hoping to get to know him better. There was something about the man that screamed powerful yet he hadn't tried to use that on any of them yet. "Have you been with Lorelei?"

Christian stilled and Jordan knew the answer to his question. Christian had indeed been intimate with Lorelei. It would kill his brother to know that but if Jordan had to guess, Sevan already knew and didn't like it one bit. "Lorelei and I have a unique relationship. It is difficult to explain to an outsider. Our customs and ways, while similar to that of humans, are not the same."

"Meaning you've not only fucked her, you've done it many times."

"She is to be my wife as decided by the elders and that is all I am willing to offer on the matter at the moment. Let us see to your ship. So far, the reports coming in from our FST department are bleak."

"Yeah, one of my Lt. Commanders gave me the abridged version of your Fleet Support Team's analysis. Our own system dialogistic matches and I have to agree it's not looking so good." As Jordan looked out at Alpha Brig Three, he shook his head and sighed. "The air compression chambers in all space pod docks have completely gone haywire. Our navigational system appears to be offline but we can't tell for sure due to our data analysis log's issues with staying active."

"Do you often pilot a vessel that should be in a salvage station?" Christian asked, his lip curling into a half smile.

If the man didn't fill the doorway and look as though he made a habit of breaking others in two, Jordan would have punched him just for the hell of it. It wasn't like he was a small guy in any way, shape or form but Christian had him beat. "No, I don't make a habit of that. The Alpha Brig Three is only four years old and that makes her a baby in the eyes of ship life. She's also top of the line and has passed all of her inspections with flying colors. It was weird. We were on our way to Margaidia and passed through a stream of stellar remains. Our fuel tank spontaneously cracked, leaking fuel out and into the gas from the remains, so we cut the engines, unsure if a spark would ignite a massive explosion or not."

"Stellar remains? Where? We've had no supernovas in our region of the galaxy for thousands of years," Christian said, confirming what Jordan already believed.

"What would you say if I told you that it didn't feel right? The entire event felt different, like something was interfering with us, something big and...."

"Mystical?" Christian nodded. "It would explain much. It was written long ago that when the time came for the rise against evil that great warriors would fall from the sky and old ones we'd lost along the way would return. I did not believe this legend. Perhaps I was wrong."

"Warriors would fall from the sky?" Jordan wasn't sure he liked the sound of that.

Christian nodded. "Yes. Long before the others came to be it was said that demons populated us and that warriors would soon follow. Well, the demon part was accurate. But they have all but overrun our planet in the last one hundred and fifty years. Not all are demons and evil. In fact, it is the select minority that terrifies so many villages into states of panic, leaving them prejudice to any who contain the blood of the others. I find that rather ironic due to the fact that Shamenians and natives of Sargaidia have always possessed skills and gifts greater than humans."

"The others? Care to elaborate?"

"Don't bother going into detail with the likes of him. You will waste your breath and he will retain but a tiny bit of it all."

The sound of Nina's voice, while alluring and cock hardening made Jordan see red. "Woman, stop treating me as though a human is the lowest life form in the universe."

"Stop treating me as though a woman should be barefoot and in the kitchen and we will no longer buck horns, Vasil."

"It's Jordan and you know it."

Nina smiled and blinked her eyes innocently. "Right you are and my name is Nina not woman."

"Touché."

Grinning, the vixen pushed past him and put her hand on her slender hips, leaving his cock twitching madly in his pants. "Christian, it is clear we cannot have them up and operational at the current rate of repairs on their vessel. As adamant as I am that we not allow outsiders to stay on our world after suns set, it would appear we have little choice in the matter."

"I agree. Have sleeping quarters arranged for the entire crew. Give them free access to the village but allow no outside passes to be administered to them. I will not allow them roaming out of the boundaries and ending up food for Stegian's men."

Nina nodded and glanced over her shoulder. The second Jordan locked eyes with her his chest pounded. She smiled wickedly. "You can pretend not to like me all you want, Vasil. I can smell your desire pouring off you."

"Yeah and I can smell your bitchiness, woman, so we're even." Jordan had never wanted to fuck a woman more and she knew it. Since the moment he'd stepped off the ship and watched her approach, his cock had been in a constant state of readiness.

Watching Nina in action only served to make it worse. The way she seemed to handle herself, no fear, no restraint, made his gut twist into a tight knot. Sure, Jordan was accused of the very same things when it came to issues of his own safety but that was different. He was a man, not the most beautiful creature in the entire universe. The need to protect her was almost overpowering.

Nina licked her lower lip. "Can I help you?"

"Huh?"

"You are staring at me."

"No, I'm not," Jordan said firmly but somehow still managing to sound like he was only ten years old.

Nina offered him a sly smile and shrugged. "Your eyes are locked on me and you aren't looking away. Correct me if I am wrong but is that not staring among your people?"

"Perhaps it is just called concentrating too hard where he comes from," Christian said, laughing softly under his breath.

Clearly not getting any help from Christian on the Nina front, Jordan narrowed his gaze. "I'm not staring--well, not that much anyways."

The second a smile poured over Nina's face Jordan couldn't help but grin. This woman, this compact, petite stick of dynamite had the power to break him with nothing more than a flash of her amusement. She also held the gift of being able to set his temper off faster than a Palertaire barge trader on a hot Exellion day.

Chapter Seven

Sevan stared up at the electromagnetically charged village fencing system. "With the amount of panic that wells up at the very mention of this Stegian's name and from the sight of what lengths they go to in order to keep him out, I'm beginning to think he's fifty feet tall."

"At least," Jordan said, arching a brow as he tossed a rock towards the fence. It bounced back hard and fast, nearly taking Jordan's head with it as it went. Nina appeared behind him and caught it with one had so effortlessly that both Sevan and Jordan's jaws dropped.

She smiled. "Careful, boys, it would be most unpleasant to find you decapitated by your own hands."

"See," Jordan adjusted his navy blue, off-duty, shirt collar, "told you she cared."

Nina laughed. "If caring means I will have to spend my evening gathering outsiders' heads off the ground before a child can wake to find them, then yes, I do care."

Unable to hold his laughter in, Sevan let it loose as he watched his brother do his best to play off the obvious blow to his ego. Nina walked up to them slowly, eyeing Sevan in a way that left him unsure if she was about to turn on him as well.

"You never made it to the quarters that were arranged for you, Captain."

"Uh," he murmured, drawing a blank instead of an explanation. Somehow, he didn't think she'd want to hear that he'd spent the night bunked with Lorelei, holding her in his arms and making love to her again and again as he had in his dreams.

"Want to tell us about this Stegian guy?"

"Not particularly." Her lack of emotion took him by surprise.

Sevan shifted awkwardly at first before deciding he had a right to know. "Excuse me but after the report I received about someone sabotaging repair efforts on my ship and the encounter with the were creature yesterday, I think circumstances warrant us being informed about the situation, in full."

Nina drew in her lower lip, an action he'd seen Lorelei do in many dreams. "I see. So, I take it that you believe it was one of our people that tampered with your vessel?"

"I can assure you that it wasn't one of my own." As Sevan said it, he wasn't sure he believed it. If what they had told him was correct and Stegian really did have the power to control men's minds then it could very well have been one of his own. The thought left him slightly chilled.

Nina merely smiled, not appearing offended in any way by his comment. "Captain, how well do you know your people's history?"

Jordan snickered and Sevan shot him a nasty look. He shut-up. "Well enough. Why?"

"Do you know of Project Exorcism?" she asked, arching a dark brow as she ran her fingers over a set of blue markings on her forearm. For a split second, Sevan was positive that they began to glow. It was gone so fast that he wasn't positive it was his mind playing tricks on him or not.

Jordan cleared his throat. "What does Earth's removal of supernatural beings have to do with Stegian? Of all the vessels sent out containing paranormal payloads, only one survived."

A horrible thought occurred to Sevan. He gasped, not wanting to believe it to be true. "No, brother. Only one made it to the predetermined destination. The rest were presumed lost--destroyed by the meteoroid shower."

Nina nodded. "I see that you're a fast thinker, Captain."

"Are you telling us that Stegian escaped from one of the vessels before it was torn apart?" Jordan asked, stealing the question from Sevan's lips.

"No," she let out a soft laugh, "no escape pods were necessary. The vessel made an unauthorized, emergency landing just outside of our village almost a hundred and fifty years ago."

"Nina."

Sevan looked behind him to find Christian standing there, his blond hair tied back at the base of his neck and wearing only a pair of dark brown pants. He locked gazes with Nina and the look he gave her was anything but friendly. "The man you assigned to do morning systems checks has not completed them or reported in. I sent Pheebes to look into the matter."

"Hey, Chieftain," Sevan said, not caring how sarcastic he came across. "How's your day so far? Anything evil take your mind over and try to make you hurt my wife?"

Nina and Christian both stared at him with wide eyes. It was Nina who finally spoke. "Your wife?"

Jordan tipped his head, looking past Nina and smiled as he locked eyes with Sevan. "Smooth way to let them know."

"Let us know what?" Christian asked, his already deep voice suddenly sounding even lower.

"Jacquelyn!"

Sevan glanced around and did his best to figure out what was going on. They'd all mentioned Jacquelyn several times since he'd arrived but he had yet to meet her. In an instant, a young girl, no more than twelve appeared before him. She was so close that part of her should have brushed up against him or even pushed him back. It didn't. No. The girl before him, with a head of long black hair and bright blue eyes, seemed to go through him. "What the...?"

She giggled. "It's nice to finally meet you, Brother-in-law."

"Brother-in-law?" Christian asked. "So, it is true?"

The young girl nodded. "Yes. The ritual was completed yesterday. The prophecy is coming true, Christian."

"Umm, anyone want to tell me why my hand is going through her?"

"Her name is Jacquelyn." Nina took a small step forward. "She is the youngest of the Janelles."

"She's your sister?" Jordan asked, shaking his head in disbelief.

Nina snorted. "While sharing your mother's womb did you allow the Captain to soak up all of the fluids necessary for natural thought?"

"No. Why?"

Sevan couldn't help but laugh. "Jordan, I think she was making a joke."

"Oh, I knew that."

Jacquelyn giggled again, this time disappearing quickly. Sevan felt around the spot she'd been in, finding nothing to prove anyone at all had been there.

"The place is haunted," Jordan said, softly.

"No, not haunted. Come quickly I'll show you to Jacquelyn," Nina said, appearing less than pleased with the entire arrangement. She quickened her pace and they were forced into a slight jog to keep up with her.

They followed, but didn't say a word. Long, gray corridors began to run into one another, leaving Sevan unsure where one stopped and another began. For a brief moment he was positive that they'd walked in circles but when Nina stopped outside of a large red door, she looked back at him nervously. "This, gentlemen is my sister, Jacquelyn."

Nina put her hand on the door panel. It slid open quickly. Sevan stopped and grabbed hold of the wall for support when he saw the mass of tubes, and medical equipment hooked into the tiny frame on the bed. It was barely recognizable as human. Had he not seen the tiny girl standing before him only moments earlier he would not have associated such a beautiful, radiant young child with what lay before him.

"What ... what happened to her?" Sevan asked, moving forward slowly and reaching out to touch the white sheet that covered her tiny body. The compulsion to prove that it wasn't the young girl was great. The need to know that Lorelei hadn't suffered a blow as big as what lay in the bed was greater. It was her baby sister there. The thought of that ripped at Sevan's gut.

Nina touched his hand and shook her head. "She says that it hurts when people touch her."

Puzzled, he shook his head. "How did she project her image outside?"

Nina glanced around at the machines that filled the room. "Christian built this all after we found her ... umm ... after the incident. Jacquelyn came to him first, in a vision. He is our healer, our Chieftain. With that position comes the power of the shamans and the strength of our greatest warriors. He was able to sense her near him. He knew what must be done. Her body may be useless and comatose, but her mind is very active, Captain. Of this, I am sure."

Sevan had a hard time believing that the large man who Nina had accused of attacking Lorelei could build such a thing, but it was clear by the way Christian stared at the child in the bed that his love for her was great. Had Sevan misjudged him? Had he let petty jealousy blind him to who Christian truly was?

Not wanting to think too hard about the answers, Sevan focused on the situation. Panel upon panel of computers lined the walls, each one seeming to be activated. A few screens were littered about, almost appearing random in the room but as he watched the code moved over them, he knew they were there for a reason.

He heard a giggle and turned to look at the door. Jacquelyn's apparition stood there grinning at him. Christian walked over to her and put out his arms. She ran into them and for a moment, Sevan could have sworn that she was real.

"How?"

"Christian loves me and he made it so I can still run around and play, when I want to, and...."

"Get into mischief," Christian said, pulling her head against his chest.

"I wish things could have been different, Christian. I saw Samson again today. He is well ... or as well as he can be now."

Christian stiffened at this statement, but forced a smile to his face. "Any news of pending attacks?"

"Yes, I overheard some of the others, ones that wandered near the outer edges of our village." Jacquelyn glanced at Sevan. "They spoke of the prophecy and the warriors from the sky that would come to aid in the fight against evil. Stegian tells them that the prophecy is a lie but they aren't so sure."

Christian exhaled loudly as he set Jacquelyn down to stand on her own. "I see. What else did they say?"

"Nothing," she said quickly.

Nina ran a hand over the markings on her left forearm again. "Jacquelyn."

Jacquelyn's face scrunched up and it was easy to see the resemblance to her sisters. "I hate that you can sense a lie, Nina."

"Yes, I know. Now, what else did they say?"

The young girl glanced nervously towards Christian. "They said that they know of Lorelei's mate coming from the vessel and that Stegian tried to control his mind fully but failed." She pointed at Jordan. "They know of you as well and believe you to be a great threat. Their instructions had been to kill you on sight and capture Sevan if at all possible. Stegian no longer wishes Lorelei dead either."

"What?" Christian asked, putting his hand on Jacquelyn's tiny shoulder.

"He wishes her brought to him alive so that he may have his hags drain the life force of the child she now carries. Stegian refuses to acknowledge that the prophecy is true, yet he is going out of his way to assure that the child of light be brought to him immediately."

Christian stepped back quickly, clenched his fists and tipped his head back. "Lorelei is with child?"

Oh, shit. It's about to get ugly in here.

Sevan took a fighting stance, ready and willing to fight Christian if need be. Much to his surprise the attack didn't come from Christian. It came from Nina. She kicked out fast, catching him in the gut, sending him tumbling back into a wall of computers. He struck it hard and then hit the ground. He clutched his stomach and fought for breath.

Nina came at him fast, her eyes burning with a fury he'd never seen a woman hold before. "How dare you show up here out of nowhere and use my sister? You're nothing but an outsider, an offworlder who doesn't belong here and cannot wait to be rid of us."

Sevan refused to fight back. There was no way in hell he was going to strike Lorelei's sister. She came at him again and Jordan stepped in front of her, blocking her path. "Enough."

A slow smile crept over her face as she swept her arm out. The next thing Sevan knew, Jordan was airborne. He hit the floor with a thud and moaned. Christian appeared and wrapped his arms around Nina. He lifted her off the ground as he rolled his eyes. "Nina, control yourself. Do you not see what has happened?"

She snarled. "All I see is a fast talker who couldn't even wait an entire day before sinking his cock into my sister. He used her, Christian, and now she will bear his child and spend her life protecting it from Stegian and his people while this ... this," she spat at him, "outsider goes back to his Commission life. It is my sister who will give her life for his need to sate his sexual appetite. You were to be her mate, Christian."

Christian shook his head. "No, Nina. I was not originally chosen. Samson was and I think we learned a hard lesson about pre-selecting mates from that, do you not agree?"

"Samson?" Jordan asked, rubbing his head.

Jacquelyn moved in close to him and touched his forehead lightly. A spark of light emanated from her hand and Jordan's eyes widened. "Thanks."

She smiled. "You're welcome. And to answer your question...."

Nina snarled again. "Tell them no more. They are leaving. I do not care if their ship is airworthy or not."

Jacquelyn giggled. "I never understood why Christian mumbles about the Janelle girls' tempers until now. He is right. You are the worst of the lot of us."

Jordan chuckled, earning a rather threatening look from Nina in the process. "I am not the worst of us all. Lorelei is."

Sevan got to his feet slowly, a bit achy and bruised. The woman packed a hell of a kick, that much was for sure. "Speaking of Lorelei, does she normally spend this long getting ready for her day?"

All eyes fell upon him. Nina's expression went from livid to concerned. "What do you mean?"

"She woke me and told me that she was going to get cleaned up and stop in to let Christian know that we were spending the day together. She mentioned wanting to show me the temples of Shamenia."

Christian ran quickly towards the panel at the far end of the room. He touched the pad and keyed in a set of numbers. "Attention, this is the Chieftain, all personnel report to your posts--the High Priestess is missing. I repeat. The Devi is missing."

High Priestess?

Jacquelyn nodded. "Yes, brother-in-law, Lorelei is a high priestess, a Devi as the villagers call her. She is capable of great things. Yet, her abilities make her vulnerable to Stegian."

"You don't talk like a child," Jordan said, getting to his feet.

She smiled. "Because I am not really a child. My mind has been free to wander the computer systems since the day of my attack. Christian built the system to project the image of me as I was then. It has been many years since then. If I were still walking among you, I would be approaching my eighteenth birthday."

"Still, you sound even older than that at times but young at others." Jordan reached out and touched her tentatively.

She winked. "It's a programming flaw that Christian is trying to overcome. He is a genius so he'll have it figured out in no time. I think, one day, he'll be able to build me a new body, one that will let me run and be free to roam further than the outer limits of our village."

Christian moved past Jordan and headed straight for Sevan. "Lorelei never made it to meet me this morning. We need to split up into teams to search for her. I'm unable to get a lock on her location." He looked back at Jacquelyn. "Run a scan of the village. She'll be easy to find if you search for new life forms. The child within her will trigger that."

A sick feeling crept over Sevan. "Wait, are you thinking that this Stegian guy got his hands on her?"

Nina shook her head. "Not him personally, unless he's found a way to travel about during suns up. He's a vampire and a sorcerer. Your people feared him so much so that legend tells he arrived in chains and that it was the other supernaturals aboard the vessel that imprisoned him."

Jacquelyn closed her eyes and put her hand out, appearing to scan thin air. She squinted and then gasped. "No."

"No, what?" Nina asked.

"I'm picking up residual blood spots near the fourth gate to the outer limits. My sensors indicate it is Lorelei's blood. If that's true then she is badly injured."

Sevan charged toward the door only to find Christian grabbing hold of him. "Let go of me. I'm going to get my wife."

"We are all going to get her. Trust me when I say it will take the entire group to ensure we get to her."

"What if that guy fucks with your head again? Huh?" Sevan needed to lash out at someone. Christian was the closest target. He shoved hard, breaking the man's hold on him. The beast within roared dangerously close to the surface. It felt as though it might actually break free. Unsure if he could really control it, Sevan looked to his brother with wide eyes. "If something goes wrong and I shift, don't let me hurt anyone."

"If you shift?" Nina asked. "You mean you are not straight humans?"

"No," Jacquelyn answered for him. "They both carry the gene of a lion within them. It was a recessive trait, one that had been thinned to the point of barely registering. That's why my sensors didn't pick it up when their ship entered our atmosphere."

"Then how are you sensing it now?" Nina asked.

Christian touched Sevan's shoulder and squeezed it gently. "Because the prophecy is true. The warriors that will help in the fight have been summoned to what was meant to be their home--they've come to grow into their full power and potential."

"Will we shift fully?"

"I would assume that in time you will. And I share your concern about not knowing if you will be able to control yourself the first time out." Christian narrowed his gaze on Nina. "Gather your men. Have them each cover an area and report to one another on their progress. Also be sure that each team is equipped with tranquilizers, should Lorelei's husband and the father of your future niece or nephew lose control and shift, they are to shoot him with them and get him back to the compound. He can be put in a holding chamber until morning."

Nina shook her head. "He'll never stand for that."

Sevan's nostrils flared. "Listen, lady. I don't know or care what your problem with me is but I can tell you this. I am not now, nor am I ever leaving Lorelei or our child. She is my wife and I love her more than life itself. If I become a threat to her you have my permission to shoot me in the forehead with a silver bullet."

"He means it," Jordan said, backing him up.

Nina smiled. "Good to know."

Chapter Eight

Lorelei lifted her head slightly and tried to make sense of where she was. The minute her gaze fell upon the bladed torture chair she knew right away--she was within Stegian's compound, or castle as he so often referred to it. In its hundred and fifty years it had played home to countless murders and torturous acts. In fact, only six months prior Lorelei had found herself in a similar room, only Christian had been strapped to the torture chair while Stegian fought for control of his mind.

"There is my Lorelei," a deep, familiar voice said. "I didn't think you'd wake yet today."

Lorelei did her best to sit up but her entire body ached and lying on the cold stone floor hadn't helped that any. "Samson?"

"Yes," he said, stepping over her body.

She stared at his shiny black boots and did her best to focus on them, not him. The pain in her chest wasn't from a wound but from the knowledge that the man before her had owned her heart at one point in her life but was now a puppet for evil.

"Why do you not look at me, Lorelei? Have you not missed your chosen mate?"

"You gave that right up when you...." There was no way she could bring herself to say it.

Samson laughed, sounding so very much like his brother, Christian, that Lorelei forced her guard up, afraid she'd trust or believe him. "Are you still upset about our last meeting, Lorelei?"

He bent down and for the first time in six months, Lorelei looked into the face of the man she had mistakenly trusted with her life. While Samson had Christian's same long blond hair and muscle bound body, he had a face that had often left him being razed for being as smooth as a baby's bottom. It had also been one of the many things she'd loved about him. Sadly enough, his innocent good boy looks were the reason she'd fallen into Stegian's trap six months earlier.

Samson ran his cool hand over her arm and tipped his head. "Your markings are gone. Why?"

He doesn't know?

He jerked his hand away as if she'd burned him. "He has done it, hasn't he? My brother has claimed you and planted his seed deep within you." Samson stood quickly. Sharp, dagger-like finger nails shot out as his incisors lengthened before her eyes, leaving fangs in place of his normal teeth. "Tell me, does he fuck you better than I did?"

Lorelei knew better than to answer. The thing that stood before her was no longer a Shamenian royal, it was a monster--a vessel for pure evil. Somehow Stegian had not only managed to break Samson mentally, he'd converted him physically as well. Samson now possessed his powers as a Shamenian and those of a vampire. If that wasn't bad enough, his sire had been none other than Stegian himself.

Where once there had been emerald green eyes, there now lay black pools of hate focused solely on Lorelei. She shifted a bit and cried out as the open gash on her upper right thigh pulled slightly.

Samson smiled, looking every bit as evil as she knew he could be. "So sorry about that leg, Lorelei. My men tell me it was necessary, that you tried to fight them all single-handedly. Is this true?"

Narrowing her gaze, Lorelei let it go hard. "I won't let you hurt Christian again."

"Ah," Samson tipped his head back and laughed, "It is so like you to be more concerned about others than yourself. What if I told you that my master has a new set of targets in mind?"

Sevan.

Lorelei?

The sound of Sevan's voice in her head sent a surge of hope through her. Doing her best to hide her joy, Lorelei continued to stare at Samson with a hard look.

Lorelei, baby, where are you? We're all looking for you. Jacquelyn says you're injured and it's bad.

It's just my leg. I'll be fine.

Sevan's worry was so great that Lorelei actually felt it through the mental link they'd managed to forge. True mates did that. Powerful true mates could do that and so much more.

The air around her grew heavy with the smell of stagnant water. For a moment, the scent of death seemed to coat her tongue, bringing her dangerously close to vomiting. She closed her eyes and did her best to control herself.

"Hag, what business have you here?" Samson asked.

Hag? Stegian was rumored to have a set of hags at his disposal. It was rumored that they were just as evil as he was. No Shamenian had ever lived to tell if the rumor was true or not. Now, Lorelei knew it was.

Think. How can I defeat a hag?

"The master has sent me to drain the child's life force. His power can be harnessed and used to fight the rest of the group," a shaky, old voice said.

Lorelei didn't open her eyes. Instead, she did her best to clear her mind of worry, of fear and most of all of hate. A pure mind was the only answer. If the hag fed off power, energy and emotion, Lorelei needed to be a blank slate.

Concentrating, the things around her seemed to amplify. The cold, hard stone floor now seemed to have a distinctly musty order. She'd smelled something similar as a child. The lagoons near the edge of the red sea were known to emit odd odors dependent upon the way the winds blew. Stegian's castle wasn't near the lagoons.

What was going on?

Opening her eyes, Lorelei found herself surrounded by overgrown foliage in shades of red, green and yellow. The red leaves, so long as they weren't attached to a tree with a sage green trunk were safe. If they were and she was somehow nestled in a patch of poisonous ollenna trees then she wasn't much better off than she'd been in Stegian's dungeon. It was still a mystery how she'd even ended up outside to begin with. Could her own, inborn powers have kicked in and removed her from harm's way or had it been the baby?

Concern for the safety of the child she now carried kicked in and Lorelei struggled to sit up. Pain rippled through her upper leg, causing her to cry out. The slightest ruffling in the bushes behind her told her she wasn't alone. "Who's there?"

"Me," Jacquelyn said, appearing next to her quickly. The young girl put her hand out and covered the wound on Lorelei's leg. "This is deep and it's infected."

"I'll heal."

Jacquelyn's penetrating gaze suggested otherwise. "I'm picking up traces of ollenna poison. You might have cut yourself on one of their razor sharp thorns when struggling or...."

"Or they could have deliberately put it in my wound." Lorelei bit back tears as she held her cry of pain in as well. "Bloody hell, Jacquelyn, I've not the strength to heal myself of something that major right now and I can't possibly walk back to the compound."

Jacquelyn nodded. "I know. I've been trying to reach Sevan and the rest of them but Stegian is going out of his way to jam technology. He knew we'd come looking and he knew they'd need my help."

"Yeah, but did he know I'd end up out here instead of locked in a torture chamber with Samson?"

"Did he hurt you again?"

Lorelei snorted. "No, but a hag came into the room with the intent of draining the baby's life force."

"How did you end up here?" Jacquelyn asked. "You just appeared out of nowhere and my sensors instantly picked you up."

"That, I don't know."

* * * *

"What do you mean she simply vanished?" Stegian asked, his jaw tight and his gaze hard. The urge to kill something was great. All that stood before him was one of the hags and Samson.

Samson shook his head, still appearing shocked by the entire affair. "Master, she simply closed her eyes and vanished."

"She came into her full powers," the hag said, looking back at him with milky-white eyes.

To his knowledge, the hags were all blind but somehow, they managed to see. The one before him smiled, revealing a mouth full of missing teeth. "It is the third eye, master."

"And did this third eye prove useful when the prisoner was escaping?"

Her already pale, light green skin seemed to lighten even more. Stegian couldn't help but pride himself on the fear he could instill in others. "I await an answer."

"N-o," she said, shakily.

"I see." Stegian took a step forward. "Would you please enlighten me as to why I should keep you around? Samson fights on the front lines, killing Shamenians and Tegmen. What is it you and your sisters provide?"

The hag tossed her head back and shrieked as Stegian thrust his power out and through her ragged body. Her skin began to sink in on itself as he drained her body of its power.

The cell door blew open and the other two hags appeared. Stegian smiled, licking a fang as he did. They stopped instantly. "Master, we have located the Janelle woman. She lies near the lagoons. An energy force is with her. We believe it to be both natural and unnatural."

"Meaning?" He released his hold on the hag for a moment to hear the others out.

"It means that the woman is somehow emitting extremely high levels of energy and that something else, we do not understand what, is aiding her."

"The prophecy," Samson whispered. "It's coming true."

There was a time when Stegian dismissed theories containing ancient prophecies. That was until he held the scrolls in which they were written and had a vision so clear that it did the unthinkable--it terrified him.

"I shall go to the lagoons, Master," Samson said.

"Take several others with you." Stegian stared at the converted Shamenian. "Do not think yourself better than an offworlder."

Chapter Nine

"Jordan, do you read?" Sevan repeated into his headset. "Damn thing isn't working."

"It's not your equipment, it's the others. They can jam electronics. That's why Jacquelyn could only reach so far to find Lorelei. They make it almost impossible for her signal to come through. Every now and then she gets the best of them, but it doesn't happen too often," Nina said, her back to him.

"Can I ask you something?"

"You want to know who the others are," Nina said, stopping on the worn path. "You don't seem to believe what Christian and I have already told you."

"Yeah."

"We spoke the truth, Captain. The others are your world's nightmare creatures. The ones you gathered up and shipped away. We are not lying when we say that they are a result of Project Exorcism."

Sevan's eyes bulged as he thought back to all he knew about Project Exorcism. It had been called that due to the nature of the cargo being gathered and shipped out-- vampires, werewolves, witches, anything that wasn't human was either forced into hiding, killed, or placed on containment ships.

The deal had been struck with the paranormal leaders, allowing them to pick the planet they would relocate to. They were given the choice of five, but only allowed to choose one. Five ships were loaded to capacity, only one arrived at the destination. The other ships were thought to have perished in the meteorite shower that occurred shortly after take off. No one had heard from them since they'd departed all those years ago, each carrying nearly a hundred military personnel, several top-notch scientists and doctors, along with several thousand supernatural creatures.

"How many of them survived?"

Nina laughed. "I couldn't honestly tell you. It was our grandparents who were directly involved in the great coming." She took a deep breath before continuing. "From the stories and the records, the crash happened at dusk. From all accounts, the human crew had come under attack from a select number of supernaturals who were not pleased with the idea of being cargo sent out into space. I know that many lost their lives directly after the crash, but some were spared by the intervention of the natives that were here along with the aid of those supernaturals not believing death should come to all humans."

She slowed her pace a bit and glanced back at him. "Christian's family was the head family, similar to a royal family. The head of the supernatural rebellion overthrew them almost immediately. That was no small feat. The people, my people, the Shamenians, who have lived on this planet since the dawn of time are not as normal as the humans who'd come here with the ship. We have abilities that supersede your kind. I believe, as do many of our scientists, that we were all one once, long ago, but that we separated somehow, spreading out over six different galaxies. I also believe that the environments we inhabited pre-determined our evolution from there. This would explain why by all outward appearances we are the same as the humans.

"I believe in many ways we are similar to," she seemed to search for the right words, "the magical ones. I'm sorry I do not know your history as well as I should. Lorelei is better at this than I am. We were all educated in your ways and customs growing up. There are still a select few pure humans here, but almost all are forced to live within the safety of the compound walls for fear of being slaughtered by the others."

"Not all of the others are evil. Many have villages, children, education facilities, the works, set up throughout these lands, but even those places are not safe for straight humans. The others have taken to attacking their own kind if they believe them to be sympathizers with the day creatures. That's what they call us, you know. They can't very well call us human. We're not all the same, so they came up with that. Though, Stegian, the leader of one of the largest packs of the others refers to us as Shamenians. Why he seems to be the only one who understands is not a question I require an answer to."

"I get the sense that you're holding back on me," Sevan said, watching Nina carefully.

"I am. The Janelles carry the gene of a werepanther in us. Our grandmother fell in love with one of the werepanthers upon their arrival and together they had a child, our father. My grandfather was killed by his own kind for loving a local, a day creature. My grandmother was forced to marry her original chosen mate, and he aided in the raising of my father. This was much to the dislike of the community, but necessary all the same. My grandmother's second husband was the only grandfather we knew. He treated us well enough while he was alive. Though I do not think he liked my father much."

"Where's your father now?"

"Dead."

"I'm sorry."

Nina stopped walking and gave him a serious look. "Don't be. Lorelei killed him and I helped her."

"Why the hell would you kill your own father?"

"You've seen Jacquelyn."

The realization of what she was saying sunk in and he felt sick to his stomach. Heat flared through him and he had to stop a moment to keep from vomiting. "What kind of sick bastard does that to his own daughter?"

"The kind that is being controlled by Stegian while in full shifted form."

"Nina?" A small voice called out from the darkness.

Nina froze and Sevan followed suit. She tipped her head to the side and seemed to sniff the air.

"Nina?" The voice spoke again. It sounded a hell of a lot like Lorelei to him so he started in the direction the voice was coming from.

"No," Nina said, slamming her hand back into his chest. The wind was knocked out of him and he was left coughing to regain control of himself. She packed a hell of a punch, that much was clear.

"Stegian, has used tricks to lure us into traps before and he's famous for mimicking our voices. It's how he lured Jacquelyn away so easily. He used my voice to call her to him and then he…."

"Nina?" The voice was there again, this time weaker sounding than before. There was a shuffle in the brush off to their left and they swung around with weapons drawn.

"To hell with this," Sevan said, pushing past Nina and rushing towards the sound of Lorelei's voice. When he broke through the dense brush, he found her lying on the ground, her leg covered in blood, her face pale and her eyes locked on him.

She blinked. "Sevan?"

His heart slammed in his chest as the beast within him fought to be free. His skin tingled and his neck tightened. That was his wife lying there, hurt and scared. Yet, he was too afraid to go to her and touch her.

Nina pushed past him and he snarled, sounding so much like an animal that it shocked even him. She stilled and began backing slowly towards Lorelei. As she reached for her side, Sevan knew what she was about to do--shoot him with a tranquilizer.

Lorelei's eyes widened. "No, Nina, don't!"

"Sevan knows that he can't control the beast his first shift out, sister."

As much as he hated to admit it, it was true. Hot, searing pain tore through his hands and he watched as claws erected from them. Shaking his head, Sevan couldn't comprehend all that was happening. His entire life he'd lived with the knowledge that somewhere deep within him lay a lion. A beast with no remorse and little concern for anything beyond itself. Now, as it began to take shape it was almost too much for him to comprehend.

A sharp pinprick hit his neck and he knew then that Nina had decided to shoot him with the tranquilizer. It was then that he also realized they were not alone. Darkness swallowed him before he could shout out a warning.

* * * *

Lorelei watched in horror as her own sister shot Sevan. "Why?"

Nina glanced down at her and offered a small smile. "Lorelei, he agreed ahead of time. He told me to shoot him between the eyes if needed. At least I used a tranquilizer and not a real bullet. Christian and Jordan will be along soon. They'll carry...."

Something was horribly wrong. The feeling of evil seemed to close in on them. Lorelei struggled to her feet, grabbing hold of Nina's arm for help. "They've found me."

"I know." Nina glanced towards Sevan's lifeless body, looking as though she regretted her decision of knocking him out.

The smell of a werewolf and something else, something familiar, threatening and close. Lorelei drew in a sharp breath. "Samson."

Nina lunged for Sevan and Lorelei grabbed hold of her, afraid that she was going to try to finish what she started. "No."

"Let go! He can't defend himself."

"Oh, I thought…." She stopped not wanting to accuse her own flesh and blood of trying something so heinous.

"Lorelei," Nina said, softly. "Do you love Sevan?"

"Yes."

"He says that he won't leave, Lorelei. That he'll stay and stand by his family's side."

Lorelei held tight to her sister as she drew on the power of the earth, the Shamenian spirits of long ago and of the werepanther within her. Power surged through her veins, harder and faster than it ever had before. Her breathing quickened and her heart raced. "By gods, I think the baby is powerful as well."

Nina nodded. "Of course, she's a Janelle."

"She?"

"Just being hopeful. We have enough boys in the family."

Not wanting to think of her brothers that had been forced off the planet long ago, Lorelei simply smiled, feeling invigorated and up to the task of fighting even the greatest of Stegian's warriors. Even if that meant fighting the man she used to love.

A dark mass leaped out from the tree line and something swooshed past them quickly. The moment Lorelei saw the silver dipped arrow sticking out of a now dead werecougar's chest, she knew Christian and back-up had arrived.

Nina wasted no time. She let her claws erect and her eyes swirl to light blue. She took off, running straight ahead, clearly sensing something. Before Lorelei could comment, Jordan appeared next to her.

He glanced at Sevan and his brow furrowed. "He's not...."

"No," Lorelei said quickly. "He's just sedated. He started to shift and Nina shot him with a tranquilizer gun."

"In the middle of a battle? Is the woman mad?" He put his hand through his hair and then gritted his teeth. "Of course she is."

"In her defense, she shot him before the enemy arrived."

He tossed his hands in the air. "Well then, that makes it all better." He looked around frantically. "Where the hell did she go? Is she trying to get herself killed?"

A blur moved at them fast. In a flash, a fully shifted weretiger had its teeth sunk deep into Jordan's arm. Fearing that Jordan would lose his arm if she didn't act quickly, Lorelei let the power that had been building within her loose. It slammed into Jordan and then his attacker.

Both men went to the ground fast. Lorelei held her breath, fearing she'd killed Jordan by accident. She reached for him, hoping he still had a pulse. Something dropped down on her, smashing her body to the ground. Crying out wasn't an option. Whatever was on her had knocked the wind out her.

"That was bad, Lorelei, running out before we were finished," Samson said, pressing his body against hers.

"Get off of her!"

The sound of Christian's voice should have been music to her ears but not now. Not when Samson was so close. The last time they'd been face to face, Christian almost lost his battle to remain on the side of good.

"Ah, if it isn't my baby brother." Samson pinned her even harder. "Tell me, do you think you are finally strong enough to defeat me?"

"Not alone but together with my new friend, I think we will manage just fine," Christian said.

New friend?

Something growled, its voice deep, making the ground around her vibrate. That wasn't a panther. No. That was a lion. "Sevan!"

Instantly, Samson was thrust clear of her body. As Lorelei went to roll over the pain in her leg reached new levels causing her to bite her lip as tears dripped down her cheeks.

A ringing started in her ears and a light tingling sensation surrounded her. "Sleep, Lorelei. Sleep. All will end well here. I promise. I will watch over them all."

The soothing sound of Jacquelyn's voice coaxed her into a relaxed state allowing much needed rest to occur.

Chapter Ten

"Sevan, I can't rest if you keep doing that."

Running his hand over his wife's slightly swollen belly, Sevan tried to imagine what their child looked like within her. Hopefully, it would come out with Lorelei's looks and his temper. With her quick temper Sevan would never survive living in a house with two of them. "Mmm, I can't help it, Lorelei. I thought I'd lost you."

"I have been out of the infirmary for over a month now."

"Yes but you were in it for over a month too," he said, not letting her forget how close to death she'd come. "Losing that much blood and using that much power almost did you in, baby. I can't close my eyes without thinking about it."

She snickered, obviously not taking him very seriously. "Try watching your brother shift back and forth between a tiger and a lion. That should give you something else to focus on."

"No thanks. I can hear Nina and Jordan arguing from across the village about it. She still thinks both are inferior to the panther."

"Aren't they?" she asked, smoothing her hand over his naked thigh.

Instantly, his cock jerked to life, wanting to be buried deep within her again. He nudged her with it, doing his best to ease it between her ass cheeks without having to release his embrace.

Lorelei moved slightly, allowing him easier access to her. "Hmm, is someone horny again?"

"I can't get enough of you or this place." Sevan took a deep breath in. "This feels like home and I love it. I love you."

"I still don't understand why your entire crew refuses to leave."

Sevan smiled. "Lorelei, Earth, or rather, the portions of Earth that we're permitted to live on aren't like this anymore. There are no more trees, plants or animals around. It's all industrialized. The portions that are marked off are kept under heavy guard. This is paradise to people from Earth."

She snorted. "We have monsters that walk among us."

"So do we." Sevan eased his cock in more, nudging at the cleft of her warm ass. "Earth officials just don't realize it yet. Not every supernatural made it aboard a vessel and I can't tell you how many more have immigrated to Earth from other galaxies. They don't have a handle on anything. And if they knew that Project Exorcism didn't go as planned--that the vessels thought lost really weren't, they'd declare a state of emergency."

"But we don't know for sure that other vessels survived, Sevan," Lorelei said, adding reason to his insane ramblings.

He licked his fingers, letting an ample amount of saliva build on them before rubbing it over the head of his cock. Repositioning himself between the soft globes of his wife's ass, Sevan lined up and eased the tip of his cock in. Lorelei bucked slightly against him and moaned out.

"Uh, yes, Sevan."

Reaching around her, Sevan stopped long enough to let his hand glide over her tiny rounded lower abdomen before heading straight for her pussy. He parted her slit and began to rub her already swollen bud as he worked his cock into her more. Her tight ass fisted it, leaving him panting softly as he continued to delve into her dark depths.

"Sevan."

He placed a tiny kiss on Lorelei's neck and thrust in the rest of the way. She cried out and then reached back and seized hold of his ass. "Harder."

Never one to disappoint, Sevan gave in and began moving in and out of his mate, his wife, savoring every second of sheer bliss as he went. She was so tight. So hot. So made just for him. He knew he'd never leave her and that he'd never be able to go on living without her.

He tweaked her ripe bud, working it to the point that Lorelei squirmed and thrashed against him. He knew her body well now and knew that she was close to an orgasm. "That's it, baby. Let go. Come, Lorelei. Come."

She pushed back against him as he continued to spoon her and fuck her. The feel of her channel clamping down on his dick caused him to lose control. Sevan pushed and then held tight to her as he rubbed her clit. His balls drew up and his cock twitched a second before he released his semen deep into her.

Lorelei cried out, digging her nails into his upper thigh and holding tight as she came as well. Another orgasm ripped through him, causing him to shoot even more seed into her. "Uh, baby...."

She snickered. "Yes, darling. I love you too. Now, what do you say to a shower?"

Sevan smiled as he held his wife to him. "I think that sounds wonderful but how about a bath instead? I can rub your shoulders easier that way."

"A girl could get used to this, Captain."

"That's a good thing. I'd hate for you to change your mind and start wanting that lechranki worm again."

Lorelei's warm laugh moved through him, leaving him feeling complete. "But blood sucking worms that eat their own vomit are so very adorable, honey."

The End

FORCE OF ATTRACTION

Dedication:

Shane, here's to eleven years of ups, downs, laughs, tears, highs and lows. We should really charge admission, honey. Our roller coaster ride has been full of thrills, chills and everything I could ever hope for. Thank you for being you. Happy Anniversary!

Chapter One

"Have a seat," Doctor Marisa Langston said, hearing the door to her exam room slide shut. "Go ahead and gown up. I'll be right with you. I just need to finish up with these logs."

She ran her hand over the edges of the electronic access tab on the file, allowing a microchip embedded under the skin in her hand to access the information in them. A clear image appeared in her mind as she downloaded the day's findings into the chart log. Visions of each patient she'd seen over the course of the day rushed through her mind. As quickly as it started, the painless procedure was over.

A husky laugh sounded, accompanied closely by the scent of cedar and musk. The smell drove her wild. The man attached to it drove her insane. "Ah, Doc, I've always known you wanted me out of my pants. Hearing you say it confirms my suspicions. I told you yesterday that all you had to do was say the word and I would show you what a real man could offer you."

Marisa outwardly cringed but inwardly rejoiced at the sound of Lieutenant Commander Bradi Janelle's deep voice. The man lived to make her life hell. He seemed to take great pleasure in embarrassing her whenever possible. There was something about him that made her blood boil and her body burn in ways it shouldn't. It wasn't something she wanted to think too hard about. She was positive she wouldn't like what she discovered.

She focused on the medicine dispensing panel in front of her instead of sinful thoughts about the man behind her. "Lt. Commander Bradi, I thought you canceled your physical today. I put someone else in your spot." She let her voice go hard, knowing full well why he was standing there. Giggling was an option she had to fight not to take. While it was childish, it seemed more than called for.

Bradi cleared his throat, the tension suddenly thick enough to choke on. "I did cancel, but since someone went straight to the big boy about my file not being complete, I got a call telling me to get my ass in here. You wouldn't know anything about that, would you, Doc? I mean, you don't have any certain *pull* with the Commander, do you?"

Grinning, Marisa turned toward him, wanting to give him the impression that he didn't get to her, but he did. Everything about the man got under her skin and she wasn't entirely sure it was in a bad way either. The fact that her pulse seemed to speed with the slightest mention of Bradi's name and that her body seemed to tighten of its own accord by his sheer nearness told her more than she wanted to know. She wanted him. She could never have him. Off limits didn't even begin to cover Lt. Commander Bradi Janelle. Dark. Dangerous. Delicious. Everything she needed to avoid.

Bradi seemed to take up so much room that he demanded attention. The dark gray backdrop of the infirmary walls provided a scene that if Marisa didn't know better, she would have said it made the brave and ballsy Lt. Commander look uncomfortable. Having an aversion to hospital like settings wasn't uncommon. Seeing Bradi appear anything but in control was. He squared his shoulders and stared down at her, a challenge in his eyes.

The man was pure muscle, at least from what Marisa could tell. He'd never allowed her to examine him in the two months she'd been the ship's assistant physician so she could only guess. As far as she knew, Bradi hadn't allowed anyone to examine him in well over a year. Judging from the way his tight regulation black T-shirt fit him, his upper body was sculpted to perfection. The lower half of him didn't look so bad either in a 'great ass, large muscular thighs and an even larger bulge between the legs' kind of way, but who was really looking at that anyway?

Who am I kidding? I can't keep my eyes off him.

Bradi pulled the leather tie out of his hair and she watched in silent wonder as waves of silky black spilled over his broad shoulders. His light blue eyes locked on her as his tongue darted out. The sight of his long tongue brushing over his full lips made her hands shake from the need to touch him. On more than one occasion, Marisa had wondered what it would feel like to have him above her, taking her in ways she shouldn't even think about.

Even while she should have been focused on her job, Marisa was focused on the idea of Bradi taking hold of her, tossing her onto an exam table and having his way with her. Her pussy dampened at the very thought of him sinking his cock into her.

Stop thinking about him like that. It's wrong. Besides, he's an asshole.

Lt. Commander Bradi was different from the men she knew. So wild. So free that the idea of not being close to him to see what it was he'd do next wasn't an option. He was certainly an individual in a sea of the same. She wasn't used to men with facial hair, the Commission frowned upon it, so Bradi stood out even more than normal. His goatee was well maintained. It wasn't pointy, like some. No. His was cut close to his natural, squared jawline. It not only suited him, but added to the mysticism behind him going down on her. The very thought of his whiskers scraping over the tender flesh of her pussy left Marisa shifting awkwardly as cream continued to build.

Gods, I want him.

It'd be a cold day in hell before she admitted that to him though.

"As much as I love the fact that you felt the need to show off your non-regulation hair, I don't need that down. I need your pants down," she said, sure that her sexual suggestion wasn't lost on him. "You need your shots updated. You're dangerously close to the expiration date on your old ones and gods help us all knowing the way you bed hop. The entire ship will be full of little Janelles. We can only hope they aren't as cocky as you are. Not only that, I'll be treating bizarre cases of whatever it is men like you spread around sexually for months. You're an epidemic waiting to happen, Janelle."

"I do not have little Janelle's running around," he said, sounding a bit annoyed. "I never will."

That surprised Marisa. Bradi generally took everything in stride. He also was known to dish out way more than she liked to receive. Seeing him upset didn't sit well with her. Softening her expression, Marisa glanced up at him. "My apologies. That was uncalled for and unprofessional. I have nothing to base my assumptions on. Sorry, Lt. Commander."

He arched a dark brow and ran his hand over his facial hair. "Want a basis? I'd be happy to give you one, Doctor," he murmured, his blue gaze suddenly raking over her body slowly. Her breath quickened. "Give me one night, Doc. One night and then you can base all the assumptions you want off it, off me. But only if you promise to let me play doctor with you, too. No fair that you get all the fun. You see," unabashed, he cupped his groin, "I have the perfect thing to take your temperature with." Bradi took a step toward her, sliding his large hand up toward his belt.

Yes, have me at your mercy.

Need slammed through her, leaving Marisa no choice but to avert her gaze. Her cheeks flushed. Crawling away from him wasn't an option. Standing there while he dropped his pants before her was what her job demanded. Wanting to see all that he had to offer was something her body demanded.

You hate him. Remember?

"I've been meaning to ask you about your heritage, Lieutenant Commander," Marisa said, doing her best to stay focused. It was far from easy. Sneaking a peek at Bradi's perfect body would be so easy. She'd lain awake countless nights wondering about him when it was another her mind should have been focused on. Each time she pleasured herself, it was Bradi's face she saw in her mind, his body she imagined in her, not the man who was supposed to be there.

"My heritage?" he asked, taken aback.

"Yes, you don't look like other Corneusims I've met before."

Bradi laughed slightly. The very sound shook her to her core. "Why would I look like a horny toad warrior from the planet Cornu?"

It was as she expected. The man had doctored his medical records. He certainly wasn't the first officer to do so, nor would he be the last. Whatever reason he had for hiding must have been a good one--to make him as desperate as he'd been. "Hmm, just wondering. After all, your last blood scans showed traces of Corneusim DNA in it."

Mumbling under his breath, Bradi rubbed his strong jaw. It seemed to be a habit he only had when he was dealing with her. "Doc Graves is ancient. I bet his equipment failed again, or more than likely he just mixed up the samples."

Bradi was right, Dr. Graves, the ship's head physician was old, but not careless. Mixing up samples wasn't something he would do. Marisa decided to fight this battle with him at a later date. Right now, she planned on immunizing him and drawing a sample of his blood in the process. Marisa wouldn't submit it to the officials. No. Bradi had his reasons for hiding. She just needed to set her own mind at ease. "Ready to bare it all, Lieutenant Commander?"

He released the slight hold he had on his pants, letting them fall to his ankles and grinned from ear to ear. The absence of underwear gave Marisa a quick flash of his front side before he turned around and pulled his T-shirt up. Her breath caught and her inner thighs tightened. Hell, the man wasn't even erect and his cock was impressive. There was no way Bradi would ever fit in her.

Thank the gods I can't have him. He'd break me.

Staring at his rock hard ass did little in the way of alleviating the overwhelming need to touch Bradi. Would it be so wrong to just trace the edges of his tight body? She licked her lips imagining her fingers digging into each cheek as he fucked her. Marisa fought to maintain what little she still held of her composure. "All set?"

"I would much rather have you remove my pants next time, Doc," he said, his deep voice moving over her.

"I'm sure you would," she said wryly, trying to shake the visions from her head of Bradi fucking her. Grabbing her booster gun, Marisa moved up behind him. Placing one hand on his ass and confirming the fact that he was indeed rock hard, she released the Star Union's recommended dosage of immunizations and population control into him. He didn't seem the least bit phased by the injection.

Lt. Commander Bradi Janelle would now be disease free for at least another year and considering the stories she heard about his prowess that was a blessing. Unable to help herself, Marisa patted his bare cheek lightly and let out a soft laugh. Bradi flexed and temptation ran through her. She clutched her hands tight to avoid doing a full backside rub down.

"Have you talked to Peter today?" she asked, desperate to get her mind off his hind end.

Bradi stood quickly, pulling his pants up as he went. The second he turned to face her, he rolled his blue eyes. Running a large hand over his chin, Bradi shook his head, annoyance evident in his masculine features. "You always do that. You always toss Pete's name out whenever I make a comment that turns you on. Every time I make you wet, you throw him in my face, Doc. What? Do you think I forget that you are engaged to my best friend?"

Marisa's jaw dropped. "I do not toss Peter in your face every time you make me wet." Instantly, she cringed. As much as she'd wanted an intellectual debate, she didn't get one. No. Confirming Bradi's assumption that he made her wet never factored into the equation. She wished she could take it back.

A smug smile tugged at the corners of Bradi's mouth and Marisa wasn't sure if she wanted to kiss or kick it away. "See, was it so hard to admit that I make you horny? Come on, Doc. Just own up to it. You want me."

Snorting, Marisa reached out and used Bradi's forearm to steady herself. He didn't seem to mind so she held tight to it. She laughed and leaned into him as he chuckled with her. "Yeah, must be the Corneusim blood in you. I've always wanted a toad. What can you do with your tongue, Lt. Commander?"

"Hold the communicator," he leaned down, putting his face so close to her that their lips would touch if she dared to move, "was that a joke coming out of your mouth? It was funny, Doc, and you look damn good when you smile. You should do it more."

Hearing the warm tone in Bradi's voice, Marisa found herself edging even closer to him as tiny giggles continued to erupt from her. "Do what more?" she asked, hiccupping. The question popped out even though no part of her had intended on asking it. Something about Bradi made rational thought leap right out the window. The man had a way about him.

Running the pad of his thumb over her cheek, Bradi caught her off guard. "You should smile more. You're getting married soon. You'd think you'd be in a better mood about it."

His words cut to the bone as they were no doubt intended to. Stiffening, Marisa collected her thoughts and hardened herself to his charms or at the moment, lack thereof. She jerked back from him, unable to hide the hurt on her face. Something moved over Bradi's handsome features. He reached for her but stopped just shy of actually touching her. "Doc, I-I just wanted you to...."

Doing her best to deal with the turmoil Bradi left her in, Marisa forced a blank expression to her face, donning what she liked to call her work face. "Lieutenant Commander Bradi, my time, as well is yours, is precious, so if you wouldn't mind...."

He sighed. "Shit, don't do this, Doc. Don't clam up and go all stick up the ass on me."

"Stick up the...?" Her jaw dropped. The ringing of her communicator cut her off. She narrowed her gaze on Bradi, daring him to continue with his juvenile behavior as she answered the call. "Dr. Langston here."

"Hey sweetheart, are you done yet? I'm going crazy waiting for you," Peter, her fiancé, said in his bedroom voice. "Did you miss me?"

Marisa turned to avoid Bradi's penetrating gaze and nodded. It took her a moment to realize that Peter couldn't see her. "Yes, I think I'm done here. My last patient was *just* leaving." She heard the door to her exam room open and close. Relief should have flooded her. Lt. Commander

Bradi Janelle had left. Oddly enough, no part of her was happy about that. Suddenly, she felt bad for her brashness. "Listen, I'll see you in a bit. There's something I need to take care of before I call it a day."

"Very well," Peter said. "See you soon."

"Mmmhmm." Marisa clicked the communicator off. Tension filled her neck and shoulders as the weight of her behavior toward Bradi weighed on her. In truth, he was no worse than the rest of the male crew on board. Being one of only a handful of females on a two month deep space journey had left her the target of many deprived males, but none rubbed on her nerves the way Bradi did. No one else made her dream of him, his touch, his cock buried deep within. No. No one else aboard the vessel did what Bradi did to her.

He's driving me insane.

"What the hell is it about you, Janelle, that gets me all fired up? I have never wanted to punch a man as much as I wanted to kiss him. Why you?" She reached down to grab a file off her desk, shaking her head at the idea that she would give Peter up in an instant to be with a man who only wanted a free fuck.

Two strong hands touched her shoulders and she froze. "If I had to guess what it is you can't resist about me, I would say it's my charming personality, my devilish good looks, and the fact that I've got an eleven inch dick. Is that marked in my chart? It should be. Wanna verify that?"

Marisa spun around to find Bradi standing there with a wicked grin on his entirely too attractive face. He winked. "Want me to take my pants off again? Oh, better yet, take yours off and I'll stick you with something special." He wagged his brows. "Something that will surely give you a boost."

"Of all the nerve," she spat as she glared at him. The urge to hit him was great. She gave in to it. The second that her palm connected with his rugged cheek, Marisa hissed, wanting desperately to take the action back. "Oh gods, I'm ... Lt. Commander...."

A fire burned in Bradi's blue eyes as he locked gazes with her. Marisa felt as though she were pinned by his predatory look. Every instinct in her screamed how very deadly the man before her could be but she didn't care. She didn't fear Bradi. She wanted him in ways she knew she shouldn't.

His cheek reddened and before Marisa could stop herself, she kissed her fingertips and pressed them to hot skin, seeming to douse a bit of the fire that burned in his eyes. Tapping her ear with her free hand, Marisa pressed one of the activation points for her built-in medical chips. "Scan for damage."

Bradi stiffened a second before a pain like Marisa had never experienced sliced through her head, instantly rendering her scan of Bradi's cheek ineffective. Grabbing her head, Marisa cried out.

"Shit, sorry," Bradi whispered, as though he had anything to do with her embedded chip acting up. The feel of his large arms wrapping around her instantly helped to chase the pain away, leaving only a tiny, dull ache in its place. "You okay?"

She nodded and stared down at her hand. "That's so strange. It's never hurt me before. Ever."

"I didn't mean to use so much ... umm," he glanced away, "of my good pick up lines on you."

What?

Growling, Marisa shoved him hard in the chest. Bradi didn't budge. The man was an oaf. A certifiable space gigolo that ran through women like they were on special. Anger welled in her. The fact that he'd heard her confession, that he now knew she wanted him, drove her to the edge of reason. Afraid of becoming violent with Bradi, Marisa pointed at the door as she glared at him. "Get out now, or so help me gods...."

Instantly, his mouth covered hers. Stunned, she gasped, giving him the opportunity he needed to ease his tongue in. She lost all rational thought. Licking the inner edges of her mouth, he made her knees shake. Marisa's brain screamed at her to bite his tongue off, but her body reacted by reaching up to touch him, to pull him closer.

He tasted so good. So sweet. So divine. She couldn't get enough.

With his height advantage, Marisa had to stand on her tiptoes while he bent down to her, but it was worth it. The feel of his hot mouth pressed to hers and of his gifted tongue tracing circles around her own made her nipples harden to pebbled points. Liquid pooled at the apex of her thighs and it wasn't until she felt Bradi's hands moving up and under her shirt that she realized what she was doing--making out with a man that could own her heart if he decided he wanted it.

Yanking back from him, Marisa lost her balance and staggered. The sounds of her exam room doors sliding open sounded. She ignored them. Bradi grabbed for her and pulled her into his warm body. The need to kiss him again, to welcome his tongue in her mouth was great. As he leaned down, she thought for sure that he'd kiss her again. He smiled. "Careful now, Doc, wouldn't want you to hurt yourself."

"That's why I keep you around, Bradi. You know how to take care of what's important to me," Peter said, appearing in the doorway suddenly.

She stilled. Had Peter seen them kissing? She knew Peter well enough to know that he wasn't one to mix words or beat around the bush. He'd have said something.

Marisa's eyes met Bradi's and she saw a shadow pass over them. What they'd done was wrong. It was clear that both parties understood that. Bradi nodded and eased his grip on her. "Yeah, if nothing else, I make a good watchdog, Pete."

She wasn't sure if that was hurt she saw on Bradi's face, or if he was just toying with her so she glanced at Peter hoping he'd shed some light on it. He offered none. No surprise there. Peter rarely had much to offer in the way of insight into Bradi. He was such a sharp contrast to Bradi that she wondered how they'd even become friends.

"Hey, Commander, I thought I told you that I'd meet you in a little bit." Marisa winked at Peter, signifying she was only joking.

Walking toward her, Peter took hold of her arms a bit harder than needed and gave her a good jerk. "And I've told you before that I do not like to be kept waiting--ever."

Marisa gave Peter a questioning stare as she tried to wiggle free of his grasp. "Peter, you're hurting me," she whispered, hoping Bradi wouldn't overhear her.

He eased up a bit but gave her a hard stare in the process. Peter's normally warm personality seemed ice cold almost daily as of late. She'd noticed it more and more and wasn't sure what had prompted it. Sure, Peter was under a great deal of stress with his new position but he'd had that for two months now. The hard as nails persona had come on in the last three weeks.

Glancing down at her, Peter smiled. It was forced and void of emotion. "Excuse us Bradi, but I need to kiss *my woman*."

"Your woman?" Marisa shot back, not caring much for the reference and still upset about the rough handling. She tugged her arm free of his grasp. "I am no man's property."

"I'm sorry. I didn't mean to snap at you." Peter gave her a sheepish grin and leaned down to whisper in her ear. "I love you."

"On that note, I am leaving," Bradi said, sounding oddly even tempered considering how heated he'd been only moments earlier. "I have to check in on the command deck. We are heading into non-Commission territory and it looks like we'll have that damn meteoroid shower to contend with after all. Our scouts tell us that it's not bad, but I would advise going around it if at all possible. I think it might be safest."

Peter gave Bradi a sickeningly sweet smile and when he spoke, Marisa could almost hear the sarcasm dripping from his every word. "That is precisely why you aren't required to think--buddy. We aren't adding any additional time to our trip. We'll continue on course as planned. I'll catch up with you in a bit. Drinks and a round of cards sound good to you, too?"

"Yeah, sure." Bradi headed for the sliding doors, not once bothering to look back. It was as though he'd already forgotten what had passed between them.

How could she have allowed him to kiss her? What was she thinking? He was Peter's friend and a jerk.

Yeah, a jerk who could really kiss!

Chapter Two

Marisa laughed and put her hand between her soon-to-be husband's knees. Shifting on his lap, she wasn't about to let Peter slip through her fingers yet again. They'd been on the ship for close to two months now and in that time they'd had only a few scattered and all too brief moments together. His ever growing coldness had only served to hamper them as well.

"Mmm," Peter murmured as he snuggled his chin into her neck, covering her with kisses along the way. He pressed his body against hers and she shivered. "I want you so bad."

"We'll be landing in a few days. Once we're on solid ground, you are mine." Her body was starved for sex. Peter had earned another promotion within the Commission and although it was an opportunity of a lifetime, it meant galaxy relocation. Moving one galaxy over shouldn't have been that big a deal for Marisa, but she'd only been off Earth a few times in her life and was terrified of what else existed beyond it.

She'd heard horror stories and prayed they weren't true.

"Are you sorry that you came?" Peter asked, obviously sensing her change in attitude.

"Don't be silly. I agreed to marry you, didn't I?" It was the best answer she could come up with and it was the truth. She'd agreed to marry Peter with little to no engagement period. He received notice of his promotion and had asked her to be his wife instantly. It was the only way they could remain together, and they weren't quite ready to break up, but certainly weren't ready to commit to marriage. At least she wasn't. Only married officers were permitted to bring anyone along. They'd allowed her to come not only because they set a date to be married before they took off but because of her skills. The engagement contract she'd signed was proof enough for the Commission, so obtaining a boarding pass was easy. The only stipulation was that upon landing she and Peter would be required to wed one another immediately.

Her father had been less than pleased with her short warning and afraid that if she wasn't happy with Peter, she'd be stuck so many light years away that it'd take him months to retrieve his only daughter.

Marisa had no fears that she wouldn't be happy with Peter. No. She'd been with him for close to two years. The minute she'd laid eyes on him she'd fallen for him. He'd been hurt during a droid attack and had been brought directly into her care. The Commission had found its medical resources spread thin after a multi-universe epidemic close to fifteen years ago, so healers of any kind were asked to come forth and be trained.

Her father, fearing that if she revealed her additional inborn gifts to anyone she would be killed, had forbidden her from joining in the call. It wasn't her fault that she possessed certain gifts from birth. Gifts that could aid in healing many. She'd had to wait until her eighteenth birthday before being allowed to join the Commission. Once in, she found out quickly that being alone in a predominately male barracks wasn't the best idea for her 'condition.' It tended to become unmanageable when her passions ran deep. Marisa knew that she needed to wait until she and Peter were alone and not in the middle of space before she allowed him to enter her body and make love to her--for the safety of all on board, it had to be that way.

She could only hope that Peter would understand that she was different, more than human and that he'd forgive her for keeping it from him.

Peter slid his hand under her gray T-shirt and gave her a sultry smile. "I can't wait until we can be alone."

Knowing that Peter's body was as hot with need as her own with no end to the torture in sight, Marisa decided to change the subject. "Tell me again of Margaidia."

Peter's eyes lit up. "Margaidia is beautiful--depending on what part of it you're in. It's as big as Earth. As I told you before, I spent the first three years of my training there. That's were I met Bradi. He's originally from there you know. You'll love it. I promise. I can't wait to see you in our new home, with little ones at your feet.

"Oh, and there are lots of shops filled with dresses and the most beautiful red flowers that will look stunning tucked into your silky brown hair." Peter took a piece of her long hair, twirled it around his fingers, and pulled her closer to him. "I love you, Marisa."

"You know how to woo a girl. That's for sure." She didn't comment on the fact that he'd brought up Bradi again. She'd mentioned her dislike of the man right after meeting him, but Peter swore that Bradi was a friend. She could concede that he could be Peter's friend, but it didn't take away from the fact that the man was an arrogant jerk.

An arrogant jerk who made her knees weak and her pulse race. Without warning, the ship lurched forward and Marisa tumbled off Peter's lap. His hand was still wrapped around her hair and she screamed out as he was thrown in the other direction. Flying toward him, she put her arms out in an attempt to catch herself.

The ship leveled and Peter pulled her quickly to him. She tried to free her hair from his grip, but it only wrapped tighter around his arm. He yanked a knife from his belt and cut the long strand of hair free from his arm, only a moment before the ship jolted again.

Marisa screamed as the knife Peter held dug down into her arm accidentally. Peter yanked it out quickly. "Marisa!"

Glancing down, she saw the large gash and knew that it would require a good twenty minutes with the lancer to fix. Peter tried to pull her to him again, but she held her hand up. "Go, you're needed on the bridge. I'm fine."

"I love you," he yelled as he ran toward the bridge.

The radio on her hip vibrated and Marisa knew right away that she was being paged to help the injured. She tapped her ear to activate her built-in chip and closed her eyes.

"Show me the damage." The chip in her head immediately began to access the ship's main computers. Her mind was flooded with images of large holes in the sides of the ship. Her gut twisted in a knot as she realized that the ship was beyond repair.

Having no desire to continue to look upon her demise, she barked new orders out at the chip, "Not that damage! The damage to life forms." She had to be vague because several of the beings on board the ship were anything but humanoid.

The initial scans revealed that seventy-five percent of the crew had been killed. The picture that the ship showed her of the mess hall was enough to make her have to swallow down the bile in her throat. No one in the mess hall had survived. Startled by the horrific images that were now displayed before her, Marisa stumbled backwards and screamed out when something seized hold of her waist.

"Calm down woman, it's me," a deep, heavily accented voice said from behind her. "Your arm? What the hell happened to it?"

"Bradi?" she asked, shocked by his sudden British inflection. It sounded so natural, so right for him that she wondered if that too was part of what he hid from the Commission. "Are you okay?"

"Yeah, come on. We need to get you to a release POD and treat that wound. Dr. Graves has ordered you off the ship. He wants you at the rendezvous point to care for the wounded." He paused. "There are only a few survivors left."

"I know." Not wanting to think about the massive amount of fatalities that had flashed before her, she nodded and took Bradi's hand in hers.

His brow furrowed as he looked down at their joined hands. "It will be okay, baby. I promise."

Normally, Marisa would have snapped at Bradi, any man for that matter, angry that he'd called her a pet name. Now, it was music to her ears. Something deep within her wanted that to be true, wanted her to be his significant other. It was absurd but there nonetheless. Squeezing his hand tighter, she offered him a slight smile. "I trust you even if it turns out you really are part toad."

He winked. "Come on." Bradi pulled her down the hallway and past the medic chambers.

"Wait!" she cried out, digging her heels into the floor.

At six foot six, Bradi towered above her. When he looked down at her and shook his head, she had to take a tiny step back to fully appreciate how intimidating he could be. "We don't have time for this, Doctor. The ship isn't stable and life support is dropping as we speak. Give it another few minutes and we'll all be frozen to death or sucked into space. That's not really my idea of fun, so let's go."

"But my supplies. I need my bag! The injured will need my attention."

Bradi growled and ran a hand through his long black hair. "Fine. But I'll grab it."

Marisa wanted to protest, but knew better. Bradi was the ship's lieutenant commander and wasn't used to taking orders from anyone but Peter or the Captain himself. She still wasn't sure how he'd managed to get to his position. He stood in direct opposition of everything the Commission required an officer to look and act like. His hair hung just past his shoulders. He had a goatee, and he gave no regard to the number of times he was reprimanded for drunken brawls while on leave or layovers.

"Marisa!"

"Peter?" She spun around to find Peter racing down the corridor toward her. He put his hand out and seized hold of hers. "Where's Bradi? I sent him to get you."

Sparks flew over their heads as the ship's life support systems began to systematically blow out. Peter slammed into her and took her to the ground. Rolling with her, he pinned her body beneath him, protecting her from debris. "Are you okay?"

She nodded. Another rumble started and Peter's eyes widened. "We've got to get to the release PODs now. Where the hell is Bradi?"

The door to the med unit opened just as another explosion went off. Bradi glanced at them as an overhead beam swung down behind him. Time seemed to slow for Marisa as Peter rolled off her and tackled Bradi to the ground. The beam crashed down onto the men and Marisa pushed up hard and fast to get to them.

Fire shot up around them. "No!"

She kicked the beam with all her might. It moved slightly before wedging itself in the doorway. She covered her mouth as she saw the two men lying lifeless. Holding her hand out above Peter's back, she closed her eyes and accessed her internal chip.

"Diagnostics." Instantly, Peter's vitals appeared to her. He was still alive, but something was wrong. Moving her hand to the left, she found the source of distress. His ribs were broken and his lung was punctured. Scanning further, she realized that part of the beam must have struck his head, rendering him unconscious.

A deep moan caught her attention right before another explosion went off, shaking the entire corridor. "Pete?"

"Bradi?" Marisa called out as she tried to roll Peter gently to the side.

Dark lines covered Bradi's face and at first, Marisa feared that he'd suffered burns from the fire. He brought his hand up and wiped his face, moving the soot with them. As Bradi opened his eyes, Marisa let out a small breath when she found them uninjured.

She put her hand out and went to access her built in chip again. Bradi shook his head no. "I'm fine, baby. Worry about Pete."

Marisa's jaw tightened. "You will shut-up and allow me to worry about you, too." She accessed her chip. "Diagnostics." Running a quick diagnostics test on Bradi, she discovered that aside from a nasty bump on his head and a few minor cuts and bruises, he was fine. The second she felt another headache coming on, Marisa stopped her scan of Bradi.

"Can you help me get Peter up?" The ship jerked and the beam creaked. Marisa yanked hard on Bradi's shirt and he rolled out of the way, taking Peter with him.

Gathering Peter up, Bradi tossed him over his shoulder. He glanced back at Marisa. "I dropped your medical bag."

"I'll get it."

"No! I will come back for it."

They couldn't wait and she knew it. "Get Peter to the POD. I'll be right behind you. Give me just two seconds, Janelle. That's all I need. Go!"

* * * *

"You are the hardest headed woman I've ever met!" Bradi let out an angry growl and ran toward the emergency exits with Peter in tow. He couldn't believe the woman would have the nerve to risk her life for a bag of goodies. He damned near died retrieving it and Pete was out cold from taking a beam to the back of the head. Had it not been for Pete, Bradi knew that the beam would have crushed him.

If he'd have thought he could have managed to carry a kicking and screaming Marisa over his other shoulder, he'd have grabbed her, too.

Bradi glanced back over his shoulder before entering the first emergency POD he found. A young man, shaking slightly, sat in the corner of it. Shockingly red hair hung in an otherwise too pale face, and the boy locked like he was about to pass out. His wide eyes stared up at Bradi. Silently, Bradi cursed the Commission's decision to allow men as young as seventeen to join and laid Pete down.

"If I am not back in five minutes," he said to the boy, "push this green button here. It'll get you and the Commander to safety. Understand?"

The boy nodded.

Bradi glanced at the POD number and made a mental note that it was POD 281 before rushing back to get Dr. Marisa Langston--who had not held true to her promise to follow right behind him. She was quite possibly the most annoying woman he'd ever met and he'd met a lot of women.

A whole lot of women, he thought to himself as he ran down the corridor.

If she wasn't so damn sexy and his best friend's fiancée, he'd take her over his knee and teach her how to behave. *She'd probably sear my sac off with a half-charged laser before she'd let me near her, but hey, a guy can dream.*

The sound of a hatch locking shut caught his attention and he turned to see POD 281 disengaging from the ship. Bradi ran toward it and slammed the palms of his hands against the porthole as he watched the POD float off into space.

The little redheaded bastard panicked. I'll kill him when I get my hands on him.

The ship shook again, slamming him into the nearest wall. Something popped in his shoulder and he tried to ignore the pain as he ran for the med unit. The feeling in his arm went and he was sure it was for the best, considering.

Terror gripped his chest as he saw that flames had engulfed the doorway. "Doc!" She didn't answer. The sane part of his brain told him to turn around and evacuate the ship while he still had a chance. Unfortunately, the sane part had little control over his everyday actions or his heart. Leaving Marisa wasn't an option. The woman owned a piece of him that even he couldn't explain how she'd come to possess. But the fact was, she did and he'd be damned if he went anywhere without assuring her safety.

Jumping through the flames, Bradi rolled on the ground as he landed. Pain shot through his shoulder with each turn, but he knew it was necessary to douse any fire on him. He came to his feet quickly and drew in a sharp breath when he saw Marisa's petite frame sprawled out on the floor before him. He tried to lift her, but his arm wouldn't cooperate.

"Marisa! Get up!" He shook her but she didn't budge.

"Doc? Baby?"

Still nothing.

"Damn it, Doc, I told Pete not to bring you on this trip. I told him that no high class lady could survive the journey. I told him that you were only cut out for dinner parties and ballrooms, not life in the Commission." The need to provoke her, to rile her to the point she got up to argue with him was a necessary evil. If it worked, she'd hate him but be alive. If it didn't, Bradi was more than prepared to die with her.

She coughed and looked up at him. Every bit of Bradi wanted to shout with joy. He held back. Marisa's green eyes lit with a fury he hoped would fuel her enough to get off the ship before it exploded. She tried to stand, but was too shaky to get to her feet without his help. The minute he slid his good arm around her slender waist, she snarled at him. Wagging his eyebrow, impressed with her tenacity, he ignored her dislike of him and yanked her up anyway.

The door, now completely engulfed by flames, was out of the question. Turning them around, Bradi moved quickly toward the back exit. Marisa looked up at him, her eyes wide. She pulled free from his hold and shook her head. "We'll never make it back to Peter in time."

"We'll get to a POD, baby. Don't you worry. We'll meet up with him as soon as we are clear of the ship."

He punched the emergency release button and pulled Marisa back just to be sure it was safe. Seeing that the coast was clear, he stepped out into the hallway. Marisa didn't follow. "Doc?"

"Peter, I have to get to Peter."

Bradi rolled his eyes and grabbed hold of her hand. "I promise not to touch you beyond this, once we are on the damn POD. You'll see Pete soon enough. The guy's probably just waking up now."

Shaking her head, Marisa stared back at him with wide, haunted, eyes. "His lung's punctured, Bradi. Without my help he will die."

Bradi? She never called him by his name. This was bad.

He yanked her down the corridor, seeking the nearest escape POD. He couldn't comment on what she'd told him. The thought of Pete dying was too much for him. The man had been closer to him than his own brothers had and he would not think of losing him now.

"I'm going to kill the little redheaded bastard that took off with him," he mumbled, under his breath.

"Stop, please. We have to get to Peter!"

Bradi came to a grinding halt outside of escape POD 303. Glancing at their joined hands, he regretted what he had to do but did it all the same. Quickly, he thrust the uncooperative doctor in before him. She fell to the floor with a thud leaving his heart heavy knowing that he caused her pain.

"Why, you..." Marisa charged at him, slamming into his bad arm. He grabbed her around the waist, lifted her into the air, and pushed the green POD release button with the toe of his boot.

"Woman, do not make me knock you out, because I will!" The thought of hitting Marisa made him sick, but he wouldn't give her the satisfaction of knowing that. She stilled in his arms allowing him to take a deep breath, knowing she was safe and with him. Had she gone with Pete he'd have worried to the point of death that something might have happened to her. Why this tiny spitfire of a woman seemed to rule his every emotion was beyond him, but she did.

Marisa grew quiet and that worried Bradi. She glanced up at him, her green eyes glistening with unshed tears. "Do you think Peter's dead?"

Spitting, throwing a fit, hell, even biting were all things he could deal with, but crying wasn't something he was prepared for. The fact that he was as concerned about Pete as she was didn't help matters any. Carefully, Bradi placed his arm around her as he sank down to the floor, holding her close to him. "I don't know, baby. I honestly don't know."

Chapter Three

Marisa woke with a start and barely held back a scream. The nightmare she'd had was too vivid for her to maintain her composure. She looked around the small pod, remembering what had happened and wondered if real life wasn't actually worse than her dream. Lieutenant Commander Janelle snored softly in his sleep, and his long body looked slightly cramped in the confined quarters.

The PODs were designed to maintain minimal life support requirements to allow for maximum amount of travel time. Marisa exhaled and swore that she could see her breath before her face. Freezing, she moved closer to Bradi for warmth.

"At least the brute's good for something," she said as she snuggled in close to him. Still cold, she butted her body to his and almost jerked back when she felt a rush of heat go through her. Thinking that Bradi might be ill, she leaned up and touched his cheeks gently. As hard and as aloof as she wanted to appear when it came to Bradi, the idea of losing him terrified her.

Closing her eyes, Marisa activated her chip and requested a check of Bradi's vitals. His core temperature was a good ten degrees hotter than a normal person's and when she went to access his medical records, pain ripped through her head. The chip fizzled and left her with a migraine.

"Bradi?" She touched his face again, needing to know that he was okay.

He shifted slightly and mumbled something in his sleep. Leaning down, she listened closer as he repeated it. "I am horny and tired. Fix the first or let me sleep."

"Oh, you ... you ... animal!"

The smirk that had spread over his features died quickly. He put his back to her and winced. She knew that his shoulder still hurt him, but until he let her examine it, she'd take what little satisfaction she could get from the fact that he was uncomfortable.

"How the hell did I get stuck with you?" She attempted to get comfortable again by putting her back to him as well and failed. "Brr ... it's freezing in here."

Bradi shifted again behind her and let out a groan before wrapping his large body around hers. Everything in her mind told her to shove the big jerk off her, but her body sizzled under the weight of his touch.

* * * *

Marisa's body was tense and Bradi knew that she was thinking of tossing him off her. In truth, Bradi kind of hoped she would. He wasn't sure what made him turn to comfort her. His bad arm was vulnerable to her if she decided to inflict pain and he didn't think he could handle her calling him an animal again. If she only knew how close to the truth she was.

The feel of her curvy backside snuggled close to his body made his cock jerk. Even after narrowly escaping with their lives, Marisa still managed to smell wonderful to him and make his body hungry for hers. She always had. The first day he'd met her, he'd been drawn to her like no other female before. Something about her called to him on a primitive level and he didn't want to think too hard about it.

To his kind that type of attraction could only mean one thing. And that wasn't something Marisa would ever want to believe to be true. Bradi was having a hard enough time juggling the idea around in his head. Asking Marisa to believe she might very well be his mate, born to be his lover, his wife, the mother of his children, was insane.

* * * *

Bradi woke slowly, his joints aching and his body on fire. It was normal with his condition for his body to react to changes in the temperature automatically. It was also common for him to run several degrees hotter than a human. That was just one of the reasons why he refused to allow Dr. Marisa Langston to evaluate him. Hell, he hadn't ever allowed any Commission doctor to examine him. It'd cost him a pretty penny to pay others to forge his documents, but it was necessary all the same. Besides, he had no family so money wasn't really a concern for him.

Marisa was still sleeping and he didn't want to wake her. She looked like an angel lying there with her arms pulled up close to her chest and it took everything in him not to reach out and touch her. The cut on her arm had finally stopped bleeding but the slightest bump could easily break it open. Rolling on his side, Bradi winced when pain radiated through his shoulder.

Peeking out the POD window, his stomach dropped. There, in the distance, he saw the tell-tale aquamarine color of Margaidia, their original destination and the destination that had been programmed into all the escape PODs should there be trouble. The POD had overshot the planet and was headed on a direct path for Sargaidia, the uncharted sister planet to Margaidia, and the last place in the universe he wanted to go back to.

Bradi checked the computer and found it frozen over. Looking around the POD, he realized that the entire thing was covered with a thin frost.

Marisa.

Dropping down next to her, he touched her lightly. Her body was rigid and extremely cool to the touch.

"Doc?" he asked, shaking her gently. She didn't respond and his gut twisted. The thought of her freezing to death before he was able to get the POD operational again was a very real possibility.

"Come on, babe," he said, hoping to goad her into responding. The faint blue line around her lips told him that no amount of prodding would help. Acting quickly, Bradi pulled his shirt off and reached for her. Groaning softly from the pain shooting through him, he covered Marisa's body with his own. "This isn't enough."

Bradi worked his boots and pants off before reaching for Marisa's uniform. He'd been dying to get her out of her clothes from day one, but this wasn't exactly what he had in mind. He worked her shirt over her head and did his best not to stare at the luscious pale globes before him. Her pink nipples looked good enough to eat and everything in him wanted to sample them. The faint light from the navigational controls reflected off her pale skin and he had to be closer to her.

The nasty cut on her upper arm seemed to be holding, but the fear of breaking it open left him moving slower than he should to warm her body. Working her boots and pants off, Bradi lingered a little too long near the top of her panty line. Thoughts of Pete kept him from peeking further.

Placing his body over hers, Bradi willed himself to be hotter. His body reacted to his command and he felt his core temperature rise even more. If he had to, he'd shift forms, but the last thing he wanted was for Marisa to wake and find herself under a partially changed man. Somehow, he didn't think that would go over so well. Fully shifting wasn't an option either. It wouldn't make it any easier on her to find herself pinned beneath a black panther.

Marisa moaned and he looked down to see if she was awake yet. Her eyes remained closed, but she moved her hands slightly. Bradi tensed when he felt her fingers running over his back.

"Doc?"

"Mmm," she whispered, grinding her hips upwards.

The sweet scent of her cream filled his head. The erection, which he seemed to permanently sport while around Marisa, ached to dive into her, sample her flesh and claim her for his own. The tiny silken barrier of her panties served as a reminder that he couldn't, or rather shouldn't, take her.

She shifted a bit. "Mmm, I want you in me."

Bradi froze as she grabbed his ass. "Doc, wake up."

Cool lips met his and he fought to keep his body from responding. The minute her tongue pushed through and found his, he lost all control.

If I'm going to die out here anyway, I might as well die making love to her. Marisa is the closest to heaven I'm ever going to be.

Marisa's hands pushed between their bodies. She wrapped her fingers around his cock and he nearly came on her bare stomach. Never before had a woman's touch brought him so much pleasure, so quickly. Reason fought its way through to him. "Doc, baby, wake up, now! You don't want to do this. It's not right."

Her lips fastened onto his as she pushed her panties to the side and rubbed the head of his cock in her wet juices. "It's more than right. I want you. I've dreamed of touching you from the moment I boarded the ship."

Bradi wanted to take the time to love her as she should be loved before entering her, but he was no longer in control. The beast within could smell her cream, her sex, and the desire to mate with her was overpowering. Easing his cock head into her opening, he gritted his teeth at how tight she was. Inching in a bit more, she cried out and grabbed hold of his arms. The pleasure of her tight channel wrapped around the tip of his dick overshadowed the pain in his shoulder as he worked himself into her more.

"Oh ... yes," she whispered, kissing his face feverishly.

He savored the feel of her. "You're so fucking tight, Doc." He briefly wondered how she could be this difficult to enter when she and Pete had been together for so long, but he pushed it to the back of his mind, not wanting to think about his betrayal. This was his moment to be in the woman who'd called to him on levels he couldn't explain since the moment he'd laid eyes on her.

Marisa's erect nipples rubbed against his chest as he pushed a bit further into her. Meeting with slight resistance, Bradi hesitated. Could it be? He stopped. She'd been with Pete for close to two years, they had to have had sex--right? There was no way she was a virgin. Not the sexually charged doctor who made him weak in the knees. No.

Marisa dug her nails into his arms and thrust her head back. "More!"

Any concerns he had flew away at the sound of her command. Thrusting into her, she cried out as he brought himself to the hilt. Somehow, she'd managed to accept all of him, her channel fisting his dick to the point he wanted to come and he'd only just started.

"Gods, baby. You're perfect."

Her body eased slightly as he worked his cock almost out of her. Her pussy clenched around him like a vice as he dove back in. Each swipe, each thrust, left him growling and fighting the beast within. It wanted him to shift. It wanted to mark her. Claim her. Keep her forever.

Bradi had never had the urge to claim anyone as his mate before and he wasn't sure how to handle it. He fought to stay in control as he continued to slide in and out of her body. The beast within him pushed back with a vengeance and surfaced quickly. His incisors lengthened and his fingertips sprouted claws. Bradi was able to fight a full change, but unable to resist the lure of Marisa's milky white skin, the pumping of her blood as it sped through her veins.

"*Mine*," he growled out.

Bradi tried to fight it, but as he felt his teeth sinking into her shoulder and his cock begin to release his seed, he knew it was too late--he'd lost himself in the paradise of her body and the beast within him had assured that they would never be apart again. She was his.

Marisa's body jerked beneath him and at first, he assumed her cries were from his teeth but when she fisted her hand his hair, holding him to her, he knew it was something else. Coppery, sweet liquid filled his mouth as he continued to deposit his come within her womb, filling her to brim and twitching with each new spurt. Bradi forced his mouth from her body when he felt the tremors pouring through her. Her already pale skin seemed to glow with an unnatural shimmer. Bradi stayed above her, still nestled deep in her body, watching in awe as the light seemed to encompass her.

The light moved over her body and covered his quickly. It didn't hurt so much as it felt like someone running a million fingers over his skin. His cock jerked to life and even though it should have been sated, it wanted more. Never one to not listen to his dick, Bradi moved his hips and began to ride Marisa's tight body once more.

She grabbed hold of his shoulders and it dawned on him that no pain followed. Glancing downward, he saw that the bite mark he'd given her was completely gone. The cut on her arm was gone as well. The light around them grew so bright that Bradi had to shut his eyes. Marisa screamed out and wrapped her legs around his waist. She bucked beneath him, driving herself up and his cock in deeper.

"Uh...."

The soft moan she let out left Bradi thrusting into her more, pummeling her glorious body and paying extra attention to his lower abdomen, making sure it rubbed her clit just right. Marisa cried out as another orgasm hit her. The feel of her pussy milking him was too much and he let his body release again.

"Mine," he whispered as he filled her with even more of his seed, his essence.

The light around them died down slowly. The tiny pinging noise from the system computer sounded, indicating it was at least on, if nothing else. Reluctantly, Bradi withdrew from his mate's now warm body.

Marisa's eyes fluttered open and she looked up at him. A smile appeared slowly on her face. "I love you ... Peter."

Peter?

Bradi froze and waited for her to take it back, to claim that it was a slip of the tongue, but she didn't. Her eyes closed slowly and he heard her breathing grow shallow. He rolled off her quickly and sat up. Running his hands through his hair, he tried to make sense of it all.

Marisa hadn't been awake at all. She'd been dreaming of Pete when it was his body pleasing her. Dreaming of another man when he'd taken her as his wife. Given her his seed. His essence. A kick to the solar plexus would have been less devastating than that.

Reaching for his pants, Bradi stopped when his gaze flickered over Marisa's legs. The smell of her blood filled his nostrils and he leaned down to find a faint line of it running down her inner thigh.

"You were a virgin?" Everything clicked then. Bradi fought to keep from vomiting as the enormity of the situation hit him tenfold. He'd made love to a woman who thought he was her fiancé, who just so happened to be his best friend, and now he'd taken her maidenhood from her on top of everything else.

Could it get any worse?

Chapter Four

Marisa opened her heavy eyelids slowly and looked up to find Bradi staring out the window. "Great, so it wasn't a dream, was it?" Sitting up, she adjusted herself. Her clothes were wrinkled and she noticed that her boots were off. Glancing up at Bradi to ask him about it, she saw the look of shock on his face. "What's the matter?"

"I'm so sorry, Doc. I thought you were awake. I did not know ... I wouldn't have...."

Marisa blinked a few times in an attempt to clear her head. "Of course I was awake, you idiot. I don't run around a ship that's blowing up with my eyes closed. Geesh!"

"Right, you were talking about the ship exploding and being a smartass before. I knew that." The tension in Bradi's body seemed to leave him. It was a shame. She really enjoyed watching the muscles in his thick neck move. Surprised by her own lustful thoughts, Marisa stood quickly.

"Shouldn't we have landed on Margaidia by now? We weren't that far from it and the PODs were set to make...." She stopped talking when she noticed the forlorn look upon his face. "Lt. Commander?"

His blue eyes found her and she drew in a breath under the weight of them. "Buckle up, sweetie. We're about to enter Sargaidia's atmosphere. And you can call me Bradi, Doc, I think you've earned it."

Earned it?

"You mean Margaidia, right?"

He grabbed hold of her waist and set her down in the POD seat. Ignoring her protests, he buckled her in anyway. "Janelle? What's going on?"

He climbed into the control seat and buckled himself in as well. The POD thumped hard against an unseen force and she screamed out. Bradi's eyebrows went up as if to say, 'you ain't seen nothing yet.'

Another scream caught in her throat as he lifted the protective visor, allowing her a full view of what was before them. Shades of red, green, and blue were everywhere. Although Marisa had only been off Earth a few times in her life, she knew enough about landings to know that something wasn't right. "Bradi, aren't we going a bit fast?"

"You can say that again."

"W-What?"

"Nothing. Umm, the POD's controls froze for a bit. I barely got them up and running before we got trapped in the planet's atmosphere." He pulled hard on the steering shift as the POD began its rapid descent.

Marisa's stomach lurched as the bottom seemed to drop out from under them. The speed at which they were traveling would most definitely kill them upon landing. She said a silent prayer under her breath and reached out for comfort. Finding Bradi's arm, she settled, grabbed hold and held tight. Something about the man made her feel safer.

* * * *

Bradi risked a quick glance at Marisa and saw her reaching out for him. He thought it was to punch him, and was surprised when she not only laid her hand on him, but gave him a gentle squeeze, too. His loins burned again to be buried in her and he shifted awkwardly in the seat.

You're about to die here, buddy, he thought to himself, stealing a glance down toward his cock. *Do you think you could get your head in the game and off her for a moment?*

The red sea came into focus and Bradi cursed himself for not landing the POD sooner. He'd misjudged and thought that if he waited another hour they'd be closer to the inhabited compounds of the planet and closer to help. He'd been wrong.

"Janelle, tell me it's going to be okay again," Marisa said, squeezing his arm more and breaking his heart in the process. "Please tell me that. I need to hear *you* say it. I trust you and need to...."

Against his better judgment, Bradi gave into what she needed to hear, all the while wishing she'd call him by his first name. "It'll be okay, baby. I promise."

Marisa's grip on him tightened and he looked into her green eyes just as the sea greeted them.

* * * *

Marisa lifted her head slowly unsure if she was alive or dead. By the nasty crick in her neck, she was guessing alive. A deep cough caught her attention and she looked over to find that she and Bradi were still strapped into the POD. Blood red water surrounded them.

"Janelle, how bad are you hurt?" He didn't answer. She unfastened her seatbelt and willed her stiff body to move to him. Placing her hand on her head, she activated her embedded chip. "Diagnostics scan."

Closing her eyes she assessed the damage to his body. For a split second she could have sworn that the chip indicated broken legs, but when she checked again there was no sign of injury.

"Doc?"

Instantly, Marisa's chip scan fizzled out and pain shot through her head. Bradi touched her hand and she peeked out at him. "Hey," she smiled, happy to see him alive and responsive, "are you okay?"

"What, would you miss me if something happened? Or are you just hoping I stay alive long enough to get you to safety?" The tone in his voice made her lip curl.

"Asshole." She pushed up extra hard off him and smiled when she heard him grunt. He unlatched himself and rose to meet her. The POD creaked and the sound of cracking glass made them both turn around.

Bradi grabbed her and pulled her down to the floor. She began to protest and he kissed her lips, rendering her silent. As his tongue moved into her mouth, hers greeted it, shocking her and apparently him. He moaned and Marisa took the lead, sucking gently on his tongue.

Bradi pulled away, his blue gaze ran over her. "Take a deep breath now!"

Without thought, she did. Bradi slammed her down to the floor and his body flattened against hers. The window shattered. Blood red water poured into the POD and within seconds they were submerged. Lifting her quickly, Bradi pushed her toward the window and gave a good shove to get her through it. Shards of broken glass ripped at her legs and she had to fight to keep from screaming out in pain.

Once free of the POD, Marisa turned and waited for Bradi. He didn't come. It was then that she realized the window wasn't big enough for his six foot six inch, muscle-bound frame to get through.

The pressure in her lungs was excruciating as she attempted to climb back through the window. Bradi pushed her hard, shaking his head violently no. She had no intention on leaving him and was prepared to die with him. Something brushed past her back and she froze. Every gut instinct told her not to turn around and look, but she couldn't help herself. Turning slowly, she found herself face to face with a large yellowish eye. Upon further inspection she found it firmly attached to the largest eel she'd ever seen.

Not thinking, she punched out and caught it in the eye. It slammed against her, squishing her between the POD and its body. It pushed her hard and seemed to be trying to lift her to the surface. She fought against it, not wanting to leave Bradi behind.

Water rushed into her lungs and she felt as if someone had lit a fire in her chest. Being a doctor, she knew the process involved in drowning and she knew that it was one of the worst ways to go.

Better to be unconscious before the eel eats me, she thought to herself as the blackness swallowed her.

Bradi's senses picked up a predator near them and he could only guess what stalked them. The seas of Sargaidia were littered with creatures that even he feared. When he saw Marisa turning back for him, his heart melted. She cared whether he lived or died and that meant something to him.

Marisa's body slammed into the POD and Bradi let the beast within surface. Slamming into the side of the POD with his clawed hands, he tore his way through the metal as if it were nothing more than paper. Swimming out of the POD, he found Marisa descending slowly in the water. There was no sign of the predator he'd sensed and he wondered if his natural warning system was getting faulty. Something had hit Marisa. But what?

He snatched hold of her arm and headed for the surface. The minute their faces broke the surface, he drew in a deep breath of air and pulled Marisa to him. She gasped, coughing out water and he exhaled.

She would live. That was all that mattered.

Looking around, he found the shoreline and headed for it--cursing the fates for putting him with a hotheaded woman, who seemed determined to kill herself before the day was up.

* * * *

Marisa hissed as Bradi pulled the soaked material off her legs. The scraps that had once been called her pants seemed to go out of their way to cling to the large gashes in her legs. "Ouch!"

"Hold still and it won't hurt so much," Bradi said, scolding her like she was a child.

"Easy for you to say."

"Baby."

She growled at him. "I wouldn't have these if you hadn't shoved me through that broken window!"

"You'd be laying at the bottom of the sea dead. Would you prefer that? I could throw you back in."

Marisa reached into his utility belt and grabbed his knife. His eyes narrowed as if daring her to stick him with it. As much as she wanted to jab him in the gut, she wanted to check her wounds first. Grabbing hold of the material, she sliced it off just below her crotch line. Following suit on the other side, she smiled as she handed his knife back to him.

"There, I'm now stuck in the universe's shortest shorts, but at least they aren't flapping pieces of nothing."

"Doc." Bradi exhaled deeply. He touched her inner thigh lightly and heat pooled between her legs. He didn't seem to notice that she damned near creamed herself with just the touch of his fingers and she wasn't about to point it out to him. "This one is bad. Can you heal it?"

"Heal it? What, I don't know. Maybe. I'll need to find something to act as a needle and...."

Bradi put his hand up, motioning for her to stop. "No, I mean heal it. Not mend it."

Marisa's heart beat furiously and she fought to maintain her composure. "Umm ... I don't know ... umm ... stop looking at me like that."

Bradi leaned down and put his face directly in hers. "Listen, lady. I don't give a shit about whatever it is you don't want people to know about you, but you see these cuts?" He ran his hands lightly over her thighs, sending shockwaves of excitement through her body. "These will not only get infected, they will draw predators to us. Is that what you want? Do you want a pard of panthers or a pack of wolves to happen upon you overnight because they followed the scent of blood?"

Marisa looked around at the edge of the forest and swallowed back the lump in her throat. "How do you know that there are panthers and wolves here? A month ago you couldn't even remember your name to board the ship after you spent the night living it up at the bars and now you're suddenly a survival expert!" She eyed Bradi for a response, but he gave none. Instead, he turned to head into the woods, leaving her to sit on the edge of the shoreline--alone.

"Janelle?" He didn't stop or answer her. "Janelle, please." Marisa gulped as he stalked off into the forest. She'd only seen pictures of vegetation as strange as this and could only imagine how many plants and animals in there were deadly. The tall, black barked tree had yellow leaves that seem to sweep to the forest floors. They were massive and distinctively different from the trees in the Earth museums.

A soft splashing noise in the red sea behind her caught her attention and she turned around quickly. The head of the mammoth eel appeared a few feet off shore and Marisa found herself crab walking backwards to get away from it. The sand was softer than she was used to and she sank down into it slightly. The eel lunged forward and narrowly missed striking her as she rolled to her side.

Pushing upwards in the pinkish sand, she somehow managed to get to her feet. She ran forward, stumbling again and again because of the pain in her legs. The long jagged cuts opened more, leaving her bleeding at an alarming rate. Risking a glance over her shoulder, she hoped that she was far enough away from the water to prevent another attack. Much to her surprise the eel began to slither from the sea. It moved toward her with a speed and efficiency that terrified her.

"Janelle," she whispered, as the need to panic beat at her.

Something growled in the bushes behind her and she didn't dare turn to see what it was. From the events that had happened since crashing, she could only assume that it was bad. When she heard matching growls coming from there, too, she knew that her suspicions were correct. She was screwed.

* * * *

"That no good, insolent, ungrateful, bi...." Bradi stopped his verbal attack on Marisa as he looked for a safe place for them to camp. The suns were beginning to set and nightfall only meant that the evil things would come out and play. Depending on where they were, they might be able to make it to an inhabited village or compound within a few days walk.

He shuddered to think of what kind of reception he'd get. He hadn't spoken to his family in nearly twelve years. The terms he'd left on had been anything but pleasant. The death of his mother had left him with a sharp tongue and a fogged sense of right and wrong. He didn't think that his father would welcome him with open arms now, that much was for sure. Hopefully, he could get Marisa some medical attention and get them a ride off this gods forsaken planet.

There was no doubt in his mind that she was dying to get away from him. She seemed to hate the fact that she had to share air with him, let alone be stranded with him. It still blew Bradi's mind that she'd refused to leave him after the POD had crashed. He'd have thought that she'd have relished the opportunity to rid herself of him. Of course, she'd be left all alone on an unfamiliar planet, but still.

He heard her call his name once more, this time in a whisper and he smiled. "Let her sweat. It'll teach her not to speak to me like a dog. Now, if she wanted to bend over and let me fuck her like a...." Something wasn't right. The hairs on the back of his neck stood on end and he tipped his head to the side, smelling the air.

Panther.

Shedding his clothes quickly, he shifted into his panther form. It had been years since he was able to shift without worry and his inner beast was happy to be free. Bending down, he sniffed the ground and followed the scent of the pard. His heart hammered in his chest when he realized that the others had made a beeline straight for Marisa. No doubt, the smell of fresh blood and human was too much for them.

Bounding through the brush at the edge of the beach, he stopped when he saw Marisa stroking the top of one of the panther's heads. Stunned, he could do nothing other than watch the spectacle before him unfolding.

How had she calmed the animal?

His senses told him that this was a group of werepanthers, not normal animals. They only respected humans if they were marked and even then that didn't save them. They were also known to not attack if the victim carried the scent of a powerful warrior panther. Instantly he thought back to the pod and making love to Marisa.

Shit, I need to stop referring to it as love. Next thing I know I'll be standing on a hilltop confessing my undying devotion and.... He bit the words back in his mind before they came to be.

Focusing his mind and still in awe of the scene before him, Bradi tried to think of what would make the others yield to Marisa. Had she tapped into the power he'd seen her use? Had she managed to kill one with her bare hands, proving that she was a skilled warrior? He highly doubted it.

Coming to his senses, he walked toward Marisa slowly, in anticipation of a fight. When the other panthers only turned and snarled lightly he understood that they would not harm her. A large male panther moved in from behind Marisa and from the way it dropped its shoulders, Bradi could tell that it was thinking of exuding its power and attempting to claim her. There was no way in hell that he'd give Marisa up.

She's mine, he thought as he leapt down before her with a vicious snarl.

"Oh gods," Marisa whispered. Fear radiated off her and Bradi knew that it was him she was scared of. She looked around nervously as tears glistened in her eyes. "Bradi? Bradi, please help me. I didn't mean to upset you. Please."

Each time she called out to him, using his name, he wanted to shift back into his human form and wrap his arms around her. That would no doubt scare her more, and if the Commission ever found out that he was part supernatural then he'd be let go and possibly brought up on charges. Project Exorcism had rid the Commission of most of its supernatural problem, or so they thought. Bradi knew better, but he wasn't about to start talking.

Bradi swiped his claws out at the large male in a show of dominance and it heeded his warning. It turned and ran toward the woods, followed closely by the rest of its pard.

A piece of him longed to run with them. He missed the days when he and his siblings, well, all the ones that could fully shift that was, ran together.

He looked up at Marisa and took another step toward her. She tensed and the smell of her fear excited the beast. "Bradi, please, I'm sorry. Please, don't leave me here. Bradi, please...."

The soft plea in her voice brought the man within him back to the surface. He was ashamed of how close he'd let his beast get to attacking her. He spun quickly around and ran off into the forest to find his clothes.

* * * *

Bradi stood silently in the shadows, watching Marisa. She sat on the beach with a large stick clutched tightly to her, wiping tears from her cheeks. He wanted to run to her, hold her, and tell her that everything would be all right, but he didn't. Instead, he took the coward's approach and rustled the bush next to him with his hand to alert her to his presence.

She wiped her cheeks and righted herself. "Bradi, is that you?"

"Yeah," he said, unsure if he could offer anymore without breaking down and confessing all his secrets to her.

She sprang to her feet and ran toward him. Throwing her arms around his neck, she sighed. Bradi froze. "This huge eel came out of the water, and then all kinds of big leopards ran out at me. One knocked me down and I threw sand in its eyes. I thought it was going to rip my throat out, but it stopped and started to sniff me." She tightened her grip on him, and he wrapped his arms around her slowly, cringing slightly at her mislabeling his breed as leopards.

"It nudged me a few times before it stuck its nose right into my crotch." She flushed as she spoke.

This piqued Bradi's curiosity, as he wondered what had driven them into acceptance of her. The mark had something to do with it. She was now viewed as claimed by him, but that wasn't always a guarantee. He stroked the back of her long, layered hair and nodded to her, encouraging her to go on.

Something flickered across her eyes and she narrowed her gaze on him. "I called for you, you stubborn bastard and you never came." Her hand came up fast and struck him square across the face. Knowing that he deserved it for leaving her alone, he said nothing, but when she attempted to strike him again, he grabbed her wrists.

"Let go of me!" she cried out as she snapped her teeth at him.

He snapped back and gave her a wicked grin.

"Ooo, forget it! If your teeth broke my skin I'd probably end up with some sort of disease considering the way you run around with the ladies."

He resisted the urge to inform her that she was now considered one of his ladies, the *only* lady in fact, and that his teeth had indeed broken her skin. "I'll have you know, Doc, that I'm up to date on all my shots, or are you forgetting how you drooled over the sight of my ass as you injected me with them?"

The Commission had instituted mandatory shots for diseases and STDs to all of their enlisted, and Marisa seemed to take great joy out of throwing what she thought was his sex life into his face every chance she got. It was pointless to give the shots to him. His genetic make up didn't allow for him to catch any sort of human disease. The worst he had to fear when bedding a woman was getting her pregnant. The shots, while they contained population control additives, did nothing to lower his sperm count. It didn't matter, really. The only way he could get a female pregnant was if she was his true life mate. He highly doubted Marisa was that. Besides, she was on Commission shots too, so even if she was his true mate, not just his chosen, she'd be protected from pregnancy.

"How could I forget?" She glared at him. "And, for the record, should I cut myself on a rusty eel, I'm as good as dead. I'm allergic to the binding agents they use in the shots so I have none."

"A rusty eel, huh?" Laughing, he pulled her close to him not caring if she protested. "I'll do my best to keep you away from any more sharp objects or rusty eels."

Chapter Five

Bradi finished putting the last of the large leaves over the crude structure and climbed underneath it to join Marisa by the fire. She sat there rubbing her hands together with her knees to her chest. It gave him a fantastic view up her ultra-short shorts and he savored it. His cock stirred to life and he could almost taste her sweet skin as he watched her.

He reached out to the give the *brula* he'd managed to catch a turn to keep it from burning over the fire and he moved closer to her. She shifted and gave him a wary look. "What do you think you're doing?"

"You look cold and I'm burning up, so I thought you might want to be close to me." It was only a partial truth. Because I want to hold you seemed like too bold a statement.

"Oh," she said, moving closer to him. She looked up at the meat and cocked an eyebrow. "Are you sure that's edible?"

He chuckled. "Yes, it's similar to rabbit."

"I'm going to eat a bunny?" She sounded so innocent.

Laughing again, he turned the meat. "No, *brula*. Similar but not the same thing."

"How do you know so much about this planet? I thought you were from Margaidia."

He had to hide his delight. She knew, or thought she knew, where he was from. That meant that she'd paid attention to the details of his life. He nonchalantly turned the *brula* again and shrugged. "Well, I lived there for the last twelve years but I wasn't born there."

"Where were you born?"

He smiled. "Tell you what--I'll tell you a secret about me if you tell me one about you first."

Marisa stiffened. "I don't have any secrets."

"Fine, then neither do I."

She glanced up at him and shivered. Sliding his arm around her, he waited for Marisa to scream at him or hit him. When she did neither, he assumed it was safe. They sat quietly and watched the *brula* cook. His gaze kept going to her legs and he wished that she'd come clean about her ability to heal just so she could mend the angry cuts on her body.

"Bradi?"

"Hmm?" he asked, not wanting to let her go and praying she wouldn't ask him to.

"What happened to the ship? It was fine and then all of the sudden it wasn't."

The same question had plagued him from the moment he'd felt the first signs of distress on the ship and that had been a day prior to the crash. His gut told him it was sabotaged, but he didn't want to believe that one of his own crewmembers would do such a thing. The meteoroid shower could have been to blame, but even that wouldn't have caused the amount of destruction he'd seen on board the ship. "I'm not sure, honey."

When she didn't balk at his term of endearment, he took it as a good sign. She sighed. "I wonder if Peter made it."

He drew her deeper into his arms and was surprised when he felt her shift her body to meet his. Kissing the top of her head gently, he rocked her slowly. Marisa turned her face to meet his and when he noticed the unshed tears in her eyes, he instantly wanted to rip something apart.

* * * *

Marisa stared into the blue depths of Bradi's eyes as the firelight sparkled off them. It struck her how handsome Bradi was and she was grateful for the warm glow of the fire because it masked the faint red glow she now wore. This man who she'd assumed was a pig sat so quiet, stroking her back gently and rocking her softly. How was it that he could be so thoughtful when she'd only ever considered him for the chauvinistic candidate of the year award?

Bradi's full lips were framed nicely by his dark black goatee, and when he tipped his head slightly to look at her, she couldn't help herself. Leaning in, she pressed her lips lightly to his. His entire body stiffened and for a minute, she thought he'd push her away from him, but he didn't. When she felt his hand move into her hair, she realized what she'd started.

The kiss remained chaste at first and that bothered her. Was she not as good as the women he normally surrounded himself with? Marisa had never undergone any drastic body changes so her breasts were hers and hers alone, as was the rest of her body. At five foot five, she just missed hitting his shoulder and she knew that men tended to prefer the intergalactic supermodels to tiny packaged women like her. Didn't they?

Opening her mouth slightly, she let her tongue slide along his lower lip. She was met with a moan and Bradi's grip tightened in her hair. Pulling her head back slightly, his mouth came down hard on hers. At first, she forgot to breathe. Sure, she'd been kissed before, but never like this. Never with such raw unbridled passion. His tongue dove in and out of her mouth, mimicking mating and Marisa's legs drew together in an attempt to quell the burning between her thighs.

Bradi began to ease their bodies to the ground and she didn't fight him. She needed comfort, needed to lose herself in the moment. Guilt over her lust for Bradi tried to surface, but she suppressed it. Stranded on a strange, primitive planet with no hope of going home, she needed to feel something--anything, and for all the faults Bradi had, not making her feel wasn't one of them.

His hands seemed to be everywhere at once and she realized that she too was feeling him. Letting her hands glide over his back, she bunched his T-shirt up to feel his hot skin beneath. Hard muscles greeted her and she drew in a sharp breath as her pussy quivered. She worked his shirt over his head and couldn't believe how incredible his body was. The very thought of him fucking her damn near brought about an orgasm. She could only dream what the real thing would be like.

Bradi was always shy about letting people see him partially dressed and she couldn't understand why. "You don't have an ounce of fat on you."

Bradi chuckled and she realized that she'd spoken aloud. He bent his head down and kissed her collarbone lightly. "Mmm, I have yet to find any fat on you either."

"Oh please, my--"

He silenced her with a kiss as he ground his hips against her. The pressure of his hard shaft through the fabric of his pants was more than enough to stimulate her swollen clit. Each rub, each sway of his hips brought her closer to climax.

Needing to be closer to him, Marisa lifted her tattered gray shirt and let her bra rub against his hard chest. Bradi's hands found their way to her breasts and in just seconds, he was rolling her nipples between his fingertips, causing her to moan for him.

When his fingers slid into the top of her shorts, she tensed a bit. He stopped and looked down at her, capturing her in his mesmerizing gaze. "Do you want me to stop?"

She bit her lower lip and shook her head. "No, but I need to tell you something and you have to promise not to laugh."

His eyebrows arched as he nodded his head. "Yes?"

"I've never ... I've never been with a man before."

He nodded and placed a chaste kiss on her forehead. "We can stop until you are ready, honey."

"No," she said, a little too fast. "I'm ready, but I thought you should know so that...."

He smiled. "So that I'd be gentle with you?"

That wasn't exactly what she had in mind. "Well, I guess gentle would be nice, but more importantly, I think you should know that I wasn't kidding about not being able to tolerate the shots." The doctor within her kicked into gear. "That means that I have no form of birth control so you'll have to pull out of me before you ejaculate. I know that you had your shot but those aren't one hundred percent unless both parties are up to date. Plus, I think you should know that something odd may happen during this. I've never told anyone about this before but I come by my healing honestly. I...."

Bradi rolled off her quickly and grabbed his shirt off the ground. He turned toward the *brula* and gave it a hard twist.

"Bradi?" She sat up and drew her legs to her chest, never feeling more humiliated in her life. Marisa had been on the verge of confessing her gift to him and he'd acted this way. Climbing to her feet, she cast him an angry look. "What the hell was I thinking? Gods, I must be suffering from post traumatic stress syndrome to let you near me!"

She spun on her heels to go and shivered as Bradi spoke. "Don't go far. The forest is deadly, especially at night."

* * * *

Bradi watched her stalk off as he removed the *brula* from the fire to let it cool. He didn't like the idea of Marisa roaming around in the forest alone in the dark, but he knew that she felt like he'd rejected her. The opposite was true. He'd wanted to take her more than life itself, but the moment she mentioned that she had no manmade form of birth control he knew why the panthers had taken to her so quickly--she carried his child.

It wouldn't take her long to figure out that she was expecting and with that damned little embedded medical chip she had, she'd be able to scan the baby and know that what she carried was not human. He could jam its frequencies if she was close, but he wouldn't always be next to her. And, when the baby did arrive, assuming they survived long enough to find his family, she'd learn one day that their child was more than met the eye, as was its father--her husband.

He knew that he should confess everything to her and tell her that he was a werepanther and that they'd made love twice on the POD, but he couldn't. Not yet. He couldn't stand to think about how she'd react to the knowledge that a supernatural being now grew in her womb. Humans hated his kind and he couldn't bear to see the hurt and horror in her eyes. Granted, he'd witnessed Marisa do something miraculous aboard the POD but until she came right out and told him exactly who and what she was, he had to operate under the assumption that his wife was human.

Knowing that it wasn't safe for her to be alone, Bradi went to find her. Before long he'd have to confess what he'd done and who he was. That would have to wait. Her safety came first. Well, that and the safety of his child now, too.

I'm going to be a father.

The thought struck him hard, leaving him doubling over and gasping for air. *She's my true mate and she hates me.*

* * * *

Marisa sat at the edge of the wading pool and marveled at how the water seemed to be turquoise here. Not wanting to chance what might live in the depths, she stayed a good bit away from the water itself.

Humiliation and confusion swamped her. How could she have been so willing to give her virginity to a man she couldn't stomach being around only days before? Sure, they'd been through hell the last couple of days, but that didn't mean she had to give what she'd been saving for Peter to him.

Peter.

Guilt swept over her as she thought of how quickly after his passing she'd almost replaced him in her heart. She looked up at the planet's moons and rocked gently. "Peter, wherever you are now, I'm so sorry. I didn't mean for this to happen. I didn't plan on *him*."

Someone cleared their throat and she quickly wiped the tears from her cheeks. Glancing behind her, she found Bradi standing there. "What do you want?"

"I just came to check on you," Bradi answered softly.

"I'm fine, now go away."

He ignored her and came to sit next to her anyway. "Hmm, I see that you found a good bathing spring."

She perked up at the sound of a bath. "Bathing spring?"

"Yes, it's not nearly as warm as the hot springs that can be found on the planet, but it's safe and clean."

"Safe and clean?"

He laughed softly. "Yes, would you like to eat first or bathe?"

She was starving, but the sound of a bath was too good to pass up. "You can go back and eat. I'd like to clean up. "

"That's fine. We can bathe if you want to. The *brula's* best served cooler anyway."

Marisa tipped her head and gave him a funny look. "We aren't bathing. I am."

Bradi shook his head and motioned to the surrounding trees. "Don't you sense the danger? We are being stalked ... or watched if you will, as we speak. It's not safe for me to leave you here alone, and I'm in need of a warm bath as much as you, so it makes...."

Putting her hand up, she silenced him. "I get it, okay. Big bad ugly things roaming around equals you and I hopping in there together."

"Yes, that's the short version."

She let her toe dip into the water and her eyelids fluttered shut with the lure of a warm bath. On the ship, they'd only had access to cleansing chambers that used artificial water supplies. And, on Earth the water had been restricted for drinking only, so each home had similar chambers. Water baths were luxuries and only the wealthiest of Earthlings could afford them. The lure of actual water was too good to pass up. "Fine, but you need to face the other way."

Bradi chuckled and turned around. She couldn't help but watch him as he removed his shirt slowly. His muscles rippled with every movement and she wondered if he had to get his off duty clothes specially tailored to fit his large size. When he went for his pants, she gasped.

"Why did I have to turn around if you were going to stand there and watch me undress anyway?"

Marisa stilled. How had he known that she'd been watching him? Had her eyes borne through him so much so that he'd felt her? No. That was ridiculous. "You're so full of yourself."

He snorted and continued to undress. As hard as she tried to avert her gaze, she couldn't tear it away from him. When his firm backside was exposed, a smile moved to her face as she caught sight of his dimpled ass cheeks.

"Would you like me to turn around? You could see all of me then."

Marisa growled as she yanked her clothes off. "You arrogant, son of a...."

Two warm hands grabbed her waist as she brought her shirt over her head. Trapped part in the material and part in fear, she stood still. "Don't move, Doc. Something's close."

Images of the eel flashed in her head as Bradi eased her shirt off. Fearing what might be stalking them, she gave little thought to her nudity and turned to face him. Bradi slid his hands down her torso, causing her breath to catch, before settling on the tops of her shorts.

"We should get you out of these so you still have dry clothes tonight."

"I thought that something was close to us."

"It is," he said with a sly grin. He positioned his hand over his groin before moving to touch her.

She began to protest, but stopped when her gaze flickered down his tawny chest. She gapped when she saw the size of his cock. "My gods!"

It twitched and she jumped. Bradi laughed as he bent down before her. In a flash, he had her shorts around her ankles, and his face directly level with her pussy.

His eyes flickered closed and he swayed slightly. Fearing for his health, she touched his shoulder. "Janelle?"

"Mmm, you smell so good ... good enough to eat. Can I taste you, Doc?" His blue eyes locked on her and she knew that she should be appalled by his lewd comments, but she wasn't. She was turned on.

* * * *

"I want to run my tongue over you and lick your sweet cream. Allow me this pleasure, please." Dipping his face forward, Bradi nuzzled in between her legs. She smelled so good, a mix of vanilla and his scent. There was little doubt in his mind that she carried his child.

The harder he concentrated on her scent, the more he found it mixing to match his own. He'd never given much thought to having children, not because he didn't like them, but because he never thought he'd be able to impregnate anyone. Genetics was funny when it came to were DNA. The recipient had to be a match for the seed to take and the chances of that were so rare that he'd all but given up hope.

Bradi parted Marisa's folds and ran his tongue out and over her clit. She bucked against his face and he laughed softly. He'd always thought her to be so stuffy, so conservative that he could hardly believe that she was as wild as she was and his.

Mine? Where the hell did that come from? She'll never accept me--not when she finds out what I have done, and what I truly am.

Bradi pushed the thoughts of rejection out of his head on concentrated on Marisa. Her legs trembled with each flick of his tongue and he sensed it right before they gave out on her. Grabbing her quickly, he eased her to the ground. He parted her legs and buried his face in her pussy. She tasted every bit as wonderful as he thought she would and more. He'd never get enough of his wife.

My wife.

The words weren't ones he'd thought would ever apply to him. In all the time he'd been alive, Bradi never once pictured himself married, tied to one woman. Now, as his tongue skated over her velvety folds, lapping up her cream, he couldn't imagine life without Marisa in it.

She slid her fingers into his hair and his chest tightened. This time, Marisa was fully awake and knew that it was he, not Pete before her, yet she seemed every bit as willing as she had in the POD. Could that mean that she felt the same for him as she did Pete? Did she love him, too?

Easing his finger into her tight channel, Bradi marveled at how wet she was. He wanted to slip his dick into her and let her body clench around him as he rode her, but he needed to see to her happiness first. Thrusting his finger in and out of her tight channel he smiled as she began to pant. "You like that, don't you, baby?"

"Mmhmm," she groaned.

"Tell me that you like it, Doc. Tell me that you like it when I touch you. Tell me that you want me buried deep in you. I want to hear you say it." Bradi needed to hear the words fall from her lips. He needed some sort of reassurance that she felt something for him. The feelings he had for her were like nothing he'd ever felt before.

Marisa shifted slightly. "I ... I like it when you touch me, Bradi. And, I want you. Gods, I want you!"

Flicking his tongue quickly over her clit, he stopped to suck on it. Marisa came with a jolt, wrapping her legs around his head and crying out. The beast within him rose rapidly to the surface and he knew that he'd never be able to fight it down on his own. His claws shot forth, and his incisors let down. The rippling on his back indicated that fur was only seconds away and he knew that he had to get away from her fast. Pushing off her, he turned and rolled into the water.

Warm water greeted him upon his descent and he welcomed its aid. The beast within him struggled to be free, but he held it at bay--barely. Only Marisa could make him lose his hard-earned control. Only she seemed to be able to leave him in a permanent state of guard against shifting. If touching her brought about the change in him every time, then she'd soon learn what he truly was. A monster. An animal. A liar. The father of her child and her husband.

Breaking the surface, he glanced around for Marisa. She was gone. Panic welled in him as he climbed out of the water. "Doc?"

When she didn't answer, he didn't stop to dress, he shifted quickly into panther form to track her better. Catching her scent, he ran toward their campsite. He scanned it quickly for threats and when he deemed there was none, he shifted back into human form.

"Doc?"

Glancing around, Bradi found her lying by the fire with her back to him. Her curves were accented by the soft fire glow and he knew in that moment that he'd never be good enough for her. She deserved a saint, not an ass who left her lying on the edge of the water without so much as an explanation. Guilt swept over him as he realized that she'd taken his diving into the water as another sign of rejection. He walked slowly over to her and sat down next to her naked form.

"Marisa?"

She didn't answer. He leaned over her and found her eyes closed and her breathing shallow. She'd fallen asleep. He couldn't blame her. They'd had a hell of a last few days and she'd not eaten. The pregnancy probably contributed to her fatigue and he couldn't fight the urge to lie down next to her. Spooning her body with his, he held her tight as sleep took him as well. "Sweet dreams, wife."

Chapter Six

Marisa glared at Bradi's back as he walked ahead of her. They'd been walking all day and she was exhausted. Giving into her aching body's demands, she sat on the forest floor.

Closing her eyes, she tried once again to get her embedded med chip to work. "Scan body for signs of infection."

The chip clicked on and then instantly fizzled out.

"Doc?"

Peeking out of one eye, she growled when she saw Bradi standing close to her. She lay back on the ground and didn't care what crawled on her. She was tired and needed to sleep.

"We can't stop here. It's not safe," Bradi said, touching her leg lightly. "Are you going to talk to me? This silent treatment is getting old."

He was right. The last time she'd talked to him was by the bathing pool close to five days ago, and it had been hell staying silent. "Fine. What is it you'd like to talk about? Care to tell me how you always seem to know when something is stalking us or how you know so much about this planet?"

Bradi grew still and she gave him a fake smile. "That's what I thought. I'm tired, Lieutenant Commander, and I need some sleep. I've contracted a bug on this planet you seem to be such an expert on and all I want to do is go home."

"You need to eat."

The thought of eating turned her stomach. "I can't. Every time I put something in my mouth, it comes right back up."

"Gee, if we only knew a healer," he said wryly.

She sat up fast and glared at him. "Say what's on your mind, Janelle."

Touching her cheek, he gave her a wide smile. "You're even more beautiful when you're angry."

Stunned by his words, she turned her head. "Well, considering I only have you to keep me company that must mean I'm drop dead gorgeous all the time, since you pretty much have me in a permanent state of pissed off."

"Yes, you are gorgeous all the time," he said, as if that cleared up everything.

She was too tired to argue with him anymore. Her body ached and her stomach was in a knot. Sinking back into the forest floor, she closed her eyes. "Please, Bradi. I need to rest."

"I know, honey."

Marisa wasn't sure if it was the please or the use of his first name, but he'd finally agreed to let her rest. When his arms pushed under her, she let out a yelp. "What the hell do you think you're doing?"

He smiled down at her as he lifted her into the air. "I'm carrying you. I told you that it's not safe to stop here and I meant it."

Rolling her eyes, she pushed on his chest. "Put me down. I'll walk."

He pulled her closer to him, allowing her to take in his manly scent. "I kind of like holding you and you're right-- you need to rest."

Opening her mouth to protest, Marisa stopped when she saw the muscles in his neck moving. Fire shot through her body and she had the craziest urge to slide her tongue over the beating pulse in his neck. Wanting to lick a man all over wasn't a feeling she was used to, and it scared her. Pride made her want to walk, but fatigue and fear were in control now. Unable to fight it anymore, she laid her head on his chest and closed her eyes. She'd never admit it to him, but she kind of liked that he was holding her, too.

* * * *

Bradi ran with Marisa in his arms. It was better that she slept. It meant that he could shift partially and travel faster. He kept a close eye on her to monitor her sleeping. The last thing he needed was for her to wake up and find him covered in a coating of black fur and his eyes glowing yellow. Somehow, he didn't think she'd take too kindly to that.

He'd spent five days trying to think of creative ways to tell her that she carried his child and was his wife in the eyes of his people. Nothing seemed to be good enough and regardless what he decided to do, he knew he'd lose her.

Marisa was out of his league.

That wasn't acceptable. The fierce need to protect her, be near her, provide for her and love her was all consuming. He knew he'd never be able to let her go and that in the end, she'd undoubtedly demand to leave.

* * * *

Nina Janelle moved with a grace most human women didn't posses. She stopped in front of Pheebes, a trusted warrior among her guards. "What was so urgent that you needed to pull me away from my duties?"

"Forgive me, my lady, but I bring news that I think you should know."

She motioned for him to join her in her office. "Tell me this news."

"A group of my men, the panther pard, were returning from a scouting mission on the edges of the red sea and encountered an outsider."

"An outsider, really?" Nina's interest was piqued. They kept close tabs on the number of outsiders they permitted on the planet. Aside from the group that had arrived two months ago with her brother-in-law, they hadn't had any outsiders here for more than a few hours in decades. "Go on."

"Yes, my lady. At first they assumed the woman was alone, and they were starved for...." His eyes shifted downward. Nina knew the sexual cravings that the men had were great, yet she discouraged them from seeking fulfillment from anyone other than their chosen mates. To do so would mean certain death and not many risked that. Pheebes' admittance to the men being horny spoke volumes for the severity of what he was about to tell her.

"Go on."

"The men cornered her and immediately noticed that she bore the mark of one of our own. Thinking that she could be the mate of one of Stegian's men, they inspected further. She was with child, and they claim that she was covered in the scent of...." He stopped and stared at her.

Nina nodded her head. "Of who, Pheebes?"

"Of Bradiainn."

"You are mistaken." Stegian was an evil vampire sorcerer who had terrified her people for over a hundred and fifty years. Nina could believe that he was behind just about anything. She could not and would not believe that her brother was back.

Pheebes shook his head. "No, my lady. My men say that a large black panther surged forward and challenged them for the woman. Do you think he has been sent by Stegian to try to kill you and your sister?"

Nina's eyes widened and her heart raced. As much as she didn't want to believe it was true, she'd seen her own father turn against his family. Bradiainn had been banished from the planet by her father due to his rumored involvement with Stegian. If it was true, and he was back, he was a threat she didn't want to imagine coming up against alone. "Tell no one of this. Organize a party of five men. Bring extra horses. We shall set out in an hour. If Bradiainn is here, we shall find him."

Chapter Seven

Marisa snuggled in next to Bradi and tried her best not to get aroused. It was hard considering their close proximity. She'd also found that although she was tired all the time and had little ability to keep anything down, she was horny as all get out.

Bradi leaned over her and grabbed another piece of the fruit he called *satunie*, but looked and smelled like mango. "Here, eat."

Her stomach turned. "I can't."

"Doc, honey. You have to eat something. The ba...."

"The what?" she asked waiting for him to finish his sentence.

"The bug you have won't get better until you add food. You can't expect your body to get better when you are living off water and air only."

She laughed softly at the irony of the fighter giving the doctor advice, but knew that he was right. "Tell you what. I'll make you a deal."

"I am listening."

Biting back all of her better judgment, Marisa continued. "Give me what I'm craving and I'll eat your damn fruit."

"What are you craving?" he asked, a hint of amusement in his voice.

There was no doubt in her mind that he was going to make her say it. She rolled her eyes and swatted his chest lightly. "You." She reached down and cupped the bulge in his pants. "This."

Bradi growled and rolled her onto her back. For a moment, she thought she saw his eyes flicker to yellow, but when he stared out at her from blue orbs she knew she'd been mistaken. "Do not toy with me, Doc."

"Me, toy with you? Please. You're the one that runs away from me every time we get close." She shifted under him as he pushed his hips into her. "Listen, I know that I'm the last person that you wanted to be marooned with and I know that I'm not like your other girls, but I need...."

He dropped his lips down and kissed her quickly. "No, you are not like my other girls at all."

The harsh reality of his words hit her and she pushed at him to get him off her. "Off, Bradi. Now!"

He looked hurt as he rolled onto his side. "What did I say?"

"Like I didn't hear it enough growing up ... like I need you to rub it in."

Bradi blinked as he tried to wrap his arm around her. She pushed it off and glared at him. "You know, my stepmother never once hesitated to tell me how unfortunate I was when it came to looks and with *my condition* she said that I'd be lucky to ever catch a man's eye." She let her gaze go hard. "I wasn't blessed with enormous breasts and extra long legs. I get that I'm not a supermodel or a Bradi groupie. I don't need to be reminded by you that I don't stack up against all of your bimbos." Marisa tried to get to her feet, but Bradi seized hold of her and pulled her to him.

"I don't know what the hell your stepmother was on that made her think you were inferior in any way, baby, but she was wrong. Dead wrong. I didn't sit by gritting my teeth every time I saw Pete put his arm around you for no reason, lady. I think you are the sexiest woman I have ever...."

"You think I'm sexy?" Marisa asked, pulling him toward her. She didn't wait for his answer. She took control of his mouth with her own and moaned.

* * * *

Bradi was too shocked to do anything other than kiss her back. Marisa's mood swings puzzled him, but he knew the reason for them. Tracing circles around her warm tongue, he let his fantasies take control and he pictured her waiting eagerly by the door of their home for his return with their child in her arms. It drove him on, fueling his already overwhelming sexual desires.

Running his hands down her body, he slid his fingers into her shorts and cupped her cleft. Marisa bucked against him and bit lightly at his lips. Easing his fingers into her tight body, she began to cry out. He used his thumb to rub her swollen clit and continued to assault her neck and face with kisses.

"Doc," he whispered, a confession of love closer to falling out than he'd have liked. "You make me crazy."

Marisa's body wiggled beneath his touch and her cries of passion coincided with her sheath squeezing around his fingers. Knowing that she was coming by the touch of his hand left his hard cock oozing precome with anticipation. The need to take her was strong, but he wouldn't push her. When she was ready to let him make love to her, he would--again and again.

He pulled his wet fingers from her body and brought them to his lips. Marisa's eyes widened as she watched him lick her cream from them. Seeing the excitement in her eyes, Bradi put a finger near the edge of her mouth, daring her to taste herself. When her full lips slid over his middle finger, he nearly came on her stomach. She sucked softly and he couldn't help but moan.

"Do you like that?" she asked softly, a hint of mischief in her green eyes. He hoped it meant that she wanted more.

"Let me make love to you, Doc." It was impossible to mask the desperation in his voice, so he didn't even try. His heart stammered in his chest when she shook her head no.

"Not just yet," she panted, as she pushed hard on his chest.

Knowing that Marisa would never have the strength to budge him, he played along with her and moved onto his back. She moved over him, sending a veil of long chestnut-colored hair around them. Bending down to kiss him, she straddled his body and Bradi fought hard to keep from coming too soon.

She rocked against his cock, and he could feel the moisture from her pussy soaking through their clothes. "Doc," he pleaded.

Marisa laughed softy and moved slowly down his body. Tugging his shirt up and over his head, she looked at him like he'd always dreamed she would--with lust, passion, and he hoped, love.

She spread kisses on his chest, as she ran her hands over his body. "You're so big."

Braid chuckled. "Thanks ... I think."

"Mmm," she murmured as she ran her tongue out and over his nipple. "That's a good thing, but it's a bit distracting all day."

Sliding his hand into her hair, he tipped her head back. "Why is my being big distracting? I would have thought you would like that."

"Because, when I'm not thinking about you wrapping your large arms around me, I'm thinking about the way they'll look when you're pumping yourself in and out of me."

The boldness of her words shocked him. Marisa had always seemed so timid when sex was brought up, but now his woman was blossoming before his eyes.

My woman, he repeated in his head.

"Bradi?"

He realized that he hadn't responded to her and he ran his fingers over her cheek. "I like to picture you under me, your hair spread out, and your eyes locked with mine as I fill you with my seed." Bradi waited for her to pull away in disgust or throw Pete in his face. She liked to do that after he made confessions like that to her. She didn't.

Instead, Marisa inched her way down his body, leaving a trail of hot kisses in her wake. He was afraid to move when she undid his pants. It wasn't until she'd not only freed his throbbing cock, but had laced her fingers around it that he finally exhaled.

Running her fingers over the head of his cock, her eyes met his. Her tongue slid out and over the tip of his cock and he thought for a moment that he'd lose control and come. Thankfully, he managed to hang on. Marisa brought her hands up and cupped his sac gently as she planted kisses down the length of his shaft. On the way back up, she began to suck gently on the sides of his penis. Pleasure burned throughout his body and his right hand shifted quickly to panther form.

Carefully, he pulled his hands away from Marisa's head and was relieved to see that she hadn't noticed the change. Her full lips hovered over the head of his cock and he watched as she took him into her hot mouth. Never before had oral sex felt so good. There was something about having Marisa sucking gently on him as she stroked him that made all others seem pointless. Like a waste of time and energy.

Her sweet mouth slid up and down on his rigid shaft and the second he felt her scraping her teeth up him lightly, he moved to get her off him. "Doc, I'm going to come. Off...."

Marisa moaned and drove her mouth down on him hard and fast, sucking with all her might. Bradi's sac drew up and his body went stiff as he deposited his seed into her throat. She sucked harder, her eyes rolling back in her head, as she squeezed his dick tight.

"I love you, Doc," he said, no longer caring about his pride.

She pulled off him slowly, kissing the tip of his sated cock before looking up at him through hooded lashes. Her cheeks were stained red and she looked as drunk as he felt from their passion. "Hmm?"

"I said that I love you."

Marisa's eyes grew to the size of half dollars and she shook her head slightly. "You mean you love getting your dick sucked, right?"

Hurt by the way she'd managed to take a beautiful moment and twist it around worse than a man, he glared at her. "Doc, no. I said what I...." The sound of a twig snapping caught his attention. The hairs on the back of his neck stood on end. Quickly, he grabbed Marisa and tossed her on the ground behind him. He fumbled with his pants and managed to get them closed, before looking off into the forest. He moved quickly to his feet, but stayed crouched low to the ground.

"Bradi?"

"Shhh," he hissed, cocking his head to the side, listening for any more indicators as to where the enemy was. "Come out. I know you're there."

* * * *

What?

Marisa sat up behind him and looked off in the direction Bradi spoke. Her eyes widened as she saw a woman so beautiful that she felt as if she should look away. Waves of dark black hair spilled around her and she wore the barest of coverings. A leather-clad Amazon woman was all that Marisa could think that came close to describing her.

The woman clutched a weapon on her side and narrowed her eyes first on her then on Bradi. "Bradiainn, I had to come and see if the rumors were true."

Bradiainn?

Marisa looked to Bradi for guidance, but he remained as still as a statue. "Hello, Nina. I would say that it is good to see you again, but that would be a lie," he said, a clear British inflection evident in his voice now. It was as she'd expected. He'd been hiding it.

The vixen laughed and Marisa shivered. Nina looked at her and ran her tongue over her white teeth. "And you are?"

Bradi put his arm out and pulled her behind him. "She is not important."

Not important?

His words stabbed her in the gut. A minute ago she could have sworn that he'd confessed to loving her, but the coldness in his voice said otherwise. Hurt that she could mean so little to him, Marisa blinked back tears. She'd thought that they'd shared something special, but now she knew that she'd just been a vessel for his release and nothing more. Another one of his endless stream of women. A Bradi groupie.

"I did not ask you, Bradiainn. She has a mouth, let her use it," Nina said, glaring at Bradi, her accent matching his. "Who are you ,woman?"

Marisa shrugged her shoulders. "I'm Dr. Marisa Langston, or you can just call me unimportant, all depends on who you ask. But, hey, he got what he wanted so what should titles really matter now?" She couldn't have sounded colder or more removed from the situation if she tried.

"A doctor?" Nina asked, looking her over from head to toe.

"Yes."

"It is a truth, yet not a whole truth." Nina took a step toward her and Bradi growled. "There is more to you, Dr. Marisa Langston, so much more. What are you not telling me?"

"Leave her be, Nina. I'm warning you."

Nina let out a rich laugh and motioned for Marisa to come to her. "I would like to take a closer look at you."

Marisa made a move to go to Nina. Bradi turned quickly and seized hold of her. "No!"

Suddenly, men surrounded them. Some held swords, others guns, but all were aimed directly at Bradi. He pushed her back and began to pace back and forth before her. He took on the eerie feel of a predator and Marisa found herself backing away from him.

"Oh, Bradiainn, do you really think you can take us all on?" Nina asked, a slight smile on her flawless face.

"I won't let you take her. *He'll* not get his hands on her!"

Marisa wanted to ask who Bradi was talking about, but knew better. Nina looked at her and for a moment, their eyes met. The knowledge that if push came to shove, Nina would indeed kill Bradi hit Marisa hard. She gasped. "Don't hurt him. I'll come to you."

Bradi rounded on her. "Are you crazy? Do you have any idea what they do to women around here?"

"She's a woman." Marisa pointed to Nina.

"She is certifiable and does not count. Her judgment is nonexistent and her ability to see truths is dismal at best." Bradi snorted and shook his head. "Doc, tell me you're smarter than this."

Nina clapped her hands together and looked around at her men. "Enough, take them!"

"Excuse me," Marisa bit out.

Bradi knocked her back with his arm as two men lunged at him. He made quick work of them, sending them hurtling in the other direction. Two more charged him and one ran at her.

Marisa stared at the large man heading straight for her and let her instincts take over. She dropped down low and he just missed grabbing her. Swinging around, she knocked him hard in the back. For a minute, she thought that her eyes were playing tricks on her as she watched the man's skin ripple beneath the two leather straps that covered his otherwise bare chest. When fur sprouted all over his body, Marisa screamed out.

"Doc?"

She turned to see Bradi's attentions on her and not on the men attacking him. His blue eyes widened and his jaw went slack. Clutching his stomach, Bradi fell to his knees.

At first, Marisa didn't understand what had happened. She hadn't heard any weapons discharge, but when she saw the end of a silver blade sticking out from Bradi's stomach, she knew.

"Bradi!" she screamed, running for him.

A furred arm grabbed her around her waist and lifted her off the ground. She didn't need to look behind her to know that a monster held her. Her concerns were no longer for herself. All that mattered was that Bradi was dying.

Bradi reached for her and she felt her heart shatter into a million pieces. "Doc, I'm sorry...."

"Put me down!"

Nina ran to Bradi's side and looked up at her. "Can you help him?"

Marisa ceased to struggle. "What do you care?"

Nina touched Bradi's cheek lightly and looked back at Marisa. "He is my brother."

The thing holding Marisa let her go and she ran to Bradi. Dropping to her knees, she assessed the situation quickly. He'd been run through by the sword and she could only guess how many internal organs were damaged. Bradi fell onto his side and reached out for her. A man moved up behind him and grabbed hold of the sword.

"No!" Marisa shouted. Everyone looked at her. "If you yank that out before we get him somewhere that I can look at him, he'll bleed to death."

"Pheebes, back away," Nina said, her order stern.

"Yes, my lady."

"We need to get him to a med unit, fast. With the proper equipment I might be able to repair the internal damage and stop the bleeding, but we haven't got much time."

"It will take us at least three hours to make it back to the compound, unless he is able to...."

Bradi reached out and touched Nina's leg, cutting her words off in mid-sentence. "No."

Nina stared at him for several moments before glancing back at Marisa. "You don't know, do you?"

"No, she doesn't know," Bradi said, as he coughed. "Please, Nina ... no."

"She has a right to know, Bradiainn. If she truly loves you it won't matter to her."

Blood trickled out of the corner of Bradi's mouth and his eyes locked on Marisa. "She does not love me." His head hit the ground hard and his body went limp.

Nina turned to Marisa, her eyes wide in fear. "Help him!"

Marisa fought hard to stay calm. The urge to scream out in agony at the thought of losing Brady was hard to overcome but somehow, she managed. "Do I need to know anything about him, before I start?"

"Do you love him?" Nina asked.

Marisa opened her mouth to say no, but stopped. "Yes. I do love him."

"He is a shapeshifter. A panther to be exact. If you can heal him to the point that he can shift, he will live."

Bradi, a shapeshifter?

"Hurry!" Nina yelled.

"Leave us alone." There was no way she was going to have an audience for what she was about to try. They stood quickly and she put her hand up to stop the one called Pheebes. "Remove the sword from him."

Nina grabbed her arm and for a second she thought that she might snap it off. "You said he'd bleed to death."

Marisa closed her eyes and let her powers build. They flooded her arms quickly and she knew before she opened her eyes that her hands were glowing. It always happened that way. The white light followed close behind the feeling of weightlessness.

Nina looked at her and nodded her head. She hurried the others away from them and Marisa put her hands on Bradi's wound. Leaning down, she placed a kiss on his lips as hot tears fell down her cheeks. The gashes on her legs, that had been scabbed over but sore, pulled together. She knew it was working, but was unsure if she possessed enough power to save Bradi. She'd never tried to heal someone who was mortally wounded before, and didn't want to think about what would happen if she failed.

"I can't lose you, too," she whispered as she pushed more of her power into his body. "I don't care if you don't feel the same way about me. I love you, Bradi Janelle."

As the last of the light within her seeped into Bradi's body, Marisa felt her own waver. She'd used too much energy, too much power attempting to heal him. "I will follow you, Janelle. If you die, I'll follow to the afterlife. You stubborn bastard. I won't let you go without me. I won't. I love you and I won't let you go!" Laying her head on his chest, she wrapped her arms around him. Suddenly, she felt fur under her fingertips. Knowing that he would live, she let the darkness come for her.

Chapter Eight

Bradi dabbed the wet cloth into the pan of cool water and wrung it out. It had been a weeks worth of revelations and worrying. It felt as if a weight had been lifted off his shoulders when he and Nina had cleared up their differences. All he could think about when he'd been run through with the sword was that his father would somehow get his clutches into Marisa and hand her over to Stegian.

The very mention of the vampire made him shudder. The thought of his wife being subjected to Stegian terrified him. Once he realized that his father was no longer a threat and Nina was not in league with Stegian, he concentrated on Marisa. She'd been unconscious since she'd saved his life.

Wiping Marisa's forehead gently, he felt someone touch his shoulder. He knew without looking who it was. "Lorelei."

"Bradiainn ... Bradi. I'm sorry. I'm not used to calling you by your newfound nickname."

It felt good to hear his twin's voice. It had been so long since he'd seen her that he was almost afraid to look upon her. She'd been away when he'd awoken to find Nina at his bedside with news of Marisa's condition, negotiating with the Neatalie village and had been summoned to return. "Nina tells me that you're mated now, Lorelei."

"I am. His name is Sevan and our child grows within me as we speak."

He knew that as well. What caught his attention was the name of her mate. "Sevan Vasil?"

"Yes. Why, do you know him?" Lorelei asked.

Bradi kept his eyes trained on Marisa as he continued to try to bring her fever down. "I know *of* him. The Commission thinks he and his men are dead."

Lorelei was silent for a moment. "We guessed as much. No, they are all, or, almost all, alive and well. We offered them the opportunity to leave, but all wished to stay. They think of this as home now, and we're glad to have them."

Bradi nodded as he continued to wipe Marisa down. "Is Christian back yet?" He hadn't seen his childhood friend since his return and he hated to admit that he missed him. Losing Pete made him realize how precious and short his time with everyone could be.

"Not yet. He should be here by suns set. He'll be happy to see you, Bradiainn. You two aren't planning on blowing anything up again, are you?"

He laughed as he thought about the time that they'd accidentally set the kitchen on fire when they'd been ordered to help the kitchen staff as a punishment for wandering off into the forest alone. The Chieftain at the time, Christian's father, had seemed so angry with them, but when they'd rounded the corner after he yelled, they'd heard him laughing.

Lorelei squeezed his shoulder gently. "Did Nina tell you of father and Jacquelyn?"

Bradi's stomach twisted in a knot as he thought about his baby sister. Stegian had managed to completely control his father's mind and he in turn attacked his own children. Nina had assured him that Jacquelyn's spirit still lived on around them, that Christian had somehow engineered a way for her to appear in the form of a hologram, but his grief wasn't lessened. She'd been but an infant when he'd left. Their mother had passed while giving birth to her and he'd sunk into a depression. It didn't help that his brothers had been forced to leave the planet by then.

Guilt for having left his sisters assailed Bradi and he hung his head in shame. "I'm sorry that I wasn't here to stop Father."

She let out a small laugh. "You weren't here to stop him because we believed him over you. We believed that you, our brothers, were the ones making deals with Stegian, not Father. He had us all fooled. Had I believed you, my own twin, then none of this would have happened. I am sorry that he sent you all away. I didn't know until it was too late."

"I know." And he did know. Lorelei and he had shared an odd connection since birth. Born of the same womb but not the same egg, they had shared the powers of their parents. Lorelei had taken after their mother who had been a high priestess, where he took after their father who had been mostly werepanther. His body lacked the colorful, tribal-like tattoo markings of the Shamenians, but he could not only shift into a werepanther where Lorelei could not, he was one of the most powerful around.

He turned and looked into his sister's face and knew that she was reading him--scanning his mind. He didn't care. He had nothing to hide from her.

"You love this woman, don't you?"

Bradi nodded his head as he touched Marisa's hand. "I do."

"And she carries your child?"

"Yes."

"Then why do you look so troubled?"

"She'll never accept what I am, and even if she does, she'll never forgive me for how she came to be pregnant."

Lorelei moved next to him and put her hand on Marisa's head. "You seem so sure that she'll disappoint you. Why is that?"

Bradi looked away, not wanting to answer her question.

"Brother, just because Nina and I were blinded by lies and hatred does not mean that she will be as well. Have faith that she loves you."

The thought of Marisa loving him made him laugh. Her heart belonged to his best friend. It didn't matter that he was dead--she'd always love Pete.

"So, Nina didn't tell you everything after all. Did she?"

Bradi glanced at his sister and gave her a questioning look. "Huh?"

"Did Nina tell you how it is that you sit here before us?"

"Yeah, Marisa saved me. She gave too much of herself during the transfer of her power and now...." He couldn't bring himself to say it aloud. Now Marisa was dying.

"True, but did Nina tell you why she allowed Marisa to order them all away?" He shook his head no and Lorelei nodded. "She asked Marisa if she loved you and Marisa said yes. Nina then told her what you are, Bradi ... told her that you're a shifter, a werepanther and she still saved you."

The notion of that sounded very romantic, but Bradi knew better. The woman only tolerated him. She didn't love him. "She probably said that she loved me to get them to leave us alone. She doesn't want anyone knowing about her gifts.

And, if I'd have died she wouldn't have any way off the planet. She's resourceful."

Lorelei shrugged. "I suppose you're right, but then that wouldn't explain why when Nina ran to check on you, she found Marisa wrapping her body around yours and telling you that she would follow you into the spirit realm if you tried to leave. Do women who don't care for a man often do that?"

He stiffened, doing his best to absorb what he was being told. "She said that she'd follow me?"

"She did."

Bradi stood and took his sister in his arms. Her belly was round and he didn't want to hurt her, but he had to hug her. "Bloody hell, I can't lose her, Lorelei. I can't. She's my mate. She doesn't know it yet, but I marked her--claimed her. I can't lose my wife. I love her so much that it hurts to breathe without her next to me. Tell me what to do. I'll give my life for her. I love her that much."

Lorelei patted his arm and nodded. "I'll do what I can for her."

"No!" Bradi shouted, remembering what Nina had warned him about. "You aren't to put any strain on your body. You almost lost your child once. I'll not let you sacrifice it for us."

"Well, it's good to know that someone in the family has some sense," a male voice said from behind him. Bradi turned to find a tall blond man standing in the doorway. He tipped his head to Bradi and looked at Marisa. "She is beautiful. I can see why you love her."

Jealously hit Bradi like a train and he felt his lip curling. Lorelei laughed and patted him on the chest. "Brother, this is my husband, Sevan. Sevan, my brother Bradi."

"Good to meet you, Lieutenant Commander."

"Don't call me that. I have no title anymore. When Marisa returns and tells the Commission what I am, they will hunt me down and execute me."

"So sure that she'll disappoint you," Lorelei muttered, shaking her head. She put her hand out to Sevan and walked to him. "My brother is so bullheaded."

"Wow, a member of your family's bullheaded? You don't say?"

Bradi couldn't help but laugh. He liked Sevan and knew that the man loved his sister.

* * * *

Stegian tapped his fingers across his desk and let the information he'd just been given sink in. His long nails scraped over the wood surface and he knew that if he chose, he could shred it with one hand, but why? He wasn't a barbarian, a monster, like the Commission had tried to make him be. No. He'd risen up above their betrayal and had made an empire for himself. He'd taken this otherwise pointless planet they'd inadvertently exiled him to and made it a thriving home for others like him. It would have been perfect too, if two men and their children hadn't interfered.

Raiden Janelle and Chreathe Beauden had decided to rally against him, and lead the Shamenians and the supernatural traitors who had been aboard the vessels, herded from Earth, to stand and fight him. Chreathe was a hard kill, but worth it in the end. Raiden on the other hand had proved to be a vital pawn in his master plan and he mourned the day that his ungrateful children had put him down.

Oh, he had been one to watch, his torture techniques proved to be most invaluable.

Stegian thought about Janelle's children once more. Seven in all, they could have been the destruction of him and his men, especially since they had teamed up with Chreathe's sons. Fortunately, one of Chreathe's boys had been easy enough to mind control and had swayed to his side.

The other, Christian, now the Chieftain of the Shamenians, proved to be stronger than Stegian had bargained for. Still, his plans for the planet and then total domination were moving along accordingly. Stegian had managed to control Raiden long enough to see him send his sons away and destroy one of his own daughters.

Now, one of the Janelle boys, Bradiainn, was back and mated.

How interesting.

He'd always found Raiden's sons to be a unique challenge. They seemed to have more resistance to his psychic vampire commands than their father did and he always loved a good fight.

"Master, I bring you your food."

Stegian glanced lazily up at his loyal servant, Yunoc, and then to what would be his first meal of the day. A sexy little blonde werehyena stood before him. He couldn't remember her name and it didn't matter. He only wanted to fuck and suck her anyway.

"Come," he said with a flick of his wrist.

The girl's eyes widened, yet she came forward. Only wearing a collar, he could see her erect nipples and couldn't wait to run his tongue over them. His cock stirred to life and he put his hand out to the girl.

"Take me in your mouth and give me your wrist," he said, pulling his shaft free from his pants.

The girl moved forward and dropped to her knees, putting her hand up to him in the process. He licked along her wrist and found the perfect spot where her blood ran fast. He waited for her hot mouth to slide over his cock before he sank his fangs into her tender skin.

The girl sucked him sweetly, flicking her tongue over the head of his cock at random moments before deep throating him. She was good at what she did, but his mind was preoccupied. At some point during the suck off, he felt her loosening her grip on him, but he paid no attention to it.

His mind drifted back to Raiden Janelle's children, and the news he'd just heard. He'd wanted to get his hands on those boys for almost a decade, and now it looked as though he would. Knowing that Bradiainn had mated made the deal even sweeter. Stegian now had the advantage he needed to bring another Janelle to his knees. It was almost too easy. The next generation of Janelle's needed to be wiped out or controlled. He didn't care which it was.

"Master," Yunoc said.

Stegian looked down at the werehyena and released his seed into her mouth. She lay motionless, with her head on his lap for a moment before he realized that he was still sucking on her wrist. Lost in thought about bringing the Janelle line to an end, he'd taken too much blood.

"Yunoc, get this whore off me and throw her to the wolves. They've earned a treat." He motioned to the girl in his lap. "Oh, and bring me another girl. I feel the need to fuck something now. I'm horny. Death always seems to do that to me."

Chapter Nine

Marisa moved around the compound slowly. Her entire body still felt like it'd been trampled on by an angry herd of elephants, but other than that, she couldn't complain. The bug she'd contracted seemed to be easing up and the people here, or rather lycan/weres seemed friendly enough.

"Good morning, Marisa. How are you feeling today?"

She turned to find the blond healer and leader, Christian, standing behind her. When she'd woken in the infirmary several weeks back, she'd found him sitting in the corner of her room. At first, he'd scared the hell out of her, but once he showed her that he possessed similar gifts to her, she accepted his offer of friendship. "I'm good, and how are you today?"

"Don't you mean how is Bradiainn?"

"No, I said what I meant." She narrowed her gaze on him.

The men on this planet seemed to share a common bond-- being pigheaded. Christian winked at her and she couldn't stay mad at him. "Is there any chance that you might want to tell me why everyone's in such a hurry around here?"

"Some things are better left for your mate to tell you."

"Yeah, when I get one of those I'll be sure to ask him."

Christian put his hand on her shoulder and smiled down at her. "Go to him. He is in the training yard with the others."

Marisa huffed. "He's known where to find me for the last eight weeks. The one time I did see him, he turned and ran in the other direction. He's a stubborn jackass and I'm tired of dealing with him. When the next cargo ship leaves for Margaidia, I'll be on it. Before you say anything, know that I'll wipe my memory of this planet clean. I won't risk the Commission finding out about any of you or your secrets."

Christian's eyebrows rose. "You can do that?"

She held up her hand to him. "The med chip that's embedded in my skin has options for me to erase used information. I've been studying it when I get the chance, since you people seem to be experts at jamming it." She gave him a hard look. "And I think I can get it to wipe out my short term memory--at least several months worth."

"So, you will not only forget Sargaidia, you'll forget all that has occurred with Bradiainn as well?" Christian asked, his face void of emotion.

She patted his mammoth arm gently and smiled. "Now you're getting the picture, champ."

"I see. Does Bradiainn know about this?"

"I think that would require him to come within a twenty foot radius of me, don't you?" Marisa turned to head back to her room when she felt her stomach flutter. Glancing down, she attempted to access her med chip. It immediately fizzled out.

"Marisa, there you are!"

Marisa turned to find Lorelei coming toward her. The woman was tiny as could be, all except for the swelling mound of her stomach. She claimed that she was only entering her sixth month of pregnancy, but she looked closer to nine months. If Marisa hadn't been assisting Christian during one of Lorelei's check-ups, she'd have never believed the news.

"How are the twins doing?" she asked.

Lorelei touched her stomach and rolled her eyes. "When one stops kicking, the other one starts. I don't know how my mother did it. Three sets of twins would push me over the edge. If Sevan thinks for one minute that I am letting him impregnate me again I'll chop his...."

Christian cleared his throat and put his hands down over his groin. "Some things are better left unsaid, Lorelei."

"Men," Marisa snorted, "are all the same."

"Care to try another one on for size, Doctor?" Christian asked.

Marisa balked playfully. "Like you could handle me."

He reached for her and she stepped away. Marisa giggled. "So, slow. Is that because you're not a shifter? Are all Chieftains as pokey as you?"

Christian's eyes lit up and he laughed. "Careful, little doctor. I would hate to have to teach you a lesson."

Marisa laughed and took a fast step toward Christian, teasing him. He grabbed hold of her and spun her in a circle. "Ah ha, what will you do now?"

* * * *

Bradi walked up from the training fields with one thing on his mind--checking on his wife. He'd spent more time lurking in the shadows over the last several weeks than not. He knew he was being a coward and the fact that Nina had come right out and called him one to his face didn't help either.

Come to think of it, every member of his family, including his holographic sister had come right out and called him a coward.

Somehow, the thought of facing Marisa and telling her that they'd not only had sex but that she now carried his child, was his wife, his mate, his life, scared him to death. Being in love was the hardest thing he'd ever done. If she left, he'd never survive without her.

Bradi heard the sweet sound of her voice and followed the sound of it. He saw his sister, Lorelei, first, with her hands on her hips complaining about never letting Sevan impregnate her again and then he saw Marisa. Her long brown hair blew softly in the breeze and the white gown she wore made her look like an angel.

Laughing, she made a quick move toward Christian. Christian dodged her playful strike and swept her up in his arms. Bradi's heart stopped when the two didn't immediately break apart. The beast within him tried to rise as he watched Christian's lips come down on Marisa's. As quick as the kiss started, it ended, but the beast in Bradi didn't care how chaste it was. That was his wife, damnit.

He ran headfast at Christian with the primal urge to tear his heart out. How dare he touch his mate? How dare he attempt to lay claim to that which had already been marked?

"Bradi, no!" Lorelei screamed.

He didn't stop. Slamming into Christian, he toppled them both over. They rolled and Bradi let his claws spring forth from his fingers. He brought the tips up and pressed them to Christian's throat. "Mine," he growled out, the beast riding him too high to form much else.

Christian smiled smugly up at him. "Then it is high time you proved it."

It hit Bradi then that he'd been baited. Christian had sensed him coming and kissed Marisa to get a rise out of him. It worked. A little too well.

"What the hell are you doing?" Marisa asked, running up behind him. She pushed him hard, and he had the decency to pretend it hurt. "Get off him and suck those claws back in or whatever it is you do with them before somebody gets hurt. What were you thinking?"

"That you are mine," Bradi said matter-of-factly.

"Oh, it's about to get ugly around here. Come on, Christian. We better get out of here." Lorelei reached down to help him up.

Bradi looked up to find Marisa glaring at him. Her green eyes were livid and he couldn't recall a time when he wanted her more. She smacked him hard on the back of the head, and he bit back a laugh. "I belong to no one!"

"Not true. You are mine."

She thumped him upside the head again. "I'm sorry, but the last one must have knocked what little sense you had right out of your thick skull. I belong to no one, Lieutenant Commander Janelle."

"Actually," he said, rising to his feet. "I would much rather prefer it if you call me by my newest title."

"What, jackass?"

"No, husband." He grinned and wagged his brows. "But you're the only one who gets to call me that, wife."

Marisa's mouth dropped open and Bradi refused to back down. He'd spent weeks being afraid of this moment and he knew that it was now or never. "And while we are at it, wife, I think you should start thinking about what you want to name *our* child."

Seconds ticked by, feeling more like hours. He expected Marisa to throw a fit. When she burst out laughing, he wasn't sure what to do. "Oh, you had me for a minute there, Janelle. The husband thing was good, but the baby thing pushed it too far. Nice try, buddy. A baby requires sex. Of which, I've had none."

She laughed harder and Bradi wasn't sure what to do, so he gave into his animal instincts. Grabbing her up in his arms, he ignored her protests and headed toward his quarters.

* * * *

"What do you think you're doing?" Marisa demanded as he plopped her down on the bed gently.

"I thought that would be easy to see. I am about to make love to my wife." Bradi kicked off his boots and pulled off his pants. The urge to be in her was too great to bother with a slow seduction.

Marisa's mouth opened. Spotting an opportune moment, he leaned down and kissed her. Her fighting stopped and she kissed him back. Her mouth tasted so sweet that he didn't want to break the kiss, but needed to in order to get her undressed. He could have ripped the gown off her, but Nina had warned him that women did not take kindly to having their clothing torn to bits.

He grabbed hold of Marisa's gown and she smacked his hand. "Bradi? Have you lost your mind? You haven't even looked at me for close to two months and now you want to get me naked?"

"Oh, woman, I've looked at you. I've done nothing but look at you. I am tired of standing in the background, worried about what you think of me. I see you accepting Lorelei and Nina and hope that you can accept me, too."

Marisa snorted. "Why wouldn't I accept you? Did you hit your head or something?"

Bradi put his hand out and let his claws spring forth. Marisa rolled her eyes. "Was that supposed to scare me?"

"Does it?"

"No."

"It doesn't bother you that I'm a monster?" Bradi closed his eyes, afraid of her response. He was a solider, a trained killing machine, but the thought of Marisa rejecting him did what no enemy had done before--it scared the hell out of him. He'd gladly face down a legion of charging alien armies before having to force Marisa to acknowledge what he knew was coming--she wanted to leave him.

He felt the light touch of her hands on his face and then her soft lips on his. She pushed her tongue into his mouth and grabbed the back of his hair. He went to wrap his arms around her and stopped when he remembered that he was partially shifted.

Groaning, he backed them up and lowered their bodies onto the bed. He needed to be in her. To bury his cock in her silken depths and release everything he'd been holding. It'd been too long since he'd found release in her and his body couldn't go without it any longer. "I need you, Doc."

She moaned and lifted her arms above her head. Easing the gown off her, Bradi let his gaze travel over her luscious body. Her nipples seemed a bit darker now than when he'd last seen them and her lower abdomen had the tiniest of swells to it. He ran his hand over it and kissed her lips.

Mine, he thought to himself, possessively.

"Are you going to stand there all day, or are you going to finally fuck me?"

Marisa's choice of words hit him hard. His cock responded painfully, aching to be in her. He dropped his pants to the floor and eased over her slowly. Pushing his knee between her legs, he spread her open to him. The sight of her neatly trimmed curls nearly brought him to his knees with lust. His cock had a navigational system all its own and centered itself in the entrance to her heated core.

"So wet ... so ready," he whispered.

"So wishing you'd fuck me already."

With that, Bradi pushed into her slowly, allowing her tight channel time to adjust to his size. She gripped his arms tightly and he smiled when he felt her nails digging into his flesh.

"Bradi, stop. I don't think it'll fit ... in there."

"Oh, it'll fit, baby. Trust me." Dropping his head down, he captured Marisa's mouth. Timing it just right, he thrust his tongue into her the same time he pushed his cock in to the hilt. Marisa cried out in his mouth and he quickly began to work his body in and out of hers. Her pussy held him tight and with each pass, he felt her relaxing more and more. Soon, he pumped into her and she responded with throaty moans.

"You feel so good, Doc. So good."

She grabbed his ass and pulled on him. "Oh gods, Bradi ... oh ... yes, oh yes." Her body milked him and he couldn't hold back any longer. Wanting to share in her orgasm, he let himself go, spilling seed deep within her. Marisa stilled beneath him and then jerked to life. "Pull out."

"Why?" he asked, feeling sated and serene as the last of his semen filled her.

"I told you that I couldn't have the shots, remember? Bradi, I'm not on birth control."

He licked her earlobe and laughed softly. "Doesn't really matter now."

She pushed harder on his chest. "Get off! I can get to the infirmary and do a cleansing before your semen has time to take."

Bradi's brow furrowed. "You would wash me from your body?"

Marisa's green eyes locked on him. "I ... I don't...."

He waited to hear her confess that she didn't love him, that Pete was the only man she loved and that it was his children she'd only ever considered bearing. "It's okay, Doc. I know that you don't love me like you did Pete, but you should probably know that it's too...."

Touching his face lightly, tears came to her eyes. "You're right, I don't love you like I loved Peter. I...."

Bradi tried to breathe, but he couldn't get air to move into his lungs. He felt as if his entire world had just crumbled around him. He began to pull out of her and she grabbed his face hard.

"Damnit, Bradi, let me finish." Tears ran down her cheeks as she stared up at him. "I don't love you like I loved Peter. I love you more, way more, and if you think for one second that I'm going to trap you with a pregnancy to keep you with me, you're wrong. I know how you like your freedom and I'd never try to...."

Bradi didn't wait to hear what else she had to say. Slamming his mouth down on hers, he felt his cock twitch back to life. Still embedded in her warm body, he began to move once more.

Marisa countered his thrusts, rotating her hips ever so slightly, making him cry out in pleasure. He drilled into her hard and fast, needing to assure himself that this was real, that she was truly under him, accepting him, loving him.

They climaxed together and he didn't pull out of her until he felt the last of his seed spew forth from his body. Marisa hit him hard upside the back of his head.

"Ouch, what was that for?"

"I just got done explaining that you couldn't finish in me and you did it again. Are you really that stupid or...."

"I am in love with you, Doc." He stared down her. "Marisa, I have been in love with you since the day Pete introduced you to me. I tried to fight it. Hell, I attempted to find relief in every whorehouse from here to Earth, but I couldn't do it. Every time another woman touched me I thought of your eyes, your smile, your quick and generally sarcastic wit. I wanted to fuck you out of my mind but couldn't get my body to respond." He groaned as he admitted it all to her. "Woman, you messed with my head from day one and I couldn't figure out why. When I realized that you were my mate, I had already done something so unforgivable that I was scared to tell you."

* * * *

Marisa stared at him, her mind working overtime. "Wait, are you telling me that all those drunken trips to whore houses that Pete would tell me you'd do were...."

"Uneventful considering that I couldn't get my damn dick to respond to another woman once I laid eyes on you, Doc," he said, huffing slightly, sounding embarrassed and agitated.

She giggled.

"Yeah, it's real funny that you broke me."

Arching a brow, Marisa wiggled beneath him. "Mmm, no part of you seems broken to me, Janelle."

"Then you've not looked closely at my heart."

Bradi rolled off her and she looked into his eyes, waiting for him to explain himself. This was all so overwhelming. Marisa wasn't sure what else he could say that would shock her. Touching his arm lightly, she waited. "Bradi, talk to me, honey. Tell me what's bothering you."

He refused to meet her gaze. Instead, he took her hand in his and led it slowly down her stomach. He stopped on her abdomen. "Scan your body."

"What?"

"Use your chip and scan your body."

Marisa shifted and tried to take her hand from his. He didn't let go. "I can't, you guys make it go all screwy on me. It leaves my brain feeling like putty."

Bradi averted his eyes. "Scan, I won't interfere this time. You have my word."

Shrugging, she closed her eyes and prepared for pain. "Diagnostic scan." To her surprise, an image came up. She watched it flash before her. Not sure what she was supposed to be looking for, Marisa checked everything. The minute she found what Bradi had obviously known was there, she froze. "Oh my gods."

Bradi's hand tightened on hers. "What do you see?"

It couldn't be right. Something on the planet had to be interfering. She checked again.

"I'm ... oh gods ... I'm pregnant." Marisa triple-checked the information for errors. "This can't be right, Bradi. It's telling me that I'm in my second trimester already and I've never had ... before you, before today, I was virgin."

Bradi sighed. "We made love on the POD. Twice. I thought you were awake." He rolled away from her. "You weren't. You thought I was Pete."

Marisa lay perfectly still, as she soaked in what he was telling her. She scanned the baby closer and exhaled slowly when the chip confirmed that the child was indeed carrying the DNA of a shifter--like his daddy. She watched as the baby began to suck his thumb. Emotions of pride, joy and love swelled through her.

"Do not cry, Marisa."

Opening her eyes, she found Bradi above her, wiping the tears from her face. "I'll go, Doc. Christian will arrange for you to be taken to the nearest Commission base and you'll be free to do as you wish with our child."

Marisa felt as though she'd been smacked. "You don't want me to keep him?"

Bradi looked away and for a moment she thought she saw tears in his eyes. "Of course I want you to keep him. I love you ... wait, him? I have a son?"

Marisa let out a shaky laugh. "Yes." She ran her fingers up his neck and pulled his face down to hers. "Why did you call yourself my husband? We're not married."

"Not according to Earth ways, but the minute I claimed you on the POD and gave you my seed, you became my wife. At least in the eyes of my people." He tried to look away, but she held him tight. "Do you hate me?"

"Why would I hate you?"

"For forcing myself on you."

Marisa couldn't help herself, she burst out into laughter. He looked hurt, but she couldn't stop. "Sweetie, I vaguely remember our first night on the POD. I thought that I dreamt it all, and assumed that it was Peter, but I wanted it to be you. I've always wanted it to be you. Granted, I thought I was dreaming and would have liked to remember our first time together better, but...." A sickening thought occurred to her. "How long have you known that I'm pregnant?"

"Since the night that you were almost attacked by the werepanthers."

She smacked him hard upside the back of his head. "Damn you! You let me think I had the stomach flu all that time and you jammed my med chip, didn't you?"

Bradi grinned at her sheepishly. "I was afraid to let you find out."

"Why?"

He shrugged. "I didn't want you to reject me. I love you too much to watch you walk away."

She hit him again. "You idiot! I've already told you that I love you. What more do you want?"

He pushed her legs apart and settled his hips between them. Pressing the head of his cock into her wet core, he stilled and stared down at her. "Hmm, let me think."

Chapter Ten

"Are you sure that you want to go out?" Christian asked.

Marisa turned and flashed him a wide smile. "Never been more sure."

"Fabulous, then I think we should start our tour near the outskirts of the territory."

Marisa wasn't an expert about the area, but she'd seen enough over her time on Sargaidia to know that they didn't tend to wander far. Christian put his hand on her shoulder and seemed to read her thoughts. "Have no fear, little doctor. We have many, many hours until suns set so let us enjoy our day together. Bradiainn was most insistent that I keep you occupied. He was also very specific as to which activities I am and am not permitted to keep you occupied with. I believe that he will be most pleased with your suggestion of learning native healing techniques."

She blushed at the mention of Bradi's name. They'd spent the night making love and she'd been disappointed to find out that he had to meet Nina at the training fields at suns up. The entire compound had been on red alert after Pheebes and his men had returned with news of a pending attack by some man named Stegian.

"I can't figure this damn thing out," she said, trying again to wrap the gold cord around the loose shirt she wore, if you could even call it that. The thing barely came under her breasts and the pants they'd given her were so low riding that she feared that if they slipped down anymore, she'd be giving the world a free peep show.

Christian laughed and took the cord from her hands. "Here, put your arms up." She did and he carefully wrapped the cord under her breasts, before crisscrossing it around her waist. She felt more like she was stepping back into time and entering the Roman era, but couldn't complain. The outfit was beautiful. Christian stopped wrapping her up and ran his large hands over her stomach.

"It's so strange," she whispered, still amazed that she was going to be a mommy.

"I take it that Bradiainn has finally told you."

"I love him, and I know that he was afraid I'd take the news wrong. He didn't intentionally deceive me," she said, suddenly feeling the need to defend Bradi.

Christian nodded and took her by her arm. "I know. "

Marisa hesitated slightly before allowing him to lead her out of the room. Something was off. She couldn't put her finger on it but there was something that wasn't quite right. "So, tell me. Are all Chieftains this insightful?"

"I wouldn't know. I am the only one. My father seemed to know quite a bit, but when you are young, you believe that all adults are wise."

"What?" She eyed him closely. "You're like the King."

He nodded his head and motioned toward the guards approaching them. Marisa couldn't help but notice the intricate markings on Christian's body. The men rarely wore more than leather straps on their upper bodies and most of the time those only seemed to be places to store their weapons. Every now and then, Christian would wear a leather vest but that seemed to be on cool days. As much as she liked the idea of being surrounded by sexy men, she only had eyes for one--Bradi.

"What do all the symbols mean?" Lightly, she traced the side of Christian's arm where several geometrical markings seemed to blend into tribal tattoos.

"That particular one allows me to connect with nature."

That piqued her interest. "So, they actually do something other than accent your muscles."

The deep laugh that bubbled forth from him let her smile as he winked at her. "That they do, little doctor."

"I noticed that Lorelei has many, and that Nina has a few. Why doesn't Bradi have markings?"

"Ah, their mother was a native Shamenian, and their father a werepanther mix. With such a varied genetic makeup, each child received different skills and markings. Lorelei is a gifted healer. Nina is a warrior. Bradiainn is a warrior as well. In time, I hope that you will be able to meet the other brothers, too."

A blond guard approached and Marisa scowled. The very sight of the man from the forest made her stomach turn. Christian smiled. "Ah, welcome, Pheebes! I am pleased you have decided to join us this fine day."

Marisa wasn't nearly as happy to see Pheebes as Christian was. The man had run her husband through with a sword. Granted, Bradi was fine now, but still.

Pheebes bowed his head and put his arm out to Marisa. She looked to Christian for guidance and he nodded his head. Not wanting to disappoint the King, she did as was required, all the while wanting to rip the man's arm from his socket for daring to harm her husband. It didn't matter that they'd thought him to be in league with this Stegian character. Bradi was Bradi and she loved him. No one had a right to harm him. No one.

* * * *

Bradi blocked his sister's kick and spun around to greet her with one of his own. She caught his foot in midair and flipped him onto his backside. "You have gotten soft during your time among humans, Bradiainn."

He rolled off the rock he'd landed on and growled at her. "Not all of us were born to destroy, Nina."

This brought a laugh from her. "But you and I were, Bradiainn. I have missed you." She dropped her sword and sank to the ground next to him. "Do you have any idea where the others are?"

By others, he knew that she meant their brothers. Their oldest brothers, Demetrios and Anatolius, had been exiled off the planet three years prior to his own banishment. No one had any clue where they were, or if they were even alive. When Bradi learned of the depth of his father's deception and the amount of control that Stegian had over him, he wondered if his brothers even lived.

His younger brother and Nina's twin, Kyriakos, had left shortly after Bradi. No one was clear as to why, only that their father had insisted that he too had fallen under Stegian's control. Nina wouldn't admit to missing him, it wasn't in her nature, but Bradi knew that she did.

He tapped her leg lightly and forced a smile to his face. "I'm sure they're fine."

"What if they are not?"

"Nina," he scolded. "I managed to survive, didn't I?"

"Yes, but not all our brothers were blessed with your stubbornness, dear Bradiainn."

Bradi clutched his chest and pretended that her comment hurt. "Woman, you sure know how to warm a man's heart.

Maybe, if you learned this fine art, you would be mated, too."

"Ha, Nina, warm a man's heart? You've got to be crazy!"

Bradi jumped to his feet and let his claws extend at the sound of the intruder's voice. He eyed the man suspiciously. There was something familiar about him, yet not.

"Whoa, kitty, put the claws away. I only came to report to the boss." The tall, sandy blond-haired man looked past Bradi to Nina and winked. "Boss, consider this my report."

Nina huffed and Bradi couldn't hold back his laugh. Men didn't rile his sister, so this one was a rare find indeed. He retracted his claws and extended his hand out to the stranger. Any man who was able to get under Nina's skin was fine by him. "I'm Bradiainn, Bradi for short."

The man eyed him warily before taking his hand. Bradi caught the faint scent of weretiger mixed with a hint of werelion and didn't let his guard down. The man shook his head. "I'm not a threat. I got attacked a few months back by one of Stegian's goons and now have the ability to lick my own balls. Isn't that every man's dream?" He set his gaze on Nina and smiled. "I'm housebroken, I swear it."

Nina hissed, practically oozing rage. "Do you ever shut up, Jordan?"

Instantly, Bradi knew why the man had looked familiar. "Jordan Vasil?"

The man nodded and ran his hand through his shaggy blond hair. "Yep, brother to Sevan, and thorn in the side to Nina. How is it that you two know each other?" There was no missing the underlying question. He wanted to know Bradi's interest in Nina.

"I'm her brother."

Relief washed over Jordan's face. Bradi smiled. Nina pushed past them and headed toward the horses. The amount of energy she put into ignoring Jordan told Bradi that his sister was a far cry from hating the man, but it wasn't his place to pry.

Jordan glanced back at Nina. "Gee, boss, do you want my report or not?"

"As if you have anything remotely interesting to offer," Nina whispered.

"I'll have you know that my hearing is just fine!" Jordan shouted. "I started out as a werelion, boss. The weretiger attack only enhanced my supernatural prowess."

"You mean skill," Nina bit out.

"That, too." Jordan wagged his brows. It took everything in Bradi not to laugh at the two of them. Had he and Marisa fought like this?

Yes.

He laughed. They both glanced at him.

Jordan shook his head. "Anyway, the men I have undercover in Stegian's castle say he's got some big ass plot for revenge that involves an outsider--a female outsider to be exact."

Nina stopped what she was doing and locked eyes with Bradi. "What of this woman? Did you get a name?"

Jordan ran his hand over the back of his neck. "No, only that they call her the healer and they seem to think that not only will she make a powerful ally to them, but that she'll somehow bring your family to its knees. Something about stopping the next generation or something. Not sure what they're hoping for. Oh, maybe she's part dog, then she could eat all the damn Janelle cats."

"Shut up!" Nina shouted.

"Marisa," Bradi said, ignoring their lover's spat and rushing toward his horse. "He wants Marisa. He knows about her healing powers and the baby."

"Who's Marisa?" Jordan asked.

"His wife."

Chapter Eleven

Bradi rushed through the compound gates and dismounted his horse quickly, tossing the reigns to the first person he saw. The redheaded teenage boy who caught them looked so familiar to him that he almost stopped to question him, but was too worried about Marisa to bother.

He ran full force toward his house. "Doc?" he called out, as he burst through the door.

"She's not here. I've been waiting for her myself."

Bradi turned slowly, not believing his own ears. "Pete?"

There, in the center of his living room, stood Commander Peter Williams. Peter gave him an odd smile before taking a step toward him. "You look like you've just seen a ghost, Bradi."

"I ... we ... thought you were dead."

A faint laugh escaped Peter's lips as he turned in a small circle. "No, I'm very much alive, and I've been worried sick about the two of you." Peter rubbed his side, as if feeling phantom pain and nodded his head.

The urge to embrace his friend was great, but Bradi held back, unsure of the welcome he'd get. "We are fine."

"They told me that Marisa's been staying here," Pete said, glancing around their home. "Hardly seems like the kind of place she'd like."

Did he know that Marisa was his wife now? "How did you find us?"

Peter waved his hand dismissively. "I called in a lot of old favors and managed to find someone who could track the POD signal. It took us a bit of time, but we finally found you two." Peter put his hands out, and walked toward him. "It's good to see you. I was afraid that you were dead. I couldn't believe the preliminary reports concerning the POD when I saw them. I hoped beyond hopes that one of the life-forces that registered on the POD was Marisa. I never dreamed you made it off the ship, too. But, who was the third person?"

"Third person?" Bradi asked.

Peter's brows came together. "Yes, the POD registered three life forms on board right before its signal was terminated. Who was the third person?"

There was no one else a board the POD except for him and Marisa. It hit Bradi then--the baby. The POD had sensed the moment of conception and had included it in its signal. Bradi stiffened and waited for Peter to probe more. He didn't.

"Umm, I'm not sure. The damn thing malfunctioned and we shot right past the rendezvous point. It's sitting at the bottom of the red sea as we speak. We were lucky to land there. If we had hit solid ground, we would not have survived."

A knock sounded at the door and Peter looked at Bradi. "You going to get that?"

"What, oh ... yeah, hold on." Bradi tried to regain his composure and opened his door. The redheaded boy who had taken the reigns from him stood there looking at him. It hit him then, it was the boy from the POD. Snatching the boy's collar, he yanked him through the threshold. "Why you little son of a...."

A hand clamped down on his shoulder. "Before you tear his head off, you should know that he's Dr. Graves' grandson and he saved my life," Peter said.

"I told the little bastard to give me five minutes. He took off the second I cleared the damn doorway." Bradi ran his hand through his hair to avoid striking the kid. "I had to drag Doc further than I should have to get her out of there."

"Ceelean, tell the Lieutenant Commander that you're sorry before he decides to tear your heart out."

The boy gulped and took a step backwards. "I'm ... I'm s-orry."

"There, that's better, now isn't it?" Peter said, with a chuckle. "Now, where's my fiancée?"

"Umm, Pete, I don't know how to tell you this, but...."

"Bradi, get the door. My arms are full and Christian is loaded up, too!" The sound of Marisa calling out to was both a relief and a worry. She was safe from Stegian, but about to walk into another hornet's nest. "Janelle, the door, now! I see your horse out here. Don't make me...."

He opened the door slowly and found a large mound of plants greeting him. Assuming that Marisa was behind them somewhere, he began to unload her arms. "You should not have carried all of this."

"*Pfff*, please, these are light. You and Christian sound so much alike at times that it scares me. Oh," she said, her eyes lighting up. "You should see the healing properties in some of these. That one with the blue tint is similar to aloe, except it heals burns instantly. Christian showed me and I've got to tell you, it blew my socks off. Bradi ... what's the matter?"

* * * *

Marisa eyed Bradi. He seemed a bit pale to her Following him through the doorway, she reached for him. "Are you sick? Did you get too much sun? I told Nina to take it easy on you. I...."

"You never do stop lecturing about one's health do you, Dr. Langston?"

Marisa's heart thumped wildly in her chest. Had she just heard who she thought she did? Turning slowly, her gaze drifted first over a redheaded boy who looked even paler than Bradi and then it fell on Peter.

She dropped the plant in her arms and stared at him for a moment, too shocked to move. Christian came in behind her and stopped quickly. "Marisa, what's wrong?"

"Peter?" she asked, reaching for him, unable to believe that he was not only alive, but standing in her living room.

He caught her hand in his and pulled her to him. His embrace was strong, passionate, overwhelming. Marisa's lungs screamed for air, but her body refused to take a breath. This couldn't be happening. His lung was punctured. She thought he was dead. And now there was Bradi and the baby.

Peter cupped her face and brought his lips down on hers hard and fast. Normally, a kiss from him could bring her to her knees, but now she wanted to push him off.

"Little doctor?" Christian's voice brought her back to her senses and she ended the kiss with Peter.

Marisa touched Peter's face lightly, still unable to believe her own eyes. "You're alive."

He kissed her fingertips and drew one seductively into his mouth. She heard Christian gasp and wondered what could be going through his and Bradi's minds.

"Please," Marisa said, pulling her hand back from Peter. He looked her over and smiled.

"I guess this planet agrees with you, Marisa. You're glowing! I've never seen you look so beautiful."

Did he know?

She glanced back at Bradi and found his jaw clenched tight and his eyes blazing. "Peter, I don't know what to say. I ... I thought that you were gone. *We* thought you were gone," she added quickly, still looking at Bradi. His face didn't change and she wanted to run to him and toss her arms around his large neck. She didn't.

Peter touched her chin and directed her attention to him. "I wasn't sure that you'd survived either, but I knew that I couldn't stop looking for you, Marisa." He reached into his jacket pocket and pulled a scannable notepad out. "I brought our engagement contract with me, so if they have a Minister or a licensed uniter, we can make it official." He didn't give her a chance to respond. "Gods, I've dreamt of this moment. I've wanted to hold you in my arms and make love to you since we departed Earth. I can't wait another minute."

"Peter, I think that we should...."

He ignored her and looked at Bradi. "Who can we see about making this official? The sooner the better. I want to be buried so deep in my wife by the end of the night that this planet sends her off because she's screaming too loud."

"Peter!" Marisa shouted, shocked by his statement.

"You would need to speak with our Chieftain," Bradi said coldly, never once revealing he was her husband now.

Didn't he want her anymore? Had he changed his mind?

Peter clapped his hands and walked over to Bradi. "Great, take me to this guy and we'll get the ceremony started. Oh, and I want you to be my best man, of course."

"Of course," drawled Bradi, his gaze hard and on her.

Marisa's brow furrowed. "Bradi?"

Christian stepped forward and broke the tension in the room. "I may be of some assistance in locating the Chieftain. If you'd like I will take you out in search of him." He looked directly at her and tipped his head. She knew then that Christian had bought her and Bradi some time to talk and thanked him with a silent nod.

"Right this way," Christian said, motioning to the front door.

Marisa waited until she was sure they were gone before moving toward Bradi. He jerked away quickly and glared at her.

"I won't hold you back, Doc."

"What do you mean you won't hold me back?" She glared at him. "And what the hell was all that about? You practically handed me to the man."

Bradi laughed. "I have feared this day from the moment we got on that POD. I knew, in my heart, I knew that you would never be mine." Abruptly, he turned his back to her. "Just go, Doc."

"You think you can get rid of me that easily? You think that I'm going to walk away from you, from us, without a fight?"

He didn't move. Reaching out tentatively, Marisa touched his back. "Bradi, please don't send me away. I love you."

"Don't do this, Doc."

"Gods damn you, Bradi! I'm telling you that I love you and you're pushing me out the door. In case you forgot, Mister, I'm already married to you."

"Not according to Earth customs."

She snorted, not believing that Bradi could be so childish. "Well, guess this baby isn't really here either. I mean, you don't seem to care about our marriage anymore, am I to assume that you don't care about me or our son?"

When he didn't respond, Marisa drew in a sharp breath. "Oh gods, that's it. I was just something to bide time with. Now that Peter's back you know you can go back to your groupies." She touched her stomach. "Damn you to hell, Janelle! I will love this child enough for the both of us! I don't need you! Go ahead! Go back to it all!"

That got Bradi's attention. He turned around slowly, and she saw why it was that he hadn't faced her--he was crying. Running to him, she threw her arms around his neck and pressed her mouth to his. Bradi kept his lips closed tight, so she moved to his cheeks to kiss away the tears there. "Bradiainn Janelle, I love you with all my heart and I don't care if you want me to leave. I'm staying here with you so just get over it!"

She paused. "Well, if you do want to go back to all those women I'll...."

Bradi lifted her off the ground and backed her up against the wall. His mouth came crashing down on hers and the minute that she tasted his salty kisses, she began to cry as well. "I love you, Marisa. You hardly ever do that."

"You called me by my name."

"I thought it was only fair, you called me Bradiainn."

She stroked his long black hair back from his face and planted kisses all over his neck. "I need you in me, Bradi. I need to feel your cock buried deep in my body. I need to know that you won't leave me. That you want me here, with you."

"Pete will be back soon. We need to sit him down and explain what has happened."

Digging her nails, lightly into the back of his neck, she growled and bit at his lower lip. Her pregnancy hormones picked then to rear their ugly head. "I said that I needed you. Do your husbandly duties now before I really get pissed off."

A wicked grin spread over his face as he pushed his knee between her legs. "What did you have in mind?"

Grabbing hold of his cock through his pants, she licked up his neck and laughed softly. "How about you fucking me against this wall for starters?"

Bradi wagged his dark brows. "Mmm, how about I make love to you against the wall instead. Same results, makes me feel like a romantic guy changing the terminology."

Marisa unfastened his pants and let them fall to the floor. It wasn't so easy to get herself undone. "Err, Christian tied me up and now I'm stuck."

Bradi narrowed his eyes, as he tipped his head. The unspoken question on his face was enough to tell Marisa that her husband was a jealous man. Not that she needed anyone or anything to remind her of that.

She snorted. "Not like that ... he helped me figure out the cord thing."

He laughed as he let a claw spring forth from his fingertip. Slashing through the cord and the material, he freed her instantly. "Your breasts are getting bigger."

Marisa rolled her eyes as she stroked her husband's erection. "So is your cock."

Bradi dropped his head down and took one of her nipples into his mouth. Her body reacted with a jolt and she cried out as he sucked hard on it. Desperate, she pumped his shaft. "Please, Bradi, hurry. I need you in me."

He growled out as he pulled his head up. His eyes flashed to yellow and she knew he was fighting to stay in control of his beast. The truth was, he'd always have to fight it, and that hurt her heart. She wrapped her legs around his waist and stared into his yellow eyes. They flickered back to blue and she knew that he was struggling with his beast. "No, let it be, and let your hands go. I want you to make love to me, Bradi. No worries, no rolling away and into water."

"No." The look on his face confirmed her suspicions. Bradi had been hiding from her when he'd rolled in the bathing pool that night so many months ago. His running, his hiding who and what he was, had to end.

"Fuck me now!"

"D-o-c," Bradi growled out as he slammed into her, impaling her with his cock. He smashed her body to the wall, and sent hot juice running down her thighs. With each thrust, Bradi left the back of her head banging against the wall. It would have been painful if the feel of him buried deep within her pussy didn't feel so good.

Clawing at his back, she held tight to him as he continued to pump his hips rapidly. His back rippled and she knew that he was just this side of shifting. The thought of that should have scared her, it didn't. It turned her on. "Oh, yes, Bradi ... yes." She cried out as she felt her orgasm building.

White lights flashed behind her eyelids as her inner legs tightened. A tingling sensation moved down to her toes. Bradi snarled as he pushed her hard, one last time against the wall, and finished deep within her, spitting his seed into her.

Panting and still coming, Marisa hugged him tight as she wiggled on his still hard shaft, utilizing all the pleasure it had to offer.

Bradi's eyes shifted back to blue and he tried to back away from her. "Doc, I'm sorry. I lost control."

"Shhh," she whispered pulling his mouth to her. "It was perfect. It's part of you, Bradi, and I love you, so I love it as well."

"You are too good for me. You know that, don't you?"

Marisa moved her hips more and felt him flexing his cock deep within her. He lifted her free of his shaft and eased her to her feet. She thought he was done. When he turned her to face in the other direction and pulled her hips back, she knew she was wrong. As he hooked an arm around her midriff and took her toward the floor, she glanced back at him. "Bradi?"

Instantly, she felt the head of his cock rubbing against her soaked slit. A low rumble sounded from his throat as he ran his hands over her ass. Pulling her cheeks apart, he slid a finger dangerously close to her sensitive anal opening. "Bradi?"

"Relax, Doc. I would never hurt you."

"I know."

He pushed his finger in slowly and she felt her tiny rosette fight back against the intrusion. Bradi ran his other hand up her spine and rubbed his cock near her opening. "Relax, baby. Let me love all of you."

Working his finger in and out of her slowly, he moved his other hand around to the front and began tweaking her swollen clit. Without thought, she bucked back against him, driving his shaft into her pussy and his finger deeper into her ass. The sensation of being so full was too much and she came instantly. Bradi pulled out of her and placed the tip of his dick to her anus and slipped it in slowly.

White-hot pain tore through her body and for a second, Marisa thought she would either pass out or scream. Bradi reached back around and toyed with her clit again, as he eased his length into her more. "Push down, baby. Push down."

Marisa did as she was told and the pain lessened, quickly making way for a unique sensation that brought her pleasure. Her body tightened as another orgasm hit her. "Oh, yes ... Bradi, yes ... more!"

He pushed in to the hilt and she thought that she might explode.

"So tight ... you feel so good."

Bradi began moving in and out of her slowly, letting her ease into the idea of having his cock buried in a new location. Marisa was lost in the bliss of his tweaking, tugging, and screwing and screamed out as yet another orgasm claimed her.

Bradi slammed his body to hers and released his seed into her. Moaning in ecstasy, he draped his body gently on hers, still buried in her, and still coming.

"What the...? Marisa?"

The sound of Peter's voice caught Marisa off guard and she turned to see Peter and Christian standing in the doorway. She leaned forward as Bradi withdrew slowly. Disgust moved over Peter's face and his eyes hardened. "You're fucking our best man? My best...? Marisa? It's Bradi! You hate Bradi!"

Bradi tossed her his shirt and it took her three tries to get it on, because her hands wouldn't stop shaking. Marisa glanced at Peter and then to her husband. Bradi finished lacing his pants up and put his hand out to her. She took it carefully, and moved closer to him, needing the shelter, the safety of his arms.

Peter reached for his weapon and Christian put his hand on the man's shoulder. "I would not advise that, Commander."

Peter attempted to advance on Bradi, but Christian held him in place. "I would not advise that either."

"Well, do you advise my best friend and fiancée to fuck each other senseless?"

Christian's eyes met Marisa's and she felt color creep over her face. The man had just watched her taking it from behind. It didn't get much more humiliating than that. "No, I do not advise that, but I do recommend that mated pairs-- husband and wife as you refer to them, join as often as possible. In as many ways as they wish to. Our race is dying out and we need all the children we can get."

"Husband and wife?" Peter asked in disbelief.

Bradi stepped forward. "Pete, I am sorry. I never intended to fall in love with her. It just happened. I swear to you that the only reason I acted upon my feelings for Marisa was because we believed you were dead."

Peter snapped his head up. "What? You're telling me that you're married to her? Oh gods, when the hell...? You never would have acted on it?" Resignation moved over Peter's face. "You loved her before the crash, didn't you?"

Bradi nodded. "I will not deny it. I have loved Marisa since the moment I laid eyes on her. Some part of me must have known that she was my true mate, even from the beginning."

"I don't give a shit what part of you figured out what, Bradi. You were my best friend. You don't do that to friends."

"Peter, you had little respect for Marisa. How many times did you ask me to cover for you when you were screwing someone else down in the private's quarters? How many times did you tell me that although Marisa was," Bradi put his hands up and made quotes with his fingers, "a looker, she wasn't your type, but her family's money made it all worthwhile?"

Marisa's mouth fell open as she listened to Bradi accuse Peter of such awful things. Part of her wanted to think he lied, but inside she knew what her husband said was true.

Peter locked gazes with her and laughed. "Oh, don't look so shocked, Marisa. Why do you think I proposed to you without first getting to stick my...."

"Watch it, Pete. That is my wife to whom you are speaking."

"And my friend," Christian added, his tone as deadly as Bradi's.

Peter chuckled. "No, that's no one's wife or friend. That's a whore and an unfaithful little...."

Bradi was on him in an instant. He pressed his clawed hand to Peter's throat, as if daring him to say more.

Marisa ran to him and grabbed his arm. "Bradi, no. He's not worth it."

Peter's gaze fell on her. "You let a shifter fuck you? Gods Marisa, if I'd have known it was that easy to get a piece from you, I would have brought my dog along and let you suck my dick while he mounted you."

Christian ripped Peter back a fraction of a second before Bradi slammed his clawed hand down. He struck the wall, leaving a gaping hole in place of where Peter's head had just been.

Bradi growled and lunged for Peter. Christian put his hand out and white light spread forth from it, pinning Bradi in place. "Bradiainn, go and comfort your wife. I sense her distress and it is not good for her. I'll see to this ... thing."

"Let me kill him, Christian."

"No, friend. I cannot let you do that. You, of all people, understand the fine line we walk between being like Stegian's men and staying decent. Allowing you to slay this man that you once called a friend could be your undoing, and I will not let that happen."

"Thank you, Christian," Marisa said, moving up and wrapping her arms around her husband's waist.

"Think nothing of it, little doctor." He winked as he grabbed a grumbling Peter and stalked away.

"I need a bath. " Marisa tugged on Bradi. "Come and join me."

"I think I need to go out for a bit."

A sharp pain shot through Marisa's stomach and she clutched it quickly. It passed quickly and she righted herself. "Please, Bradi."

Laying her head against Bradi's back, she held him tight. "Why didn't you tell me about all the things that Peter was doing when we were on the ship? I would have walked away from him."

"And, you would have terminated your employment with the Commission and I would have never seen you again."

"You let him make a fool of me just to keep me around?" Marisa was shocked.

Bradi turned and pulled her to him. "No, Doc, I let him make a fool of himself just to keep you around and I would do it again in an instant. Come on, didn't you mention a bath?"

"Yes," she smiled mischievously, "I did, dear husband."

Chapter Twelve

"Thank you again," Sevan said, pulling her into yet another hug.

Marisa patted his back and laughed. "All I did was assist in the delivery of your boys." She glanced toward the room where Lorelei now rested.

It had been a long delivery to tell the truth, both she and Christian had been concerned about Lorelei. Her blood pressure had plummeted and they'd lost heartbeats on both babies. Two months earlier, shortly after Peter had left, Lorelei began to experience odd cramps, similar to the ones Marisa now had on a regular basis but kept hidden from everyone else.

"You did more than just assist, Marisa," Sevan said, his voice low, his tone even. "You combined your power with Christian's and saved not only Lorelei's life, but my children's as well. I will never be able to thank you enough."

"Sevan," she said, putting her hand on his shoulder. "She would have done the same for me."

He nodded, knowing it was true. Glancing back at the door, he smiled and let out a long breath. "I thought that I'd lost her there for a moment."

Marisa patted his hand and motioned to the door. "Go, sit with her while she rests."

Marisa rubbed her shoulders and did her best to let the tension out as she watched Sevan head into Lorelei's room. Strong hands moved over her own and she jumped.

"Calm down, woman, it's me."

"Mmm, Bradi," she said, rolling her shoulders under the weight of his touch. "That feels so good."

Bradi wrapped his body around hers and she felt his cock digging into her back. "I could make you feel even better. Once, you're rested of course."

"Of course," she said.

His hands slid around her and came to a rest on her very swollen belly. "How's my son doing this morning? His mommy's had a rough night and I'm worried about them both."

As if on cue, the baby kicked out hard. Bradi yanked her back to him with such a force that it knocked the wind out of her. "Was that what I thought it was?"

Marisa coughed and patted his large arms, encouraging him to loosen his hold on her. "Bradi."

"Oh, sorry." He kissed the top of her head gently. "Got excited."

She ran her hand over his and pressed down lightly on her stomach. The baby immediately pushed back and Bradi gasped. "He's a stubborn little thing with a hell of a kick."

"Have you thought about a name for him yet?"

Marisa turned to talk to her husband and the room suddenly seemed to spin around her. She swayed and Bradi grabbed her. "Doc?"

Righting herself, quickly, she smiled up at him, not wanting to alarm him. His stubble-covered jaw line was tight and she knew he was concerned about her. The pregnancy had been plagued with problems for the last couple of months, but she'd done a fairly good job of hiding that from Bradi. He had enough to worry about as it was. The added stress of knowing she wasn't doing as well as expected wasn't something she wanted to concern him with.

The spies they had in Stegian's camp had reported that his people were up to something again, so Bradi and the rest of the group had been busy preparing for the inevitable. Telling him that she wasn't sure she'd make it through the pregnancy seemed wrong to do to him at a time like this. His people needed him level-headed, not worried and grieving. One problem after another had arisen and Marisa had done her best to heal herself, but for some reason, her powers couldn't seem to fix this.

She chanced a glance down at her belly. Only entering her sixth month, she didn't hold out much hope that the baby could survive on its own if it came early. Her knowledge of the behind the scenes happenings was the reason she refused to name him. The thought of losing him already kept her up nights as it was.

"Doc? What's the matter?"

"Nothing."

"You're lying."

She really hated the fact that Bradi and his shifter sisters could sense lies. It made it extremely hard to hide the problems in the pregnancy from them. "I'm just tired, honey. Really. I need some rest."

* * * *

Bradi swept her up in his arms and headed toward the front door. One look at her told him that it was getting worse. Christian had warned him that Marisa and the baby were not doing as well as expected, but he didn't want to believe it. Marisa had told him over and over again that all was well, and that she and the baby were fine. Seeing her so pale, so sore, and so tired concerned him.

Chapter Thirteen

Bradi rose slowly from the table and glanced around the briefing room. Sevan seemed preoccupied, most likely from lack of sleep. Twins will do that to you. Jordan hadn't taken his eyes off Nina since he'd arrived, but he proved to be well versed in the art of war so Bradi let that slide. Nina was completely engrossed in the latest reports on Stegian and Christian was staring Bradi right in the eyes.

"What troubles you, old friend?"

Bradi forced a smile to his face and did his best to look as though he had no cares in the world. Christian shook his head, indicating that he wasn't buying it and Bradi shrugged. There was no way that he was about to pour his heart out about being concerned over Marisa. She'd seemed fine when he woke up this morning and had insisted that she was going to go and visit Lorelei and the new twins later today. Against his better judgment, he agreed to let her go.

"What of the news regarding Stegian's interest in Dr. Langston?" Nina asked, always one to get straight to the point.

Christian leaned forward and tapped his hand on the table. "Nina, is it so hard for you to refer to her by Marisa or even Dr. Janelle? She is your brother's mate now."

Nina rolled her eyes and smiled sheepishly. "Sorry, Bradiainn, I meant no disrespect."

Bradi waved his hand in the air dismissing it all and walked toward the back wall. They'd been gathered around the conference table for the majority of the day and had made minimal headway. They did manage to discern that the ship that had brought Peter had landed near Stegian's fortress, but other than that, they were at a loss.

"Relax," Christian said, appearing next to him. "Pheebes is guarding Marisa."

"I know. I just can't help but worry about her. Things are not as they should be with her pregnancy."

"I know." Christian drew in a deep breath and patted Bradi's back.

No part of him wanted to ask the question that had to be spoken aloud, but he had little choice. He had to know. "Will she live, Christian?"

"Are you not concerned about the child?"

Bradi slammed his fist into the wall, dangerously close to Christian's head. All eyes fell upon him, but he didn't care. "Of course I am concerned about my son, but I cannot lose my mate, my wife, my world. I can't lose either one!"

"It may come down to a decision, and I believe that Marisa will choose the baby, Bradiainn."

"I know." Bradi hung his head, hoping that no one would notice the unshed tears in his eyes.

"If she instructs me to save the child and not her, then I will abide by her wishes, old friend."

Bradi nodded, unable to offer anything further to Christian. He knew that Christian would honor whatever Marisa wanted and he knew that he hated the fact that the possibly of having to pick between his wife and his son was fast becoming a reality.

Closing his eyes, Bradi did something he hadn't done since his mother was alive--he prayed. For a moment, he could have sworn that he heard the sound of a young woman giggling. He knew Nina's voice and that wasn't it.

Looking up, he searched the room for signs of her but found none. "What the...?"

Christian's lip twitched. "It would appear my upgrades to Jacquelyn's computer interface may have been successful after all."

"Her what?" Bradi asked, still searching for signs of the girl.

Lorelei and Nina had explained in detail that Christian had hooked Jacquelyn's body up to machines after she nearly died at the hands of their father. They told him that Jacquelyn could manifest into the holographic form of the age she had been when the attack occurred. Since he'd arrived home, he hadn't seen his baby sister do anything of the sort. No. He'd spent many a day checking in on her vegetable state, her body in a bed, barely recognizable as human--more machines, wires, artificial life than anything else.

Something had gone wrong shortly after Sevan and his vessel had arrived. Jacquelyn had apparently rushed in and saved Lorelei's life and that of her unborn child. In the end, whatever Jacquelyn had done had proved to be too taxing on her body, her mind and she'd shut down, gone into herself.

Christian had spent a great deal of time tweaking her machines, building new technologies that he was sure would help ease the strain the old ones placed upon Jacquelyn's human body. No one but Christian thought it would work.

Hearing the faint echo of a young woman's laugh again, Bradi began to rethink doubting his childhood friend. If Christian had succeeded, even just a tiny bit, then Bradi's baby sister, who, according to Nina, had been locked in the age of twelve for years would now be permitted to virtually age at her correct pace.

* * * *

"Tell me, witch, what news have you?" Stegian asked, as he approached one of his favorite old crones.

She tipped her head and lifted her arms upwards. "Ah, I drain the child of its lifeforce as we speak. Every day I take more and more."

"Why is it not dead?" He grabbed her arm and jerked her to him. "I do not wish to have to kill you, but I will."

With her face this close to his, he could smell her stagnant breath. His stomach turned at the sight of her wrinkled, pale green skin and hairy chin. She gave him a wide, milky-eyed stare and he knew that she looked into his soul, or what little was left of it. "You fear the coming of the child. Why?"

"I fear nothing."

Her foul breath brought bile up in his throat and he needed blood to wash it down. Lacing his long fingers around her neck, he tipped his head and smiled down at her. His power poured through him and he watched with a sick satisfaction as her skin pulled back from her bones. She shrieked out and reached for him. Before she was able to touch him, he let her go. Her face returned to its normal, ugly mess as she panted. "Master ... I drain the child to near death each day, but its mother's healing powers bring it back."

If what the crone said was true then this child would be born not only part werepanther, but also with the power of a healer like no other. That was not acceptable. He'd spent too many years building his empire here to allow another generation of daywalkers to threaten him. "Then we shall kill the mother."

"Master," Yunoc said from behind him. "They keep the compound tightly guarded and the women are watched constantly.

Stegian turned and put his hand out toward the door. "I know the perfect bait."

Chapter Fourteen

Marisa walked slowly toward Lorelei and Sevan's home. She didn't need to look behind her to know that Pheebes followed her. He'd been trailing her for the greater portion of the day. She knew that he meant well, but it was annoying all the same.

"Can't you go to lunch or something?" she called out.

"No, I have sworn to protect you and that is what I shall do."

"Fine, but could you at least take a break to eat and bring me something while you're at it? I'm craving just about anything sweet so take your pick and I'll eat." She turned to see him closing in on her.

"As much as I would love to assist you, Doctor, I was instructed to stay with you."

"By whom?"

"Too many names to list. I can assure you that all have your well-being on their mind."

Marisa didn't like the idea of a permanent babysitter, but couldn't deny that after the stories she'd heard of Stegian, the vampire terrified her. "The suns are high in the sky, Pheebes, and you yourself told me that the compound is safeguarded to notify you all of suspicious weres, so why can't you take a minute to bring me lunch? Oh, I bet Lorelei would be thrilled to have someone bring her something as well. She's nursing twins and needs all the nourishment she can get."

Pheebes seemed to mull over her words. His gaze darted toward the village and she knew that she had him. Laying it on thick, she ran her hand over her swollen belly. "Oh, the baby kicked. I bet he knows that uncle Pheebes is going to make his mommy happy."

"You will go straight to the Devi's home?"

If Lorelei hadn't told her that the natives called her Devi, then she'd have been lost. "You have my word that I will go straight to the Devi's house."

"Very well. I will meet you there."

She exhaled as she watched Pheebes walk away. He was a kind, handsome, man but the thought of him acting as her shadow for the rest of her life scared the hell out her.

With a light skip in her step, she headed for Lorelei's.

"Marisa."

She glanced over toward the compound fence looking for signs of life. Something moved in the brush and she was just about to scream when Peter walked out. His clothes were tattered and torn, and his hair was a good deal longer than when she'd last seen him.

"Peter?"

His eyes locked on her and she felt as though someone had punched her in the stomach. Clutching herself, she staggered toward him. "Peter, I thought you'd gone."

"Marisa, you have to help me. I tried to board my ship and these things attacked me. They're coming for me ... help me, please."

She eyed him warily. It seemed odd to her that Peter, a man who prided himself on his fine upbringing, would have enough survival skills to last in the wilderness for eight weeks, but she couldn't in good conscience leave him out there with the likes of Stegian's goons.

Running to the nearest security gate, she stood before its scanning screen and let it see that it was her. The gate slid open quickly and she motioned for Peter to come. He took a few steps toward her, then tumbled to the ground. Instinct took over and Marisa raced toward his fallen body.

She dropped down next to him attempted to roll him over slowly. He swung around and knocked her to the ground. Landing with a thud, pain shot through her back. "Peter?"

Peter's blond head of hair appeared above her and he leered down at her. His eyes seemed to scorch her with no more than a look. When he got to her swollen belly, his eyes narrowed to slits. "Get up."

Marisa opened her mouth to yell for help, but stopped when she felt something cold and hard pressing against her stomach.

"One sound and I will cut this abomination from your body, Marisa."

Unsure if he was telling the truth or not, Marisa froze. Peter touched her neck, the blade still in his hand, and ran his rough fingers over her skin. His touch used to bring her joy, now it made her skin crawl. There was something about him, something different. It was his eyes. Where once they were brown, now they were gray.

"So, soft, Marisa ... always so soft," he whispered.

She didn't dare move. Whatever had happened to Peter had left him wild, untamed, frightening.

"You'll come with me." When she didn't respond to his command he put the knife to her throat and sneered at her. "He promised I could have you."

Who? The question was on the tip of her tongue, but she knew better than to ask it.

Marisa stiffened as he jerked her to her feet. Wanting to run, shout, anything that would grab the attention of the villagers, she twisted slightly, preparing to run.

Peter seized hold of her hair and yanked her back to him. His hot breath hit her cheek as he spoke. "I will gut you, Marisa ... know that. And when your screams bring Bradi, the others that lurk around me will hold him down and make him watch as I cut you to pieces, then we will tear him limb from limb. It is as the Master wishes it to be."

The Master? It hit her then who he spoke of. "Stegian," she whispered.

"Yes."

* * * *

Bradi took another sip of wine and rubbed his temples. If they continued to sit in here spinning their wheels they'd be too old to go after Stegian. All he wanted to do right now was attack and assure that his family was safe.

The door to the conference room burst open and all eyes went to it. When Bradi saw Pheebes standing there he knew that something was wrong. "What has happened? Is it the baby?"

Pheebes paled and shook his head no.

"Then speak." Christian commanded.

"She is gone."

"Who is gone?"

"The lady doctor. She was hungry so I went to retrieve lunch for her, and she was to go to Lorelei's, but she never arrived." Pheebes said, hanging his head in shame. "The pard men are tracking her scent as we speak. I did not stay to see what they found. I thought that you would want to know."

Bradi couldn't move, couldn't breathe. Christian grabbed his shoulder and it was all the jolt he needed to run out the door.

* * * *

Marisa pulled at her wrists to free them, but the manacles on them would not give. Each time she pulled, they only got tighter. Her feet barely touched the floor as it was, so she stopped struggling. She did her best not to think about the sound of the mice scurrying about around her. The sound of boots scraping over the floor grabbed her attention.

"Ready to surrender yourself to me?"

Marisa didn't recognize the voice, but had a good idea of who its owner was. "I'll not give you an inch, Stegian."

In a flash, something was behind her, touching her, rubbing against her. She bit back a scream and kept her eyes forward. Cool hands gripped her neck and she felt fingernails digging into her skin.

"Ah, I know that you will taste divine. I do so miss a woman who tastes as good as she feels when my cock is in her, and you do want my cock in you, don't you, Healer?"

She wanted to ask how he'd managed to pop up behind her, but she didn't. "No."

He rubbed against her back and she felt his erection digging into her skin. "The answer to your question is magic. I have always had the gift to wield it, but it was not until I became what you see before you that I truly knew how to use it."

"Hmm, I haven't seen anything before me, Stegian," Marisa said, shocked that she'd let that slip out.

A cold laugh sounded behind her and she shivered. "I see why Raiden's son likes you."

Stegian moved around her slowly, but she didn't turn her head to look at him. Instead, she let her eyelids flutter closed. "You believe me to be hideous, do you not?"

Marisa saw little point in lying to the man. "I have no idea what you look like, but I've heard of the things that you've done and those are heinous crimes that are inexcusable."

He grabbed her chin and she felt his hand warm a bit to the touch. "Look upon me, Healer. Let me see myself through your eyes."

"*Nooo.*"

He tightened his grip on her. "Look."

There was a certain push in his voice that she could no longer ignore. Opening her eyes slowly, she looked upon him. At first she thought it a trick--another use of his magic, because the man she looked upon was not hideous. In fact, he was far from it. His long brown hair was pulled tightly back from his face leaving nothing obstructing his high forehead, strong jaw, and gray eyes. He was tall, taller than she thought he'd be and a hell of a lot bulkier too. Why she had assumed that he'd be this hideously thin monster with scales was beyond her, but he was a far cry from it and that made him even scarier.

His lip pulled into a smile. "I am pleased to know that you find me attractive, Healer. Most fear me so much that they do not dare look upon my face for fear that I will capture their minds with but a look."

"Can you do that?" Marisa asked, fearing that she too would succumb to him.

"With most, yes, but not you."

"Why?"

He laughed. "That I do not know, but I find it intriguing."

"Why do you do it?"

He moved closer to her and touched her face lightly. "Why do I do what?"

"Why do you hurt the Shamenians?"

Stegian bent down and Marisa sucked in her breath as his lips came to her face. He flickered his cool tongue over her skin before flashing her an unnaturally white smile. "Because I can."

"There's a mature answer."

He grabbed the back of her hair and jerked her head back. "You would dare to speak back to me?"

Someone ought to, she thought to herself.

He tapped the side of her temple lightly and smiled. "I can hear you."

Great, gorgeous, psycho, and a mind reader.

"I like you, Healer, and I am not prone to liking anyone."

"Like me enough to let me go?"

"I wish I could, but you see, I need to eliminate Raiden's line, and the quickest way to do that is to keep you until Bradiainn comes, kill him, and then I am afraid that I will have to kill you as well."

"No!" someone shouted.

Stegian turned and then looked back at her. "It appears that you have a rather brave admirer."

"You promised that I could have her."

"Peter?" Marisa asked.

Peter moved up toward her and seemed to drink her in. It was unnerving and very un-Peter like.

"What did you do to him?"

Stegian laughed and shrugged. "When he landed near my home, I greeted him as an honored guest. When he returned from his visit with you enraged, I helped him free himself of his inhibitions."

"Meaning, that if he feels the urge to fuck you like a dog then he will," Stegian said. Marisa tensed at his words and looked at Peter. "I can stop him, Healer. I control him now. All you have to do is agree to help me and I will not allow him to harm you."

"Pfft, you said you were going to kill me. Geesh, remember your threats before you go making promises."

Stegian lowered his mouth to hers and she pulled her lips in, not wanting to kiss him. He didn't seem to care. Squeezing her cheeks hard, her lips puckered out. His cool lips pressed down on her mouth. His tongue flickered into her mouth and she considered biting it. He tightened his hold on her cheeks and she knew that he was scanning her thoughts.

How a man who seemed as though he could have it all turned so violent was beyond her. It was clear by his actions toward the Shamenians that he could not be redeemed. It seemed a shame, because her gifts had always given her the ability to sense others like her, healers, and she sensed that in him. He had the gift to restore life, but instead had decided to take it--as often as he could it seemed.

Stegian dropped his hand from her face and backed away from her. He wiped his mouth and let his finger linger over his lip. "Your powers are strong to be able to persuade me so easily."

"Persuade you? I didn't ask you to kiss me." She wanted to smack his face, but her bound hands prevented that. The blood had long since drained, her hands were now numb.

Peter moved closer and looked as though he intended to touch her. Stegian's hand shot out and he grabbed Peter by the throat. "Do not touch her."

"She's mine."

"No, she is not."

"You said you wanted the baby dead and I could have her!" Peter spat.

Stegian backhanded him, sending him hurtling into the wall. Marisa closed her eyes tight, not wanting to see what Stegian would do to her now. "I ... regret," he seemed to choke on his words, as if he'd never spoken even semi kindly to a soul in his life, "having to do this, Healer, but the child cannot be allowed to survive."

Marisa bit back a cry and just stared at him.

"Hag."

There was a bright light and an old woman appeared before them. "Yes, Master?" Her eyes appeared to be covered with a white film, yet they fixed on Marisa. "Oh, you have brought the child closer for me to drain."

"Drain?" Marisa asked.

Stegian's face dropped. "Do what you must, Hag." With that, he stormed out of the room.

Marisa found herself wanting to call him back. It was odd that the leader of evil had seemed less of a threat to her than the old woman and Peter. Glancing over her shoulder, she saw Peter climbing up. His eyes locked on her as he wiped the blood from his mouth.

Heat flared through her stomach and brought Marisa's attention back to the old woman. The woman stood with her hands out, chanting something softly. Cramps rippled through Marisa's body and she cried out.

Peter pushed his body against the back of her, and she felt his erection. Lifting her dress in the air, he pulled her hips back to him.

"Please, Peter, stop this. Stop her ... she's hurting the baby," Marisa cried out as pain shot through her body.

"No," Peter said, his voice harsh. "She's ridding you of that abomination." He clawed at her hips and rubbed his body against hers. The hag's eyes lit like fire and an orange light shot forth from her to Marisa's stomach.

Marisa screamed out as her stomach cramped. A loud growl caught her attention as the weight of Peter's body was suddenly ripped from her. Waves of blond hair spilled around her and she looked up to see Christian standing before her. She tried to ask him where Bradi was, but when she heard another growl, she knew.

Christian cut her wrists free and caught her as she fell forward. She clung to his arms, and cried out as another cramp ran through her. "The hag ... she's doing this."

"Sevan, stop the witch!"

Bradi moved off Peter's limp body and focused on the old woman before him. He watched as Sevan charged her, his sword drawn. The witch cackled and turned a hand out to him. Sevan's body flew through the air and Jordan did a partial change, catching his brother before he hit the ground. The witch turned and looked at Christian. She put her hand up and Bradi leapt into action, snatching up Sevan's sword and bringing it down hard and fast. The witch's arm went one way and her body went another. She screamed out, but Bradi didn't stop his assault. She was the reason his baby had suffered.

With a flick of his wrist, he turned the sword around and backed into her, effectively ramming it in to the hilt. He pushed her off the end of the sword and turned to Christian. He held Marisa's still body in his arms.

"She is dying," Christian said, softly.

Jordan and Sevan moved up next to him. Jordan's face said it all. He was sure Marisa was dying as well. "Let's get her home."

Bradi scooped his wife up in his arms and drew in a sharp breath. She was so weak, so unlike herself. Christian touched her forehead and her eyes closed slowly.

"Thank you," Bradi said, knowing that Christian had just eased Marisa's pain.

Epilogue

Bradi sat with his head down, afraid to move. His life had changed so much in a few short months. The rustling of a chair moving behind him caught his attention. He turned and smiled as Christian sat down.

"How's she doing?" Christian asked.

"You tell me. She doesn't seem to have changed a bit in the last week. How can that be?" Bradi looked down at Marisa and touched her cheek gently. She hadn't moved since they'd brought her home and everyone was doing their best to stay out of his way.

"She's only at rest because I keep her that way." Christian exhaled. It was clear to see the Shaman cared for Marisa. As it should be.

"I know."

"She'll live and be able to have more children."

Marisa's eyes popped open and she looked from Bradi to Christian. Bradi stood quickly and touched her forehead. Her fever was gone. He looked up at Christian with wide eyes, relieved she was awake but scared something else might be wrong. "I thought you were willing her to rest."

"I was." Christian said, seeming as shocked by Marisa's awakening as Bradi was. It was rare for Christian to be caught off guard with anything relating to medicine or healing. He was an expert. A man born to the art.

Marisa's gaze went to her stomach and Bradi saw the pain in her eyes. Her breath caught. "Oh gods ... no.... Bradi, no."

"Shh, Doc, it's all right. Everything is all right."

Her head shook violently. "No, it's not all right. The baby?"

"Nina!" Bradi called out, needing to see his wife at peace but wanting to yank her up from the bed and hold her close. Gods how he missed her.

The door to the room opened and he heard his sister there before she even spoke. "Bring in my son, Nina. It is time he met his mommy."

Marisa covered her mouth and each tear she shed chipped away at his heart. "You didn't keep him ... did you?"

Bradi was shocked by her question. "Of course I kept him. He's my son--our son!"

Nina came back into the room and Bradi turned to see her carrying the baby wrapped up tightly in a blue blanket. Pride welled in him, just as it had done every moment he looked upon his son. "Here you go," she said, handing the child to Bradi.

He took his son gently and looked down into his eyes. "He has your eyes and my hair."

Marisa sat up on the bed, but then backed away from him, seeming beyond hesitant. As if she didn't want to accept what was before her eyes. "He's alive?"

"Of course he's alive, Doc. What the ... oh, honey, you thought that I had kept him and that he was ... oh, sweetie, no. He's perfect." Bradi sat of the edge of the bed and held the baby so that she could see him. "He's not only alive, but healthy and right now, asleep."

Marisa let out a half sob and reached for the baby. "But how? He was too early and under so much stress."

Christian cleared his throat. "Excuse me, I know this is a moment for the two of you, but I think that I might be able to clear this up for Marisa." Bradi nodded his head. "Your healing power surged once we brought you back with us. At first we thought that you were dying, but once the light cleared we realized that you were not only fine, but had saved the baby. And in the process, had removed him from your womb, and strengthened his heart and lungs. He is part shifter so he naturally is stronger than a normal human baby, but Marisa, whatever you did brought about a perfectly healthy baby boy. I was just telling Bradi that I can find no evidence of scarring in your uterus and you should be able to have many more children. Now that the hag is dead, they will not be drained of their life-forces."

Bradi watched his wife's eyes light up as she held their child and he wrapped them both tightly in his embrace. "We weren't sure that you were going to wake up. You didn't show any signs of coming around."

Marisa pressed her lips to his and he felt them trembling. "I love you so much, I couldn't go where you weren't."

"I love you, too." Bradi touched her cheek and looked down at the baby. "And you too, little man."

"Does he have a name?" Marisa asked, tears streaming down her cheeks.

"No, I wanted you to name him."

She smiled. "I'd like to name him Eli Bradiainn Janelle."

"Eli?"

Marisa looked hurt. "You don't like it?"

Bradi shook his head. "No, it's a fine name. I just wondered what made you pick it."

She laughed. "Oh, it's in honor of the first thing to welcome me to your home planet. A giant eel."

"Giant eel? Where?" Christian asked.

"In the red sea that we crashed into," Marisa said, holding their child tight to her bosom, where he belonged.

"Interesting. I had always thought him a myth. Remember when our fathers told us of the ancient guardian of the waters? The one that protected the innocent?"

"Yes, they said it was an ... eel," Bradi said, stunned that Marisa had seen it. Laughter welled up inside him and he was left no choice but to let it out. "Eli is a perfect name for our son. If he is anything like his mother he will become a legend as well."

THE END

Printed in the United States
56939LVS00002B/283-288